WAIFS AND STRAYS

BOOK ONE

THE CAT LADY CHRONICLES

HELEN HARPER

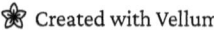 Created with Vellum

For all the cats I've ever known but especially Winky, the perfect ginger love who was such a comfort when I was young; Cat, who didn't belong with us but was determined to stay anyway; Hugh, who was always hungry; Cassie, who was so scared; Black Cat, who was ferociously feral but who gave me his last few hours; Scout, who's been here the longest and who puts up with so much; Mavis, who eats everything and anything; and Lara Croft, who won't let an adventure or a rodent pass her by.

CHAPTER
ONE

Everything was just peachy until the day a teenage werewolf showed up at my door.

I'd spent the better half of the morning coaxing She Who Hisses out of the bush in the far corner of my tiny front garden. Progress with the large, black, feral female had been slow over the last few days. When she'd given me her name on Sunday in return for some kibble, I'd been certain her attitude towards me was softening. Unfortunately, she seemed to have decided the reverse and that offering her name had been an aberrant show of weakness on her part. As a result, she had resolutely refused to look at me ever since.

Under normal circumstances, I'd have left her in peace; not every cat wants a home of their own and it's important to respect their wishes. However, She Who Hisses was sporting a nasty, pus-filled abscess on her hind quarters and I knew that if she didn't receive proper medical attention soon it would be the death of her, especially with winter approaching.

I'd left a trail of tasty tuna titbits and maintained a healthy distance to make sure she didn't feel trapped. I'd been holding my position for almost thirty minutes and she'd quested forward on three separate occasions, her whiskers quivering and her nose twitching. I'd have her on the fourth attempt, I was sure of it.

The bush rustled and I held my breath. A black paw popped out, and another. They were followed by the pale pink of her nose. Here we go.

'I'm not trying to harm you,' I told her softly. Her head pushed forward and her yellow eyes blinked at me. I smiled. 'Hello, gorgeous.'

A shadow fell between us. She Who Hisses growled once and threw herself out of the bush, darting to the side to scale the wall and leap away before I could grab her. She moved so fast I had no time to react. *Goddamnit.*

I let out a hiss of my own and, standing up, threw a withering glare at the intruder. 'Get off my land, you tool!'

The teenager blinked at me with slow, uncomprehending confusion. 'Huh?'

I waved a frustrated hand in the direction of She Who Hisses, even though the cat was no longer visible and likely wouldn't return for hours, if ever. 'You scared her off,' I ground out. 'I was trying to catch her.'

He blinked again. 'For food? There's not much meat on a cat.'

I stared at him in disbelief.

He coloured. 'I heard a rumour that's what people in this part of town do.'

Eat cats? 'Which people?' I demanded.

The kid shrugged. 'Just ... people.'

My eyes narrowed at the idea that anyone would even consider munching on a feline, then I exhaled as logic overtook my anger. This wasn't exactly the most salubrious neighbourhood in the magical city of Coldstream. It had garnered the nickname Danksville, and those of us with a sense of humour had appropriated the name and used it with pride. I supposed there would always be those who made up stories about its inhabitants.

From the kid's expression, he knew nothing beyond that one ridiculous whisper. There was little chance it was true; nobody would really eat a damned cat.

I muttered under my breath, spun on my heel and stalked towards the house. That was when he finally sprang into action, lunged after me and grabbed my elbow. Big mistake.

I snarled, snapped my hand back to grip his forearm and twisted hard. He released his hold on me, dropped to one knee and screamed. It was an astonishingly high-pitched sound for a werewolf already at the tail end of puberty. 'Bitch!'

'Only one of us around here is a canine and it isn't me,' I told him. I let him go and continued on my way.

'Wait!' His voice was strangled. I ignored him. 'Please.'

I stopped in my tracks and looked over my shoulder. 'What?'

'I'm here about the flat.' He rubbed his arm as if he were afraid it might suddenly drop off. 'Is it still available?'

I'd only advertised the vacant flat the previous day by placing a small advert in the classified section of the *Coldstream Courier*. I wasn't even sure that I wanted a new tenant – the last one had left the place in a mess and I certainly didn't need the money – but it was helpful to maintain my position as a landlady to satisfy the unspoken questions from my nosy neighbours about where my money came from.

Curiosity finally got the better of me. I turned, faced the boy and gave him a closer look. He was tall and gangly, although there was evidence of the man he'd become one day from the way his chest was starting to fill out. Sadly for him, at the moment it made his body look out of proportion, more like a badly carved puppet than a living, breathing person.

It had been ten days since the last full moon but his wolf was still gleaming out of his skin, his beast form lurking directly beneath his acne-ridden pores. His shaggy, dark-brown hair was long enough to brush against his shoulders and didn't appear to have seen a hairbrush or a comb since Michaelmas, but his face was clean – as were his expensively tailored clothes. He certainly hadn't bought his shiny trainers here in Coldstream, and his gold watch looked like a family heirloom that was worth more than most of the houses on this street.

'How old are you?' I asked.

'Nineteen,' he answered quickly. He'd clearly been expecting the question and the lie fell from his mouth with prepared speed.

'You're fifteen years old,' I said. 'If that.'

He scowled. 'I am not!' I waited and he looked away. 'I'm sixteen,' he mumbled.

Although he was probably telling the truth, he had folded far too easily for a sixteen year old. His cheeks were mottled red with embarrassment, but he was trying to mask more than mere shame. Interesting.

Suddenly I suspected there was more to his story than an angry rebellion against his parents. 'What's your name?'

He hesitated, as if weighing up the merits of another lie. 'Nick,' he said eventually. He drew in a breath. 'And I've got money. I'm not looking for charity.' He dug into his pocket, withdrew a wad of cash and held it out to me.

'Put that away!' I barked. He had a damned death wish. This was *Danksville*; nobody waved that sort of money around here unless they had a personal army as back-up – and even then they'd be taking a risk.

'It's six months' rent up front,' Nick said, with the edge of a whine. 'My money is as good as anyone else's.'

He'd obviously misunderstood my reason for telling him to put the cash away. Who *was* this kid? And where had he got all that money from? I sighed, then nodded towards the front door. 'Come on,' I said, hoping I wasn't going to regret it. 'Let's talk inside.'

~

I put on the kettle and pointed at the kitchen table. Nick took one look at it and stepped back, crowding the doorway with his lanky frame. 'Is there a problem?' I asked.

He gestured wordlessly towards the old fruit bowl which contained not fruit but the curled up, gently snoring, ginger-furred form of He Who Must Sleep.

Ah. I nodded. 'He doesn't mind werewolves. He'll barely notice you.'

As if on cue, He Who Must Sleep opened one lazy eye and gazed at Nick then closed it again and gave a brief sigh.

'What is it with you and cats?' Nick asked, relaxing slightly.

There weren't enough hours in the day to answer that question so I offered my stock response. 'They keep me company.'

'Uh-huh.' He stayed where he was in the doorway, still flicking nervous glances in He Who Must Sleep's direction, then he swallowed hard and stepped bravely into the kitchen. He pulled out one of the wooden chairs and perched on the edge of its seat. When He Who Must Sleep continued to ignore him, his shoulders dropped and he relaxed some more.

I looked down. She Without An Ear was preparing to wind herself around Nick's legs. When she rubbed her head against his calf, he glanced down and froze. 'She won't bite you,' I said. 'As long as you—'

He reached down nervously as if to stroke her. She Without An Ear whipped round and snapped at his fingers. Nick yelped and drew back.

'—don't try and touch her,' I finished.

The boy straightened up and folded his arms tightly around his body.

'If you have a problem with cats, you can't rent the flat,' I said. 'The cats come and go through the whole building as they please. Although there are four flats, only two of them are habitable at the moment – this one and the one directly upstairs that you're asking about.'

'You'll let me stay?' Nick asked, his eyes flaring with hope.

I gave him a long look. 'I'm considering it.'

'I love cats!' he declared. I raised an eyebrow. He shrugged. 'I can learn to love them.' His voice rose at the end of his sentence so I wasn't sure whether he was asking a question or offering a statement. I suspected that neither was he.

'You don't need to love them, you only need to co-exist with them.'

'Then I will do that.' He held out his hand as if it were a done deal.

I made no move to shake on it. 'I haven't agreed yet.'

His mouth curved into an arrogant smile that gave me another flash of his lupine genes. 'You will.'

Yeah, probably, but he didn't need to know that. I maintained a tight frown until he dropped his hand and his smile melted away. I hadn't lost all of my skills; that was something.

'I'm sorry I called you a bitch.' Nick bit his lip. 'And I'm sorry I scared that other cat away. I'm sorry that—'

I held up my hand and his voice faltered mid-sentence.

Good. I had no desire to hear a string of apologies that he likely didn't mean. 'First I have questions,' I said sternly, 'What are you running from?'

His face took on the aspect of a sullen adolescent. 'Nothing.'

'In that case,' I shot back, '*who* are you running from?' He didn't reply. I softened my tone. 'This is my home. If I'm going to let you live in the same building, there are things I need to know for my own well-being as well as yours.'

He appeared to consider this. 'Fine,' he said eventually. 'It's my uncle. He wants me to join his pack but I'd rather be a lone wolf.'

Hmm. Lone werewolves were scarce, far scarcer than most people realised. Typically, children were bound to a pack by the time they could walk, a simple, painless ritual that went some way to ensure both their safety and the pack's future. Disentangling from a pack was a far more complicated process and certainly not something I'd want to get involved in. I'd immediately be accused of unlawful interference, and no pack would allow an outsider to even consider such a thing without considerable bloodshed. I enjoyed a quiet life these days; stirring up werewolf politics was not on my agenda.

'I cannot—'

Nick interrupted me. 'I'm not bound – I'm not in a pack. I don't have to be. And I've got a friend who's not in a pack. He has a great life. He does what he wants – he doesn't have to abide by stupid rules.' He tilted his acne-ridden chin defiantly. 'Besides, I'm not from Coldstream.'

Now *that* was even more interesting. It also explained the shiny trainers.

'I know the rule is that Preternaturals usually live here,' Nick went on.

It was more of an unwritten rule than a law, but he was

right. Birds of a feather flock together and almost every Preternatural in Britain lived in Coldstream. Once upon a time it had been a sleepy village but now it was a sprawling city filled with magical beings of every type. The deep enchantments that had settled into the bones of the border between Scotland and England had drawn us here, together with the idea of living in a like-minded community. Very few Preternaturals chose to live elsewhere.

Nick shrugged as if it were not a big deal. 'My parents wanted to try a different life. They left their packs and Coldstream before I was born. We lived in Glasgow until this summer.'

'Both your parents are werewolves?'

His expression closed off. 'They were. They died last month in an accident.'

Oh. 'I'm sorry,' I said gently.

His body was stiff. 'Why? You didn't know them.' He folded his arms across his chest defensively. His pain was obviously very raw and very deep; he was clearly still grieving deeply.

I inclined my head in acknowledgment of his feelings. 'Your uncle—' I began.

'He has no claim on me! He doesn't know I'm here and he probably wouldn't care if he did. All I want is some peace and quiet to live out my life. I don't want a pack and I definitely don't *need* a pack. I'm fine on my own.'

I suspected that what Nick needed was time to come to terms with his parents' deaths. He suddenly looked very young and vulnerable, although I doubted he wanted to be seen that way.

I drummed my fingers on the table and decided to meet him on his own terms; the rest could come later, when he was ready.

'Okay,' I said briskly. 'I need two months' rent as a deposit, which will be returned to you at the end of your tenancy once any property damage has been taken care of. Water and electricity are included in your rental payments, which must be paid on the first of every month. Miss a payment and you're out.'

The pain in his eyes had been replaced with relief. This was what he wanted, to be treated like an adult and not handled with kid gloves. 'No parties,' I told him. 'No guests after 10pm. Do you have a job?'

'I'm going to look for one first thing tomorrow.' He was grinning now, his smile stretching from ear to ear.

'Fair enough. What questions do you have for me?'

Nick blinked: it didn't appear to have occurred to him that he had the right to ask questions of his own. 'Uh ... your advert said the flat was furnished?'

I nodded. 'There's a sofa, a table, four chairs, a cooker with a built-in oven and a bed. There's no washing machine but there's a laundrette at the end of the street.'

His brow furrowed; it would have been cute if I hadn't felt sorry for him. He was a man-child pretending to be an adult. 'Bedding?'

'I can arrange some for you before night falls.'

He was on a roll. 'And a television?'

It was a rare evening when you could get any sort of signal here, and the same went for the internet. Something about the magic that was bound into Coldstream messed with both of them, although the old landline telephone system worked well enough. Despite his upbringing, Nick ought to have known that.

'No chance,' I told him. 'And no point.'

'Fucking Coldstream,' he muttered.

I affected an offended expression. 'No swearing!'

His eyes dropped. 'Sorry.'

'Just don't do it again.' I tried not to smile. 'Any more questions?'

He was silent for a moment. 'Just one,' he said eventually. 'What's your name?'

This time I didn't try to hide my grin. Better late than never. 'Kit,' I told him. 'Kit

McCafferty.'

CHAPTER
TWO

L ess than twenty-four hours passed before they came for him. They were faster than I'd expected, even allowing for the scent-driven skills of werewolf trackers.

I was in the garden pruning the old rosebush that had chosen to bloom all year round and keeping an eye out for She Who Hisses when the first one appeared.

She didn't attempt to hide. She stalked down the road towards the house and took up position on the other side of the street, leaning against a lamp post and watching my every move. I ignored her. She wasn't a threat, not yet.

By the time I was gathering the cuttings into a bag, another werewolf had joined her; now two sets of lupine eyes were following me. I ignored the prickling sensation on the back of my neck.

Dave, the old druid who lived in the small house next to my larger property, hobbled out of his front door. He hawked up a ball of phlegm and spat it in their direction before leaning over the rickety fence that separated us. 'Somebody ought to do something about them,' he said.

I guessed he wanted me to be that somebody but I wasn't

stupid enough to rise to the bait. 'Morning, Dave,' I said cheer-fully. 'How are you today?'

He scowled in response. I didn't take offence: the deeper the scowl, the stronger Dave's affection. As an ex-con who'd done serious time for armed robbery, he hadn't smiled for decades and I suspected those particular facial muscles had atrophied.

'Several of your wee furry bastards have been shitting in my garden again,' he said.

'My apologies for that,' I offered, although I wasn't really sorry at all. Cats were going to cat. 'I'll pick up a repellent spell at the market later today.' A spell would be enough to keep them off his patch; it was a small price to pay for a quiet life.

As if on cue, He Who Crunches Bird Bones appeared through a gap in the fence on the other side of Dave's garden. He raised his white head, looked around, then sauntered to the centre of the small lawn and squatted, cat fashion. I met his green eyes for a moment before returning my attention to Dave. 'Is there anything else I can pick up for you while I'm out?'

'Wolfsbane,' he grunted.

'That's illegal,' I said. As he well knew.

'And?' Dave looked again at the two werewolves across the road. 'Trilby usually has some under the counter.'

Trilby sold everything under the counter, but I had a were-wolf tenant so wolfsbane would not be a solution. I patted Dave's shoulder. 'I'm sure those two won't hang around for long.'

His lip curled. 'Not if they know what's good for 'em.'

I wouldn't disagree with him on that point. I waved a brief farewell and returned my attention to my rosebush. There was a hedge witch at the market who'd take the cuttings off my hands and give me a few quid in return. I didn't care about the money but it was useful to remain on good terms with everyone in the community.

I tied the bag carefully. When I glanced back up, the two werewolves had vanished. A second later, I knew why.

'I slept in,' Nick said, with an abashed expression as he wandered outside. 'It's later than I thought.' He shielded his eyes against the sun. 'Thanks for the breakfast. You didn't have to do that.'

I'd left some orange juice and cereal outside his door. A lot of cereal – he was a teenage werewolf, after all, and he could probably eat a horse for breakfast. As Mrs Jones down the street kept a couple of Shetland ponies in her garden, it seemed wise to pre-empt any more neighbourly disputes. Given Nick's upbringing in the confines of normal human society in Glasgow, the ponies were probably safe but I didn't want to chance it.

'You're welcome,' I said. 'You've not had the chance to go shopping yet so I figured breakfast was the least I could do.'

He coughed delicately, which was out of odds with his personality. 'I am not very, uh, adept at cooking.' He ran a discomfited finger under his collar.

Nick was going to have to learn to be more direct. 'You'd like to borrow a cookbook?' I asked. 'I have several. You're very welcome to them.'

'No, I, uh, I...'

We could be here all day. I took pity on him. 'You'd like me to cook for you as well providing a roof over your head?'

His relief was palpable. 'Yes! I'll give you extra money. And I'm not fussy, I'll eat anything.'

'Even cats?' I asked.

He laughed nervously but at least he'd realised I was joking. 'Anything.'

It wouldn't be hard to cook larger portions, and cooking for one was always a depressing prospect. 'We can come to some sort of arrangement.' I waggled my fingers at him. 'But that will include cooking lessons. You have to learn how to feed yourself.'

He nodded happily. 'Thank you.' He beamed. 'You're not that bad for an old lady.'

I choked. I was forty-one.

The breeze shifted and the few rose petals I'd not managed to bag skittered across the garden. Nick's brow furrowed, his head jerked up and his nostrils flared as, somewhat belatedly, he caught the scent of the two werewolves.

So he wasn't a natural tracker. All werewolves possessed scent-tracking abilities but some were more adept than others and Nick clearly didn't fall into the adept category. I filed that information away and watched as he scanned the empty street with roving, restless eyes.

'Is something wrong?' I asked casually.

He didn't hear me so I repeated the question more loudly. This time it registered. His expression cleared as the breeze died down and he lost the scent. He shook his head, his shaggy hair flapping. 'No.' He shrugged. 'S'all good. I'm going to head out, if that's okay. I want to start looking for work.'

He didn't need my permission but I nodded anyway. 'Good luck.'

The moment he'd disappeared around the corner, the two watchers returned. Now I understood their game and I also understood why Nick had ended up in the dodgy part of Coldstream instead of one of the better neighbourhoods. He had enough cash to pay for a decent place but I reckoned that his uncle's pack were intimidating landlords to ensure wee Nick had nowhere to go. They wanted to back him into a corner so he felt he had no choice but to return to the furry fold of his family. They didn't want him to know they were interfering and they were giving him the illusion of choice; that meant those two were here for me, not Nick.

They'd start with a little intimidation, escalate to bribery then resort to violence if they didn't get their way. I sighed; I'd suspected it would come to this. I only had myself to blame for getting involved and letting Nick stay. I should have known better.

He Who Crunches Bird Bones abandoned Dave's garden for mine. As he wandered over his tail flicked from side to side to project his annoyance, then he blinked at me and gave a small, questioning miaow.

'You're pretty tough,' I told him. 'But you're no match for those two.'

His tail flicked harder.

'I mean it. Leave them to me. They won't hang around for long.'

He Who Crunches Bird Bones glared at me and I glared back. His fur bristled then he stalked away in a huff.

I mentally revised my day's schedule. There was a confrontation looming. If I wanted to avoid any of the five cats who lived with me getting involved, I ought to take control of the situation. It was time to vamoose.

I set off for the riverside market, my shopping bag slung over one shoulder and my bag of rosebush cuttings in my opposite hand. I'd barely taken three steps when the two werewolves peeled away from their side of the road and started to follow me. I reckoned that they'd accost me directly by the time I reached the McBarry house on the corner.

I lost my own bet; I'd gone less than twenty metres when I heard the trundling footsteps of an approaching wirry cow. I grimaced; with the events of the morning, I'd forgotten what day it was.

I spun on my heels and narrowly avoided colliding with the female werewolf, who was closer than I'd realised. Her expression was one of blank astonishment as, for a moment, she obviously thought I was about to engage in a fist fight right there on the pavement. Instead, I gave her a rueful smile.

'Sorry,' I said. 'Bin day!' I darted past her and her companion and rushed back home to haul out my rubbish bin and deposit it at my front gate.

I didn't really need to run: this particular wirry cow was old and she took her time lurching from house to house, but I wanted to get my rubbish out before the werewolves thought to stop me. It would be a pain in the arse if it piled up for another week. There were enough rats in this part of town as it was, and I didn't want to deal with the cats dragging any more small grey corpses into the house than was absolutely necessary.

I was slightly out of breath by the time I was done. As I passed the werewolves for a second time, they watched my progress with narrowed eyes. The wirry cow was already at the next house, chewing noisily on some broken glass while pawing through the remainder of the rubbish with a hungry eye.

Wirry cows could – and would – digest practically everything except plastic. It was for that reason very few plastic items were found in Coldstream. Naturally some plastic did appear, often left by visitors or newcomers like Nick, and it was astonishing what floated in via the River Tweed, but it was rare to purchase anything made of plastic within the city limits.

People used to complain about that, even though there was no way that a normal bin lorry could ever navigate most of Coldstream's narrow, winding streets, but nowadays most folk were proud about the absence of plastic. Various dignitaries from the less magically endowed parts of the country often visited hoping to learn some environmentally friendly tips that they could take back to their own communities. Like the rest of us Preternaturals, however, wirry cows preferred to live near the magic bound into Coldstream's earth. They'd never leave.

'Hi, Maggie,' I said as I passed her.

She stopped chewing long enough to snuffle at me, and I reached up and stroked her long nose. She shivered in delight before gently nudging me out of the way. Maggie had priorities and if I wasn't food, I wasn't one of them.

Patting her rump, I sidled past her and Maggie obliged by moving sideways until the road was completely blocked by her massive furry body. The werewolves would be trapped behind her for several minutes, which was good news. Although our confrontation was inevitable, it would be nice if I could get my shopping done before any blood was spilled.

I started to whistle and picked up my pace; if my luck held, there would still be some fresh morning loaves for sale.

CHAPTER

THREE

Close to 700,000 souls lived in Coldstream, so there were plenty of places to shop. The open-air market by the River Tweed was by far my favourite, even when it was blowing a hoolie and there was sideways hail. The ground there managed to be both sludgy and slippery, the aroma was often less than appetising, and you had to keep one eye on the murky depths of the river because there were numerous sharp-teethed creatures living in the water who'd take any opportunity to steal your shopping right out of your hands. Or grab a small child.

However, the market was also one of the few places in Coldstream that boasted a wide-open view. The river stretched in both directions, and the swathes of farmland, trees and small isolated buildings across the water and the border with England provided a treat for eyes used to crowded streets and higgledy-piggledy stone buildings.

It was true that not all the stallholders were friendly – in fact, some made a point of being as rude as possible – but they were honest to a fault. I've never heard of any of them trying to rip off a punter. For me, there was also considerable comfort in familiarity; I knew who these people were and I'd never come across any of them during my previous line of work, which counted for a lot.

I dropped off my bag of rose cuttings and spent a minute or two perusing the hedge-witch's wares before buying a small bottle of enchanted repellent that would keep the cats out of Dave's garden. It would also discourage birds, mice and insects but Dave wasn't interested in maintaining a healthy ecosystem so I figured that didn't matter.

Next I loped over to the baker and managed to snag his last seeded loaf together with several tasty-looking pastries that I suspected Nick would appreciate. By the time I was at the butcher's stall and considering the merits of a venison haunch, the two werewolves had caught up to me – and they were no longer interested in keeping their distance.

'I suppose you think you're clever,' the female hissed in my left ear before taking my arm.

The male appeared on my right and took hold of my other arm; they were clearly planning to frogmarch me out of the market. It was rare for anyone to be so brash and open with their violent intentions in such a public place.

The butcher, a muscular troll called Natasha with a penchant for swirling enchanted tattoos, sensed she was on the verge of losing a customer and took umbrage at the were-wolves' presence. 'Oi!' she bellowed. 'Leave that poor woman alone!'

I almost grinned. Poor woman. That was me.

'This doesn't concern you,' the male wolf growled. His voice was so deep and croaky that he sounded as if he'd swallowed a frog. I decided that Ribbit would be a good name for him.

I glanced at his lankier female companion. She had pursed her lips in an extraordinary duck-like fashion so I christened her Quack.

Natasha was not going to be intimidated by a pair of were-wolves. She placed her hands on her hips and glared at them. 'You're not regulars! You can't storm in here and harass people! You've got no right.'

I wondered whether that meant she'd have looked on their tactics more benevolently if they attended the market more frequently; anything was possible where Natasha was concerned.

I widened my eyes and affected a tremor. 'I've not done anything wrong,' I said quietly. 'I'm only doing my weekly shopping.'

Several of the other stallholders were eyeing us with interest. I spotted two young witches carefully lower their shopping bags to the ground and roll up their sleeves. This could end badly for the werewolves but fortunately, Ribbit and Quack had come to the same conclusion. They exchanged glances over my head and dropped their hands.

'We meant no disrespect,' Ribbit croaked.

Quack nodded. 'We only want to talk to her.' She paused then let her black coat fall open to reveal the silver insignia emblazoned on her chest.

I stiffened. I didn't need to examine the design to know what it meant: only one werewolf pack dared to use silver to advertise its family name. It wasn't that the colour was dangerous but by using it, even in embroidery, they were declaring they weren't afraid of anything. Nothing would stop them from getting what they wanted.

Shocked whispers rippled through the crowd. 'MacTire. They're MacTire wolves.'

Arse. Nick could have mentioned which pack his uncle hailed from – then again, I could have asked. It hadn't occurred to me it would be the MacTires and that changed things considerably.

I cleared my throat. 'Let me finish my shopping,' I said. 'I have to get some meat, then grab some veggies at the grocer's. Oh, and I'll pick up some fish for my cats at the fishmonger. I'll meet you for coffee at Black's.' I was going to have to talk to the werewolves sooner or later so it might as well be in a comfortable chair whilst I drank the best brew in Coldstream.

Suspicion clouded Ribbit's face. 'Twenty minutes,' I told him and looked at Quack. 'I give you my word.'

There was another sharp intake of breath from the onlookers. Metaphorically, I'd dropped to the ground and displayed my belly; then again, I was only a middle-aged woman with no weapons who was wearing old clothes covered in cat hair. My submission couldn't be *that* surprising.

'Fine,' Quack said. 'Twenty minutes.' She bared her teeth. 'Or you belong to us.'

Unsurprisingly, I was ushered to the front of the queue at the other stalls; nobody wanted to be the reason why I didn't show up at Black's on time. If I hadn't had other concerns, I'd have been touched.

I presented myself at the homely coffee shop with several minutes to spare. As soon as I walked through the doors, I was pointed towards the back where Quack and Ribbit were waiting. From their relaxed body language, they'd decided that the hard part was over and they'd won. The smart thing to do would be to give them their victory but unfortunately I wasn't always smart. Besides, something about Nick and his pain had tugged at my heart strings.

I sat opposite them and leaned forward. 'I did as you asked. I'm here. What do you want?'

They gave matching smirks. 'There's no need to sound so antagonistic, Ms McCafferty,' Quack said.

Ribbit nodded. 'Yes. Ms *Kit* McCafferty. We know who you are.'

I managed to avoid rolling my eyes; they knew my name but they had no idea who I was.

'Why don't you order a drink and then we'll discuss the matter properly?' Ribbit went on. 'Some chamomile tea, perhaps, to calm your nerves?'

I decided to play to type even though I really wanted a coffee. 'Sure.'

Within seconds an anxious waitress had placed the tea in front of me. I took a sip, scalded my lips and returned the cup to the table. 'So?' I asked. 'What do you want to talk to me about?'

Ribbit spoke first in a soothing, patronising tone. 'We know you're a nice lady and you don't mean any harm. You collect cats and you help strays. That's good of you.'

Quack took up the thread. 'But there's one stray that you're going to have to let go.'

I widened my eyes. 'Not She Who Loves Sunbeams? Please – she's been with me for years. She's an old cat, she doesn't deserve to be out on the streets.'

It took her a full moment to appreciate I was being disingenuous. MacTire werewolves were supposed to be intelligent but I was starting to revise that opinion.

'We're talking about the boy,' she said icily. 'He can't stay with you. You need to go home and tell him you've changed your mind. Tell him he has to leave.'

'I can't do that.'

'Tell him you need the space for more cats,' Ribbit said.

'Or that you're allergic to werewolves,' Quack suggested. 'We don't really care. Just make sure he's out of that flat by nightfall.'

My bottom lip jutted out. 'There are a lot of scary creatures on the streets at night. He might get hurt.'

'He won't,' Ribbit assured me. 'We're looking after him. Nobody will go near him.'

'He's not your concern, Ms McCafferty,' Quack added. 'You don't have to worry about him.' On cue, they both grinned at me; it wasn't particularly reassuring.

I picked up my cup and took another tentative sip. 'I'm afraid that I still can't do as you ask. I told him he could stay. He can leave any time of his own free will but I won't kick him out.'

Ribbit reached into his coat and took out a bulging wallet. 'Five grand,' he said. 'In cash.'

It felt like he was low-balling me. 'Sorry,' I said. 'But no.'

Quack nudged him. 'She deserves more than that for her trouble,' she chided, before upping the ante. 'Ten grand.'

My expression didn't alter. 'That's very generous of you.' Ribbit smiled again and started to take out the money. I shook my head. 'I'm not agreeing. I don't want your money.'

'Spend it on some cat food. It must be expensive keeping all those kitties happy. It'll go a long way towards looking after them.'

'They're already happy.' I eyed the cup of tea and decided to abandon my efforts to drink it. I took a small white handkerchief from my pocket and dabbed my mouth. 'I'm not taking your money. And the boy can stay as long as he wants.'

They weren't smiling now. 'How much?' Quack asked with a hint of a snarl. 'How much will it take? Because you don't want to make enemies of us, Ms McCafferty.'

I stood up. 'No,' I said simply. 'I don't want to do that.' I nodded. 'Have a good day.' And with that, I strolled out of the coffee shop.

Naturally they followed, nipping at my heels so closely that I could feel their hot breath on the back of my neck. I headed away from both the market and my home; there were a few quiet streets within walking distance where we could bring this nasty business to a head.

'Don't do anything stupid, Ms McCafferty,' Quack said.

Ribbit agreed. 'Help yourself by helping us. The boy means nothing to you.'

I turned into a narrow alley and walked past a series of brightly coloured posters advertising events for the upcoming winter solstice when all Coldstream residents were granted a public holiday. 'And you mean nothing to him,' I said pleasantly. 'You ought to accept that.'

The words were barely out of my mouth when one of the werewolves slammed a fist hard into the spot between my shoulder blades. My money was on Ribbit rather than Quack – he seemed the type of guy to hit someone when their back was turned.

I was sent flying and landed face first onto the dirty cobbles, and it was certainly Ribbit's hand that grabbed a hank of my hair and yanked my head upwards to spit words in my ear. 'You should have taken the money.'

Probably.

I jerked my leg up and kicked his knee hard enough to make him release his grip on my hair and howl. I sprang upwards and spun in mid-air to face him. My ribs were bruised from my fall and I was already panting. When had I gotten so out of shape and unused to pain?

I grimaced, then threw up a hand to block a blow from Quack. She snarled and threw another punch. I ducked and narrowly missed it. My reflexes definitely weren't what they used to be, and that was galling.

'I think you dislocated my knee, you bitch!' Ribbit shrieked.

I raised an eyebrow: it wasn't dislocated, it was probably

barely bruised. I raised my leg and kicked his other knee and this time there was a sickening pop. *That* one was dislocated.

He collapsed, a writhing, howling pile of whine. One down. One to go.

Quack was staring at me as if I were a psychopath. I had plenty of empathy for my fellow man – or woman – but if you came at me from behind you had to take the consequences. It was rude. With that thought in mind, I eyed her height. This would hurt, but it would be worth it.

Most people think a headbutt involves smashing your forehead into your opponent's forehead, but an effective headbutt requires you use the strongest part of your skull and slam it into the weakest part of your opponent's face. Depending on your species, that's usually your crown and their nose. The move wouldn't have served me well if it had been a full moon and Quack had been in wolf form, but at that moment it was all I needed. And I was shorter than her, which gave me a useful advantage.

I launched my head forward with all the force I could muster and broke her nose. All in a day's work. Maybe I wasn't so rusty after all.

Bright-red blood streamed down her face, but Quack was stronger than her friend; despite the pain and obvious humiliation, she wasn't ready to quit. Her eyes were full of venom – and she'd located a knife from somewhere in the folds of her jacket.

She meant business. She jabbed it forward, slicing the blade through the air with unerring speed. I was caught off-guard and the tip caught my cheek, piercing my flesh. It hurt more than it should have done and I wondered briefly if the metal was coated in poison. It was the sort of daft thing I'd expect from inexperienced fighters like these two, although I reckoned I *deserved* to die horribly after allowing myself to be cut with such ease.

I sighed, snapped forward and curled my hand around her wrist, squeezing it tight. Quack cried out and dropped the knife. There: that was better.

I bent to pick it up so I could examine the blade for signs of a poisonous coating. As I did, I caught sight of two slitted eyes watching me from behind a pile of damp cardboard boxes. It was She Who Hisses. She must have been hanging around the market searching for easy pickings around the fishmonger's stall.

I kneed Quack in the stomach so that she collapsed beside Ribbit, then I pocketed the knife and moved away from the moaning werewolves. It was time to coax a kitty. Perhaps this day wouldn't turn out to be so pathetically shite after all.

CHAPTER
FOUR

Nick was sitting on the doorstep when I returned home and heaved myself through the garden gate. He Who Roams Wide was lying on the grass less than three metres away. As a large black tomcat with a brazen attitude, not much fazed him, not even a twitchy teenage were-wolf. He was similar to He Who Must Sleep in that regard, even though they had little else in common.

The cat ignored my entrance but Nick leapt to his feet in alarm. 'Jesus!' he exclaimed. 'Have you been in a fight?'

My clothes were dirty and torn in several places. There was at least one deep scratch on my cheek and several on my hands and arms, but nothing about my appearance was related to my fight with Quack and Ribbit. My current state was all down to She Who Hisses.

I pulled a face. Nick darted to my side and grabbed my arm as if to help me stumble into the house. My glare intensified and thankfully he got the message and released me. I was perfectly capable of walking.

Sensing my displeasure, He Who Roams Wide lifted his

head and looked at me. 'Yes,' I told him. 'It was She Who Hisses.'

The cat blinked. 'No,' I said through gritted teeth. 'She ran away.' *Again.*

His tail flicked and he lowered his head back to the ground.

Nick squinted, his confusion obvious. 'She Who Hisses?'

'The black cat you scared away yesterday,' I explained.

'That's her name? She Who Hisses?'

I nodded.

'Weird name. Why don't you call her Hissy or something more normal?'

'Like what?' I asked drily. 'Tiger? Blackie? Socks? She Who Hisses is what she calls herself. Cats are perfectly capable of christening themselves.' I pointed. 'That's He Who Roams Wide. The least I can do is show them respect by using their preferred names.'

Nick took a step backwards. 'Ms McCafferty,' he said. 'Do you ... talk to cats?'

He was remarkably naïve, even given his upbringing away from Coldstream. 'Doesn't everyone?' I asked mildly. 'And I think *we're* on first name terms now, Nick. Call me Kit.'

He continued to eye me as if I were crazy, though cat-lady crazy, not murderous maniac crazy so I supposed it could have been worse.

'Anyway,' I said, 'how did you get on with your job hunting? Did you have any luck?'

His expression transformed. He bit his lip and nodded, putting me in mind of a small child clutching a stick of candy floss. 'There's a construction crew working out of the Glebe,' he said, naming the warehouse district that bordered Danksville. 'They've agreed to take me on probation. It'll be scut work but the money's not bad and it might lead to better things.'

'Uh-huh. What's the name of the crew?' I'd have to check

them out and make sure they were above board; there were plenty of unscrupulous people around who'd be happy to take advantage of a kid like Nick.

'The Crushers.'

They didn't sound very friendly. Did the name mean Skull Crushers or Candy Crushers? My mouth tightened but Nick didn't notice.

'The foreman is a bloke called Tommy. He's half-ogre, but he's really nice. He gave me a tour of the site and said that they've been looking for someone like me to join their team. I'll get three hundred a week until I pass probation, then it'll go up to five hundred.'

That wasn't a bad deal for someone of his age without any experience or obvious family connections. It could be above board – or they could be hoping to use young Nick as a sacrifice to appease any nasty creatures that were lurking around which-ever warehouse they were working on. I'd find out.

Such dark thoughts weren't plaguing Nick, who was hopping excitedly from toe to toe. 'I like the idea of building things,' he beamed. 'Creating something useful. *Contributing*.' His eyes shone. 'I can do this, Ms McCafferty. I can be good at this.'

'Kit,' I said to him. 'Not Ms McCafferty.'

He didn't hear me. His expression had taken on a distant gleam as no doubt he imagined himself designing and building skyscrapers. I softened further. This, I decided: this was the reason I was fighting his cause. He deserved to forge his own path and experience life for himself.

'My dad would be really proud of me,' he mumbled.

'Yeah,' I said. 'I imagine he would be.'

～

I PICKED up the pile of mail that had landed on my doormat and flicked through it with a disinterested eye: three bills, and a whole heap of junk mail advertising a series of druid-led yoga sessions; a subscription service for a range of useless magical ingredients, and something exhorting me to spend the winter solstice at Crackendon Square. It was all rubbish.

I dropped the letters and flyers into the bin without another thought then I put away the shopping and busied myself tidying up before schooling Nick in the art of peeling potatoes and chopping onions in preparation for dinner. He approached the tasks with gusto, even though the onions made him cry harder than I had when She Who Loves Sunbeams had given birth to a litter of four poorly kittens who didn't make it through their first night.

Before too long it occurred to me that I'd forgotten to pick up tomatoes during the excitement of the morning's activities, so I sent him to buy some. Tears were still streaming down his cheeks. It was quite a sight as he lolloped off, a bag in one hand, a pastry in the other, a contented grin and a lot of crying. At least the boy was happy to be making himself useful.

Once he'd gone, I went outside to put down food for the neighbourhood ferals – my motley crew would eat later. As I did every afternoon, I replenished the water bowls and laid out several plates of cat food. Usually the cats were waiting, ready to pounce as soon as the food was down, but today there was no sign of them. Even He Who Roams Wide had vanished.

Something was up. Unfortunately, I suspected I knew what it was.

There was no sign of any werewolf watchers but just because I couldn't see any of them didn't mean they weren't out there. I stepped away from the food, went to the gate and peered up and down the street. At first the way seemed clear, then I glimpsed the car trundling in my direction.

Only the uber-wealthy drive in Coldstream because something about the innate magic in the city makes cars break down frequently. Maintaining them is an expensive process, and keeping a petrol-driven vehicle is next to impossible, although electric cars tended to be more affordable. Or so I'd heard.

I rarely travelled far enough to make owning a car of any description worthwhile. Since I'd left my last job, I'd had no reason to stray from Coldstream. If I needed to head into the city centre, I jumped on a tram and walked the rest of the way. Trams were reliable and there was no chance of being diverted down an unusual road only to end up stuck in a too-narrow street. Given the powerful coven of witches who ran the tram network, there was also far less chance of random hijackings even in this dodgy neighbourhood, and for that I was grateful. There was nothing quite like the experience of being trussed up in a corner by a bunch of violent, spell-wielding idiots to ruin your day.

The car rolled to a halt outside my gate. Its windows were tinted so I couldn't identify the occupants, but that didn't stop several of my neighbours from twitching their curtains and gawping. It had been a long time since a car had driven down this road, so it would be the talk of the street for days to come. To be honest, it was a miracle its wheels were still intact; there were enough deep potholes in Danksville to rip most tyres to shreds.

I watched warily while the driver's door opened and a woman stepped out. Her authority and power were obvious: she held herself in a manner that didn't so much suggest 'don't fuck with me' as 'please fuck with me because breaking every bone in your body will make my day'. I already liked her.

Quack and Ribbit must have been the Z-list of MacTire werewolves but this woman, with her sleek black hair, perfect poise and clever green eyes that didn't miss a trick, was definitely A-list. These werewolves really wanted Nick back in the fold.

She carefully adjusted her cuffs as if she didn't already know I was watching her then lifted her head and smiled at me. Her smile didn't reach her eyes but her expression was more professional than threatening. 'Good afternoon, Ms McCafferty,' she said and gestured to the car. 'Please step inside. I'd like to take you for a drive.'

No, thanks. 'I was brought up not to speak to strangers,' I said. 'And I don't want to go for a drive.'

I caught a flicker of amusement in her face. 'It's not a question of what *you* want, Ms McCafferty, it's what *we* need.'

'Is that the royal "we"?' I asked.

On cue, the rear passenger doors opened and two burly male werewolves stepped out wearing identical dark suits. They gazed at me as if I were a tasty morsel; one of them even licked his lips.

'No,' the woman said. 'It's not.'

I considered my choices. 'I'm still declining the offer,' I told her.

I expected the two suited goons to rush forward and try to bundle me into the vehicle but the woman surprised me. She nodded and reached into the car for something, though she didn't pull out a weapon or produce a threatening spell; what she pulled out was a cat carrier.

I stared at the carrier, then at her. Well played, scary lady. Well played. I had to hand it to Quack and Ribbit as well. Despite their injuries, they must have been paying greater attention to me in the alleyway this morning than I'd realised.

From inside the carrier, two very annoyed yellow eyes shone balefully in my direction. She Who Hisses lived up to her name and hissed.

'How about a trade-off?' The woman pointed to the carrier.

'Two hours of your time for...' her mouth tightened '...this delightful creature.'

I sighed. Score one to the werewolf in the power suit.

∼

The goons left the carrier with She Who Hisses inside my front door, which suggested they expected to return me later in the day – or that's what they wanted me to think. Either way, I played nice and climbed into the back seat.

'You know,' I said, as they sandwiched me between them like a slice of ham, 'it's faster to take the tram.'

Nobody deigned to answer; they'd gotten what they wanted and were no longer interested in conversation. The woman put her foot down and expertly reversed the vehicle. If I'd been hoping to witness the shiny car getting stuck down a narrow street, I was going to be disappointed because it was obvious she knew what she was doing. In any case, by the time she'd manoeuvred into a forward-facing position, the goons had plonked a velvet hood over my head. To add to my irritation, they tied my hands together. It felt like overkill but I knew better than to complain.

I could have spent the journey trying to work out where we were heading but I already knew. I leaned back and figured I might as well take the opportunity for a catnap. I performed far better when I was well rested, and one should never miss the chance of a little snooze.

I must have slept more deeply than I'd intended because one of the goons had to shake me awake when we arrived. They hauled me out of the car and half-dragged, half-pushed me into a building. I sensed wooden floors and wide hallways.

Hands pressed down on my shoulders and I was forced into a chair; only then was the hood yanked off my head.

I blinked and looked around. I was in the centre of a large room with shuttered windows, a roaring fire and lots of solid-looking furniture of the sort that was handed down through generations rather than purchased on a budget for the short term.

'She fell asleep on the way here,' Goon One announced.

From behind me a smooth voice drawled, 'Did she, indeed? Either she is very stupid or very confident.'

'Or very tired,' I said aloud.

There was a short laugh. 'That's also a possibility.' There were footsteps then their owner walked around and faced me. Alexander MacTire, head of the MacTire pack. I'd expected as much.

'Greetings, Ms McCafferty,' he said. 'You've been causing me some problems today.'

I looked him up and down. He held his wolf well; truthfully, if I hadn't already known who he was, I'd have questioned if he were a werewolf at all. His hair was dark, albeit peppered with shots of silver, and his skin was tanned. While I didn't get the same sense of simmering potential from him that I'd got from the woman, he exuded authority. This was someone who was used to being in command and who enjoyed the role of leader. But I already knew that.

'Do you like what you see?' he asked, raising an eyebrow.

I managed a shrug. 'There's not much of a resemblance between you and your nephew.'

'He favours his father. His mother was my younger sister.'

'Did you have her killed?'

MacTire looked genuinely astonished – and he wasn't the only one surprised by my question. The nearest goon back-handed me with enough strength to send me flying off the chair and I landed on the floor with a heavy thump. Ouch.

To give him his due, Alexander MacTire was at my side in a second to help me up while glaring at his minion. 'We don't do that,' he said with quiet menace. 'Leave us.'

'Boss—'

MacTire didn't bother repeating himself. I felt the temperature in the room drop several degrees, then there was a rustle of fabric followed by a near-inaudible whisper. 'Yes, boss. Sorry, boss.'

There were footsteps then MacTire and I were alone. 'My apologies,' he said, gently returning me to the chair and untying the rope around my hands. 'My people can be somewhat over-zealous at times.'

Uh-huh.

'But you have to admit that your question was very rude – more than rude, in fact. For a mere cat lady, you tread a dangerous line. I loved my sister and I liked her husband. Both their deaths were the result of a tragic accident.' His voice hardened. 'I am not in the habit of killing off my family members.'

I didn't comment. MacTire watched me for a moment before taking another chair and sliding it opposite mine. He took off his jacket, placed it carefully on the chair back and sat down. 'Who are you?' he asked softly.

'My name is Kit McCafferty.'

'I know your name. I want to know who you are.'

He was a lot smarter than Quack and Ribbit. 'I'm exactly what you see. A middle-aged cat lady looking for a quiet life.'

He didn't miss a beat. 'If that were true, you wouldn't have slapped down my people this morning.'

I snorted. 'It's not my fault your werewolves are useless. They have far more confidence than skill.'

'Not any more.'

I inclined my head. 'Then I'm glad to have been of service. However, you don't want to know who I am, Mr MacTire, you just want your nephew back.'

He leaned back in his chair. 'Nicholas needs a firm guiding hand. He needs to be with me, with *family*.'

'He doesn't want to be in your pack.'

'Right now he doesn't know what he wants. He's still grieving for his parents.'

'Exactly,' I shot back. 'You need to give him space and time. Anything else and he'll resent you. You don't want that.'

MacTire linked his hands. 'He only showed up at your door yesterday. What's your angle? Did you lure him to you?'

I almost laughed. 'I'm not that kind of person. He saw my advert and he answered it. Nothing more, nothing less.'

'Then why do you care what happens to him?'

I shrugged. 'I'm a sucker for lost souls.'

He continued to eye me, his dark eyes glittering. 'Nah,' he said eventually. 'I'm not buying it. This is what is going to happen, Ms McCafferty. You are going to leave here unharmed, and in return you will tell my nephew that he is no longer welcome to stay with you. I will take care of him. He will be safe with me.'

'Like his parents were?'

For the first time Alexander MacTire's mask cracked. 'As I've already told you, that was an accident,' he bit out. 'I want Nicholas where I can keep an eye on him to ensure there are no *more* accidents.' He was too smooth and too practiced for me to judge his sincerity.

My best move would have been to walk away. I didn't know Nick, I certainly didn't owe him anything and his uncle might be telling the truth about having his best interests at heart. But nobody should be forced into a situation against their will;

nobody should be pushed into a life they hadn't chosen for themselves.

'Unfortunately accidents happen,' I said after a few moments' thought. 'And they seem to happen regularly to the MacTire pack. You became pack alpha when your father met an unhappy,' I paused before emphasising the word, '*accident.*'

'My father died of a heart attack,' he said stiffly.

'Mmm.'

His eyes flashed with anger but I ploughed ahead regardless. 'You asked who I am, Mr MacTire. I really am a middle-aged cat lady but I've not always been that person. I retired from my job three years ago.'

His brow furrowed. 'Aren't you a little young to retire?'

'My previous employer requires everyone to hang up their proverbial hat at the ripe old age of thirty-eight. They have their reasons for enforcing that rule – good reasons, mostly.'

MacTire's anger had been replaced by wariness. 'Who was your previous employer?'

I smiled. 'Eagle Enforcers and Liquidators – EEL. Our paths have crossed before, Mr MacTire, although you probably weren't aware of it because we didn't meet in person when you hired EEL four years ago. In fact, you were one of my last clients. I'm the person who helped your father with his ... heart attack.'

I lowered my voice and took a breath. Here we go. 'That's how I know his death wasn't an accident. He wasn't ill, he was the picture of health until an hour or so before his passing. So while you might not be in the habit of killing off family members, you have done so at least once. His death was at my hands but it was on your orders.'

MacTire didn't so much as twitch. 'You're an assassin,' he breathed.

'As I said,' I murmured, 'I'm retired.'

CHAPTER
FIVE

I suspected it was rare that Alexander MacTire was unsettled. He loosened his tie, stood up and started to pace around the room. My eyes tracked his movements; I was curious about what he'd do next.

To be fair, he'd had good reason to order the hit on his dad, even though it was a highly unusual move to make on your own alpha. Pack leadership didn't necessarily follow a direct genetic line; typically the most powerful werewolf was chosen to become leader, not the one with the closest family links.

It wasn't ambition that had caused Alexander MacTire to request a contract on his father. Alexander MacTire's reasons hadn't been because he craved a pay rise or a new job description.

While it wasn't up to me to judge my clients' choices, I had always been allowed to refuse jobs and there were plenty over the years that I'd turned down. I'd always researched my targets thoroughly, not only to find out why someone wanted them dead but also to ensure I wasn't being set up. I had trusted my employers at EEL, but everyone makes mistakes and they expected me to double check. I had been one of their best killers for a reason.

To put it mildly, Bruce MacTire had been a bastard. He'd abused his wife – Alexander MacTire's mother – and the string of women he'd had affairs with over the years; given his horrific treatment, they were lucky they were still alive. He had led his pack with an unerring dogmatism towards war with two of the other powerful werewolf packs in Coldstream and sent several young werewolves to their deaths as a result.

There were numerous allegations of brutality against him, including stories of children he'd hurt. He'd been one of those men who didn't care who he damaged in his quest to achieve power, and he'd only been interested in that power for power's sake.

Despite all his faults, however, werewolves were a loyal bunch and it was testament to Alexander MacTire's strength of character that he'd ordered the hit. Breaking pack loyalty, even when it was justified, was incredibly rare. I'd heard it caused real physical pain. Also, if it ever got out that his own son had ordered their alpha's death, the rest of the pack would be obliged to take action against Alexander MacTire, whether they wanted or to not. Werewolves were weird that way. No doubt that was why he'd hired EEL instead of killing his father himself.

Alexander MacTire had plenty of reasons to keep me quiet. None of his werewolves cared about me but they would care a great deal if I told them what I knew. If he'd inherited any of his father's less savoury genes, he would no doubt try to kill me there and now – or at least he'd try to. It would be his safest move.

After pacing the same piece of floor several times, MacTire stopped and turned to face me. 'EEL pride themselves on their vows of secrecy. If they found out that you're talking openly about this...'

He went up a notch in my estimation; at least he wasn't trying to deny his culpability. 'I'm not talking about it openly, am I? Nobody else is in this room and you already know what you did. I'm breaking no vow and neither shall I.'

He took three strides towards me and got into my face. His breathing was controlled and measured but I knew he was seething. 'Is this why you took in Nick?' His snarl was quiet but menacing. 'Because of this? Because of me?'

My heart rate ratcheted up and my imaginary traffic lights flicked from green to amber. I was in dangerous territory. 'I didn't know who Nick was to begin with. I didn't realise you were related until those two idiots approached me this morning.'

He pulled back and folded his arms across his broad chest. 'What do you want, Ms McCafferty?'

'It's not about what *I* want. It's about what *Nick* wants.' I sighed. 'Look, barely anyone except my ex-employer knows what I used to do for a living, and that knowledge gives you power over me. I don't want anyone coming after me because of my past work.' I kept my voice calm and reasonable. 'I'm not threatening you – I am no threat to you at all. I'm simply trying to help a confused kid sort himself out.'

He didn't speak. I took that as a positive step and continued. 'I could kick Nick out and he'd wander around Coldstream for a few days then either return to you – and spend the rest of his life resenting both you and the pack – or vamoose without a backwards glance. Lone werewolves rarely live long, especially if they choose to leave this city. If you give him some breathing space, he can think through his options and make a decision about his future with a clear head. It might not be the decision you want, but that's up to him. In fact, if he knows you're giving him the time he needs, he'll think more of you. You're not your father – and you can't scare him into making the choice you want.'

MacTire growled. 'He's young and often foolish. One stupid move and he'll get himself killed. For the sake of my sister – for *Nicholas*'s sake – I have to keep him safe.'

I read the subtext: because he hadn't been able to keep Nick's parents safe; he hadn't kept his own baby sister safe. This had nothing to do with control and everything to do with grief. The same raw pain I'd seen in Nick was in Alexander MacTire, simply buried deeper.

'I've already proved my capabilities against your werewolves. I can keep Nick out of trouble,' I said gently. I paused. 'Well, most trouble.'

'You probably can.' MacTire ran a hand through his hair. 'I can't bribe you?'

'Nope.'

'I can't intimidate you?'

'Nope.'

'I can't kill you?'

I grinned. 'You can try.'

He didn't smile back.

Something inside me gave way: I wasn't only a sucker for lost souls but also for sob stories. 'Give him a month,' I said. 'Give him the time alone that he's craving, then take him out for dinner. See which way the land lies. You'll likely find him more amenable once he's had a chance to experience life on his own terms.'

A muscle throbbed in MacTire's jaw. He knew I was right, he just didn't want to admit it. 'If anything happens to him...'

'He'll be fine.'

MacTire gazed at me. 'One month. After that I will reassess the situation.'

I released a breath. 'That's your prerogative.'

'Alright.' He looked away. 'You should leave before I change my mind.'

As I stood up, my mental traffic lights flicked back to green. That had gone better than I'd expected. 'Thank you.'

'I'm not doing this for you.'

'I know,' I said simply and started to walk away. I hesitated at the door and turned back to him. 'For what it's worth, not all your people are useless. The woman who brought me here...'

'Samantha.'

'Samantha. She would have done well at EEL.' It was the highest compliment I could give.

MacTire seemed to understand that I was trying to acknowledge the power within the pack and, by default, that the power he commanded made him someone to respect. He nodded stiffly.

And with that, I left.

～

I WAS FORCED to go through the rigmarole of wearing the same dark hood when I was driven away from the MacTire property. I knew exactly where the house was located – I even knew its weak points. After all, four years ago I'd broken into that very house to kill Bruce MacTire.

I had to pretend otherwise, however, so I suffered the indignity of being rendered sightless. At least the MacTire wolves didn't tie my wrists this time – and neither did they bother driving me all the way home.

They dropped me off at Crackendon Square, hauled off the hood and shoved me out of the back seat so I stumbled onto the cobbles. I blinked hard to adjust my vision and relaxed. They'd done me a favour by dropping me near a tram that ran back to the edge of Danksville only a short walk from my house. I'd be home in no time. Only a few people were waiting at the tram stop as I ambled over to wait.

I had been fortunate that Alexander MacTire had listened to me and that I'd remained in one piece. While I definitely possessed well-honed, hard-won skills that could get me out of many dire situations, and I'd faced him with the serene confidence of a winner, I was far from invincible.

I could take two werewolves – if they were like Quack and Ribbit I could probably take half a dozen – but against the likes of Alexander MacTire, Samantha or the many MacTire werewolves who doubtless resided in their grand house? I wouldn't have a hope, not without considerable preparation. No matter how good you are there is always someone better, and greater numbers almost always beat greater skill.

I wasn't the only lucky one because today's venture was very good news for young Nick. I hoped he'd appreciate his freedom and use his time to make the right decision about his future. I mentally patted myself on the back. I'd done good.

I leaned against the wall next to yet more posters advertising the upcoming solstice and glanced down the street. A horn blasted and a moment later the tram shoogled into view, shaking its way towards the stop. Sparks danced around its snaking form as it slowed down. I'd long since suspected that those purple flickers of light were an artifice used by the witches who ran the tram system to remind commuters of the built-in magic that kept them safe. What you saw in Coldstream was often not what you got.

I reached into my pocket for the tram token that I knew was buried there, and which I always carried with me for an eventuality such as this one. As I moved my head, I caught a brief glimpse of another werewolf standing about fifty metres away underneath the awning of an old antique shop. He wasn't looking in my direction but, from his stiff body language, I suddenly sensed that he was there for me. I had no proof, but my gut instinct had served me well over the years and I wasn't about to mistrust it now.

It didn't make sense that he was a MacTire wolf because Alexander MacTire had cleared me – at least for the time being – and the MacTires knew where I lived, so they didn't need to follow me around. If they were going to tail anyone it would be Nick; despite my assurances, they'd want to ensure his safety.

I chewed my bottom lip and took out the token. There were several ways to test the wolf and my paranoia and I opted for the simplest one.

I fiddled with the brass token then, with a show of clumsiness, I let it tumble from my fingers onto the road. I let out a sharp cry of dismay and lurched forward to grab it.

A couple of the other people waiting called out.

'What are you doing?'

'The tram is coming! Get out of the way!'

I ignored them and the approaching tram and stooped to pick up the token. As I did so, I turned my head; the waiting passengers were watching me with morbid fascination. I suspected that at least some of them were hoping to witness a bloody mess as I was run over.

The one person who wasn't watching me was the damned werewolf, who continued to studiously avoid looking in my direction. That settled it: he was definitely following me.

I scooped up the token and jumped back in the nick of time before the tram creaked to a halt at the spot where I'd just crouched down. The witch driver glared at me; the last thing he wanted was to deal with my corpse on his tram tracks.

I offered a sheepish shrug by way of apology and took my position at the back of the queue while I sifted through an array of mental images in an attempt to identify my erstwhile follower. I'd only caught a glimpse of him but I'd seen enough to register his face. He had bright-red hair shorn close to his skull and his skin was only lightly tanned in the manner of a true ginger. He had a crooked nose, suggesting it had been broken at one point and not healed properly, and his clothes were baggy to conceal his physique. The fact that he didn't want to display his physique told me that he was either incredibly skinny and weak or completely the opposite, and I suspected the latter. I was also certain that I'd never seen him before in my life.

I shuffled up the queue and waited for my turn to board. Just before I stepped up, I heard footsteps behind me. He had decided to get on the tram with me and, no doubt, track me all the way to my front door. I caught a faint whiff of unwashed clothes overlaid with vetiver, woody, leather notes bound together with a hint of citrus, before I hopped onto the tram and handed my token to the scowling driver. Then I paused.

The werewolf followed me and gave his own token to the driver. I squeezed into a narrow spot at the front, forcing him to pass me by, then I coughed loudly, spun round and leapt off the tram just as the doors started to close.

I landed on the pavement and turned in time to see the driver's irritation deepen but the werewolf only stared at me from the other side of the window showing no discernible emotion. The horn blasted again and the tram trundled away with the red-headed werewolf still aboard.

I exhaled. I had no more tokens with me. So much for public transport; I was going to have to walk home instead.

CHAPTER
SIX

I kept my wits about me during the long hike through the streets of Coldstream in case the werewolf had jumped off at the next stop and doubled back. If he were a tracker, he'd already have my scent in his nostrils and he'd locate me within minutes.

Although it was unlikely I could disguise my scent, I skirted close to several stinking open drains. If I'd had any money on me, I could have detoured to a witchery store and purchased a masking spell to conceal myself but unfortunately, although I was smart enough to always carry a tram token in my pocket, I didn't always carry cash.

There was no sign of the werewolf, though, and that in itself was curious. If he wasn't a skilled tracker then why would someone have sent him after me? Surely any of the packs that were curious about me would have used somebody who could stay close – unless, of course, whoever had ordered Mr Red to follow me had underestimated my abilities even more than the MacTires had done.

Without more information, it wasn't a problem I could solve. Maybe the werewolf had happened to be passing the

MacTire stronghold and seen my hooded body being bundled in or out of it and followed to satisfy his curiosity. He might have already lost interest. Whoever he was, I wasn't going to lose any sleep over him. I told myself to be proud of my day's achievements and pushed him out of my mind.

It was late evening by the time I turned onto my street. My feet were sore and I was longing for a hot bath. I heaved myself along the last few hundred metres and turned into my front garden. Before I did anything else, I had to deal with She Who Hisses. The gnarly cat would not be happy.

Dave waved at me from his window and I felt a brief rush of warmth. He wasn't stupid enough to have gotten involved in my abduction but he'd kept an eye out for my return. I waved back and he scowled; all was right in the world.

I opened my front door and stepped inside, desperately pleased to be home. Part of me hoped that Nick had taken the initiative and finished the cooking we'd started that morning but there was no aroma of home-cooked food, delicious or otherwise. There was, however, a very angry cat in the carrier near my feet and a large paper bag filled to the brim with the tomatoes I'd asked Nick to buy.

I left them where they were and focused on my more immediate problem. She Who Hisses was already emitting a low-pitched growl and I could see a line of black fur standing on end along her spine.

I sighed and scooped up the carrier. 'I'm sorry,' I told her. 'This wasn't the way I would have chosen to do things but it will be for the best, I promise you.'

She glared at me, her narrowed eyes promising dark vengeance. I cooed at her and hauled her into the kitchen where nothing had been touched since I'd left earlier in the day.

I pushed aside the chopping board and the prepped onions and carrots and got to work. From my special cupboard I selected several dried herbs then reached to the back for a sprinkling of magical enhancement powder. That ought to do the trick – at least I hoped it would.

I wasn't particularly skilled in spell-craft; for one thing I wasn't a witch, and it was rare for non-witches to be able to cast anything useful on spec. But witches were business people and they were happy to sell their wares to anyone who needed them, so I maintained a healthy supply of magical medicines. I only needed an extra sprinkling of weak magic to bring the ingredients to life and I could manage that much.

I chatted to She Who Hisses as I worked. 'It really won't be that bad,' I told her as I measured out the ingredients. 'First I'm going to send you to sleep...' she gave a low screech of righteous indignation '...though not for long,' I assured her. 'Ten minutes at most.'

She yowled again, although there was less fury in it this time.

'Then I'll apply an ointment to that nasty wound to sort out the infection. You'll be healed in no time.'

The kitchen door creaked as He Who Must Sleep nudged it open with his paw. He yawned, wandered inside and looked up at me. I knew that all five of my cats would have kept their distance from She Who Hisses while I'd been gone because they wouldn't have trusted the cat carrier to hold her for any length of time. Now I was back, they'd wend their way to me, hungry and annoyed that I'd missed their usual dinner hour.

'I'm guessing you've been snoozing away in the back all day long,' I said.

He blinked at me lazily then stretched. She Who Hisses watched his every move with undisguised malevolence.

'Where are the others?' I asked. He Who Must Sleep blinked again.

I shrugged and returned to my potion, rubbed the mixture

of dried herbs between my fingertips then scattered them over the cat carrier. I received a furious hiss in return but fortunately the herbs were still potent enough for it to be short-lived. There was a thump as She Who Hisses collapsed.

Now I had to work quickly. I unzipped the carrier and carefully lifted her out. Her fur was dirty, suggesting that she'd had a particularly hard time lately and hadn't been inclined to groom herself. Laying her on her side, I examined the wound before I set about cleaning it.

The edges were ragged and I reckoned she'd been attacked by something; hopefully it had been a wild animal and not a Preternatural who'd decided, as Nick had suggested, to put cats on the menu. I cleaned away the pus and the dried blood then gently rubbed in the special ointment and murmured a basic incantation.

He Who Must Sleep started to purr, indicating that the magic was filling the room. That was good. As long as She Who Hisses didn't try anything stupid, the wound would heal within hours.

Her eyes were starting to twitch so I hastily completed my ministrations, picked her up and carried her into the small back room. I made her a warm bed with some blankets and left a litter tray, plenty of food and several empty boxes that she could hide in or behind if she wanted to. She could stay there for twenty-four hours before I released her back into the wild. I already knew she wouldn't choose to stay with me; She Who Hisses was not that sort of cat.

When I returned to the kitchen, He Who Must Sleep had jumped onto the windowsill and was staring into the garden. I followed his gaze; all four of my other cats were outside, perched on the wall, their eyes wide and their ears pinned back.

I washed my hands and ambled outside to talk to them. 'She's been taken care of and she's locked in the back so she won't disturb you. You can come in for dinner. I'm sorry I'm late getting it to you.'

None of them made a move and I frowned. I'd taken care of plenty of feral cats in the past: there was one large tom cat called He Who Fathers Many Litters who'd been so badly injured he'd stayed for a full week and kept half the street awake at night with his furious protests. Although they'd kept their distance, none of my house cats were bothered by his presence, so what was the problem with She Who Hisses?

I put my hands on my hips. 'She won't hurt you and she's going to recover quickly,' I reiterated. 'There's really no need to worry.'

That was when He Who Crunches Bird Bones raised his head and looked pointedly towards the first floor of the house. My stomach dropped as I realised that the cats' wariness had nothing to do with She Who Hisses; it had to be related to Nick. He Who Must Sleep was still staring at us from the kitchen window. He was the only one who hadn't noticed anything, probably because he'd been fast asleep.

'What is it?' I asked as snaking tendrils of dread filtered through my body. 'What's happened to him?'

The four cats dropped their heads and avoided my eyes. As I stared at them, I belatedly noticed the long black mark on She Without An Ear's left flank; it looked like an acid burn. He Who Crunches Bird Bones had a similar wound on his tail.

I glanced around and spotted the same mark scorched into the ground. Somebody had been here – somebody had attacked my cats. I hissed and moved over to them. The wounds were shallow and would heal quickly but that didn't make me feel any better.

Quickly returning to the house, I jogged up the communal stairs until I reached Nick's small flat. The smashed front door was hanging off its hinges and my anxiety intensified tenfold. Oh no: this was not good at all.

Tension made my limbs feel stiff and awkward as I went inside and the iron scent of lupine blood reached my nostrils. I had a horrible premonition that I was going to walk into the living room and find Nick's dead body. I swallowed hard. I didn't want this but I had to see the truth for myself.

I held my breath as I walked down the small hallway then paused and tilted my head. Whatever had happened here was over; there was nobody inside the flat. Nobody alive, anyway.

I closed my eyes briefly then stepped into the living room and looked around. No Nick and no body, though there was a puddle of blood in the middle of the floor and the outline of several splatters along one wall that someone had tried to clean up but which had left a mark on the fresh paintwork.

Moving more quickly, I checked the rest of the flat. The kitchen was untouched; it didn't look as if Nick had even crossed the threshold. There was nothing untoward in the bathroom so I moved into the bedroom. The bed was unmade and there was a pile of clothes on the floor, but nothing to suggest anything dramatic had happened. The action, whatever it was, had occurred in the living room.

I returned to the scene of the crime. Although there was a fair amount of blood, it wasn't enough to signify a death: half a pint, I reckoned, less than any normal person would donate in a blood bank.

My brow furrowed and I knelt down to examine the bloody puddle more closely. Whoever it belonged to had been standing here, been attacked but hadn't moved from this spot.

I twisted my head and checked the rug; it had been replaced after the last tenant so the pile hadn't yet properly settled. There was the imprint of a very large footprint. I couldn't be certain – it was only a damned rug after all – but it looked far too big to be Nick's.

I lowered myself to the floor and sniffed it delicately. I didn't possess even a whisper of vampiric heritage so I had to concentrate hard to be sure, but when I caught a whiff of earthiness I knew that the blood had definitely come from a werewolf. Whether that werewolf had been Nick or not remained to be seen.

I straightened up and squashed any thought of the earnest, grieving boy in order to examine the scene with an analytical eye. I had never been part of a clean-up crew or visited a crime scene, but I'd been responsible for plenty of tableaux like this. I had more than enough experience and I knew what to look for.

I swivelled to my left and gazed at the faint stains on the wall, looked down once more at the puddle then back at the wall. Hmm. None of the furniture had been disturbed so there hadn't been much of a fight. Whatever had happened in here had happened quickly. And yet...

Wrinkling my nose, I leaned in to the wall. Whoever had tried to clean it had used the lemony detergent I'd left in the flat when I'd cleaned the place after the last tenant had departed. I was forced to get so close that the tip of my nose almost brushed against the stain – but I registered the lingering scent of blood beneath the sweet aroma.

I walked backwards through the flat to the battered front door then re-traced my steps for a second time as I ran a series of possible scenarios in my mind.

Somebody had come to the door, somebody who knew exactly who Nick was and where he was staying. They hadn't knocked or rung the doorbell but had kicked in the door and marched straight into the living room where Nick had probably been lounging on the sofa. He'd jumped up when his assailant had entered the room and lashed out in self-defence. That accounted for the spray of blood on the wall – and why it had been cleaned up and the blood on the floor hadn't.

Blood could be used for all sorts of things and it was wise not to leave any of your own behind. Any witch worth their salt could use fresh blood to establish someone's identity; if they were canny enough, they could even place a curse from a distance on the person it had come from.

After Nick had made his move to defend himself, the mysterious assailant must have struck at him in return, quite possibly with a knife, slashing his skin, creating a deep wound, and then grabbing him as he bled. The attacker obviously hadn't cared too much about the blood that Nick had left in the living room. However, there was no blood in the hallway or on the stairs so it was more than likely that they'd also knocked him out and taken the time to bind the wound, probably to disguise any trail. Then they'd hauled him out of the flat and away.

No doubt He Who Crunches Bird Bones and She Without An Ear had tried to prevent the getaway and Nick's assailant had probably thrown magical acid at them as a form of defence. Both cats were fast and knew how to avoid predators, but they were lucky they'd escaped with only minor wounds.

Nick's wound was unlikely to have been a mortal one, though that didn't mean he was still alive. He could have been dragged off and killed elsewhere. Thankfully, the fact that he hadn't been killed in the flat suggested that his assailant hadn't *wanted* to kill him – at least not yet.

I tapped my finger thoughtfully against my bottom lip then I left the flat and returned to my own place where all five cats were waiting. 'I don't suppose any of you could tell me exactly who nabbed Nick?'

They all miaowed in turn. They'd alerted me to the problem and, as far as they were concerned, any immediate danger to their own charmed lives had passed. Now they expected recompense in the form of tuna before they could even begin to consider anything else. Cats have priorities – and only a fool ignores them.

I nodded understandingly and dealt with their wounds first, gently cleaning them to encourage the healing process before I gave each moggy a reassuring pet and laid down their bowls. Leaving them to their dinner, I nipped next door. Somebody had to have seen something.

It took Dave several moments to open up. 'What can you tell me about the visitor who dropped by this afternoon?' I asked as he scowled at me from his doorstep. He was obviously preparing to settle in for the night; he was wearing his worn tartan slippers and clutching a tumbler of amber whisky.

He grunted in confusion. 'You're the one who got into their damned car. What can *you* tell me about them? Since when did you have friends in high places who own cars?'

I ignored his questions. 'I'm not talking about those visitors. I want to know who came after them when I was out.'

All he offered me was a blank expression. I muttered a curse and left him on the doorstep.

Next I crossed the road to talk to Mrs Miller across the street. She rarely left her house so she'd almost definitely know who'd been round. In sharp contrast to Dave, when she opened the door her face was wreathed with smiles. 'Kit! Come in! Come in! How lovely to have a visitor!'

No way. Mrs Miller had a sprinkling of faerie blood; her great-grandmother had been a true faerie of the Summer Court, and although Mrs Miller's genes were considerably diluted she still possessed more power than I was comfortable with. If I moved across her threshold, she'd ply me with tea and scones and somehow several days would pass while she kept me talking.

It had happened once before, not long after I'd moved in,

and I'd vowed it wouldn't happen again. I strongly suspected that her husband, who never left their home at all, had been a travelling salesman whom she'd invited in decades ago and who still hadn't managed to leave. He seemed happy enough whenever I saw him, and the one time I'd enquired whether he needed help to escape he'd smiled benignly and told me without any trace of compulsion that he couldn't imagine a better life than the one he had. I'd left him to it; his situation wasn't for me to judge.

'I can't stay,' I told her, double-checking that my toes weren't touching her doorstep. I didn't apologise even when her face fell; despite her friendly exterior, she knew exactly what she was doing every time she invited somebody into her house. 'I only wanted to ask who visited me earlier today.'

Mrs Miller's eyes widened. 'There was a *car*,' she breathed. 'An actual car! A woman was driving it – I think she was a werewolf. She had dark hair down to about here.' She indicated the nape of her neck. 'And there were two muscly werewolves with her. I thought I saw you get into it, dear.'

'I did,' I said. 'I'm not talking about them. I want to know who came after that.'

Her face clouded with the same blank confusion that Dave had displayed and my stomach flip-flopped. 'Mrs Miller,' I asked carefully. 'What did you do this afternoon?'

'I had lunch with Derek,' she said cheerfully, referring to her husband. 'Carrot soup that I made myself. Then I did ... stuff.' She bit her lip before brightening. 'Now I'm talking to you.'

'What stuff did you do?'

Yet again she looked baffled. 'Just ... stuff. Do come in, dear. I can tell you all about it, if you like. I'll pop the kettle on and we can chat.'

'No, I really can't stay.' I was already backing away. 'Thanks for your time, Mrs Miller.'

'Sure, Kit.' She waved at me. 'Come round next week for the solstice. I'll be at Crackendon Square in the morning but I'll be back here for lunch with Derek. You should join us.'

Not a chance. I waved, hoping that would satisfy her for the time being, then turned on my heel and returned to Dave's front door. This time he opened it before I could knock. 'What now?' he growled.

'What did you do this afternoon?' I asked.

He stared at me. 'Why the fuck do you care about that?'

'Humour me.'

As he stared harder, his scowl deepened and his eyes shifted. 'I...' He stopped. 'None of your damned business!' He slammed the door in my face.

I stepped back and ran a frustrated hand through my hair. Suddenly it was very obvious what had happened: whoever had attacked Nick and kidnapped him had employed a forget-me-not spell.

Some spells were easy to cast: any Tom, Dick or Harry could wander into a witchery store and buy the ingredients and knowledge to make a minor healing spell, such as the one I'd employed on She Who Hisses. Only a real witch with a powerful coven at their back could fix internal haemorrhaging or serious injuries, but there was plenty of magic accessible to virtually everyone. A masking spell of the sort that I could have used this afternoon to avoid being followed was another example, although it would have been more expensive than the enhanced herbs I'd used to help She Who Hisses.

Some of the spells that most people could employ were ruinously expensive and therefore rarely used; any spell that messed with somebody's mind usually fell into that category. Casting spells that affected the physical world was one thing but interfering with the psyche was on a whole different level because, regardless of the cost, there was no guarantee that you wouldn't turn your target's brain into jelly.

I had made a great deal of money as an assassin but even I would baulk at the price of a forget-me-not spell. There had only been two occasions in my illustrious career when my clients had signed off on the cost of such magic and the job had offered no alternative. Even then, EEL hadn't permitted me to wield the spells myself; they kept a talented witch on the payroll to administer them. I could still recall her white face and the beads of sweat on her forehead the last time she'd cast a forget-me-not spell for me. Despite being the most skilled witch I'd ever met, even she'd been terrified of getting it wrong.

Whoever had hurt Nick and abducted him had no such fears, and they'd employed a forget-me-not spell on my neighbours as if it were as simple as turning on a light. If I knocked on the door of everyone who lived nearby, I'd probably receive the same response: complete bafflement over what had happened here this very afternoon.

It was extraordinary that anyone would contemplate doing such a thing to so many people. I couldn't even begin to imagine what young Nick had done to warrant such attention.

CHAPTER
SEVEN

After visiting three more of my neighbours and confirming my suspicions, I returned home with a heavy heart and a churning mind to consider my options.

I made myself a cup of strong coffee while She Who Loves Sunbeams nuzzled my arm and did her best to keep my spirits up. He Who Crunches Bird Bones eyed me worriedly from the corner, and even He Who Must Sleep stayed awake and tried to groom the inch of bare skin around my ankle with his rough tongue to raise my mood. It was an indication of their anxiety – and mine – that they remained awake.

The obvious suspect was Alexander MacTire. MacTire was wealthy enough to afford any number of forget-me-not spells. He could easily have sent another wolf to grab Nick while I was in his drawing room having a chat. It would serve him well to blame me for the abduction because it would provide him with a logical reason to kill me.

Nick could re-appear in a few weeks' time, whole and well and completely bound to the MacTire pack, while Alexander MacTire would no longer have to worry about what I might reveal about him. He'd wave a hand and murmur an 'oops' about my death then a heartbeat later he'd forget me and get on with his life. With Nick in tow, whether he wanted to be or not.

'It's twisted,' I told the cats, 'but theoretically possible.' I shook my head. 'I'm not convinced, though. I believed MacTire when he said he'd give Nick more time, and he doesn't seem the sort of person to come up with such a convoluted plan.'

He Who Crunches Bird Bones squinted at me and I scratched his chin.

'I could try a tracking spell to locate Nick, but I don't have the right ingredients here – and let's face it, anyone who has the wherewithal to employ a forget-me-not spell will have masked their trail at the same time.'

I sighed. 'But I do need to rule out MacTire completely before I look at the other suspects.' I thought of the construction crew that Nick had mentioned and the mysterious red-haired werewolf who'd tried to follow me home. There were several avenues to consider.

I drained the coffee cup in one long gulp; sleep was out of the question tonight and I needed all the caffeine I could get. I knew what I had to do. Whoever had taken Nick and hurt him was going to rue the day they'd been born.

COLDSTREAM WAS a different city once the sun went down because plenty of Preternaturals were nocturnal. In a bid to appear as normal as possible, I'd avoided night-time excursions since I'd retired and moved to Danksville, though I still relished the dark. You could take the woman out of the assassins but you couldn't take the assassin out of the woman; there would always be a kernel of a killer inside me – and killers love the night.

Although there was cloud cover, I still covered my hair with a dark woollen hat. When I'd been working I'd had to appear as nondescript as possible so it was dyed a dull shade of mousy brown. These days it was a vibrant shade of purple, which was great for standing out in a crowd and fit my image of an eccentric cat lady but wasn't conducive to staying under the radar. I'd already removed my shiny jewellery and dressed in ninja black so that not even a glimmer of moonshine could glint across my body.

I had intended to donate most of my old working clothes to charity when I had the time. Now, as I felt the familiar fizz of anticipation burst through my veins, I wondered if I'd deliberately held onto them in the hope of an event such as this one. Old habits died hard.

'And old assassins die even harder,' I whispered as I looked at my reflection in the mirror. I gave a humourless grin; nobody had said I couldn't be cheesy.

I double-checked my equipment then abandoned the mirror and popped my head into the room where I'd left She Who Hisses. I caught a glimpse of her flicking tail from behind one of the boxes. Despite her anger, she'd eaten a decent amount of the kibble I'd left. I nodded approvingly and closed the door. A good appetite was a good sign.

He Who Roams Wide was waiting for me at the front of the house and I knew that She Without An Ear would be keeping an eye on the rear. Although we knew that what had happened to Nick hadn't been their fault any more than it had been mine, they were making up for what they perceived as their failure to guard the house. We were all out of practice these days but there was no point saying that aloud; words were easy to deliver but feelings – and guilt – were far, far harder to deal with.

When I walked down the garden path and out of the gate,

He Who Roams Wide followed me. As soon as I stepped onto the dirty cobbled street, He Who Crunches Bird Bones slunk out and took up the position of watchful guard in front of me. His white fur meant that he was visible to anyone who passed by, which was the point.

I tipped an imaginary hat in his direction and indicated to He Who Roams Wide to wait, then I nipped into Dave's garden and dropped a sealed envelope on his doorstep – it was my insurance and my instructions if I didn't return. In the event that I came home hale and hearty, I'd pick up the envelope long before Dave saw it and he'd never know that I'd designated him as the executor of my last will and testament. It paid to be prudent, however, especially when one had cats to look out for.

Satisfied, I went back to He Who Roams Wide. 'Ready?' I asked softly. He offered me a quiet purr of acquiescence and we set off.

I didn't see a soul until I reached the end of my street, although there were plenty of lights on in the houses I passed. He Who Roams Wide and I moved silently – at least I'd not lost all of my skills. We padded to the crossroads and looked up and down to check the way ahead. I was still concerned that the red-haired werewolf was watching my every move but there was no indication he was there; in fact, nobody was around apart from a ban sith wailing outside the block of flats on the corner.

He Who Roams Wide took point and sauntered towards the howling woman. When she paused mid-wail and reached down to scratch his ears, he responded with a delighted chirrup. I didn't acknowledge her: the last thing I needed right now was to become the target of her shrieks.

I crossed the street and stopped at the tram stop. Right on cue, a tram trundled into view. The tram witches kept them going all night and they were often busier in the wee hours than they were during the day.

This time I was prepared and had plenty of tokens to choose from. I dropped two into the driver's outstretched palm and beckoned urgently to He Who Roams Wide because I knew the driver wouldn't wait for a cat. Fortunately, the sleek black tom understood and hastily abandoned the ban sith's scritches in favour of joining me on board. Before the doors slid shut, the ban sith resumed her wailing. Nobody in that block of flats would be getting much sleep tonight.

I snagged a seat halfway down opposite a well-dressed man reading a newspaper. He Who Roams Wide stared unapologetically until the man looked up and blinked in surprise. He smiled. 'Cute cat,' he commented. 'You've got him well trained.'

'It's more like the other way around,' I said.

The man laughed heartily even though my remark hadn't been that funny and reached out to stroke He Who Roams Wide. My cat, however, wasn't in the mood for any more petting. Denied the opportunity to unsheath his claws, he ignored the outstretched hand and turned instead to the other tram passengers with a look that suggested he was daring them to challenge his presence. When nobody came forward to complain, he sniffed and hopped onto the seat next to mine.

'Disappointed?' I asked. I nodded towards the next tram stop. I'd already seen who was waiting to board. 'I wouldn't worry. You'll have your fun soon.'

The next man who heaved himself on board was huge, though not in terms of height: he was probably only five feet tall. He was incredibly wide, however; his shoulders spanned at least two feet and he had to step sideways like a crab to fit through the tram door. Maybe he was somehow related to crustaceans; he was certainly red enough in the face to bear more than a passing resemblance to a cooked lobster. I'd have assumed he had some troll or ogre blood, but I'd never seen such a vertically challenged version of either species.

It wasn't the man who engaged He Who Roams Wide's interest, it was his dog, a slavering, three-headed beast that was as wide as its owner.

Although I was a cat person, I liked dogs; there was something to be appreciated about their biddable nature, plus I had a lot of time for a waggy tail. This dog proved an exception.

This particular monstrosity wasn't a natural creation: some witch's coven with more interest in profit than sense had poured magic into several generations of puppy litters to create it. No doubt they'd marketed it as a nod to the fabled dog Cerberus, though the hideous furred thing shouldn't have been allowed to exist. I didn't blame the dog, just the arseholes who'd made it and the idiot owner who'd probably paid a fortune for him.

I kept that thought in mind when the dog's nearest head caught wind of He Who Roams Wide and started snapping and growling in our direction. The other two heads followed suit and suddenly the man was straining to hold the dog's leash. If his hand slipped, the dog would bound forward to rip He Who Roams Wide to bloody shreds. Or try to.

'Who the fuck brings a cat on a tram?' the man bellowed. Several of the nearest passengers were already on their feet and moving towards the back of the tram. When the well-dressed man next to me shot me a concerned look I smiled serenely, but unfortunately that only enraged the newcomer further.

The tram driver engaged the controls and we jolted forward, making the dog's owner wobble despite his low centre of gravity. He lurched towards me, all three dog heads snapping, growling and drooling.

He Who Roams Wide licked his paw delicately. The only sign that the dog's presence discomfited him was a faint puffing up of the fur around his tail. I knew exactly what he was thinking and I hoped the dog was ready. 'Don't hurt him too much,' I murmured.

He Who Roams Wide pretended not to hear. He stood up, flattened his ears against his head and fixed the three-headed dog with a narrow-eyed stare that promised death.

The man gaped as the barking and growling faded away. The middle head gave a small whine whilst the other two heads dropped their gaze, then the dog lowered its body to the floor in submission. It had taken seconds, and He Who Roams Wide hadn't so much as extended a single claw. As was often the case with success, it was all about self-belief and attitude.

Unfortunately, the dog's owner was less impressed. 'What the fuck did you do to my dog?' He glared at me as if I'd cast some sort of subduing spell, which I clearly had not.

'Your dog is fine,' I said calmly.

'Look at him!'

I glanced down. Yep, he looked fine to me apart from the three heads, and there was nothing I could do about those. He was even wagging his tail, admittedly more from anxiety than happiness, but even so...

'You shouldn't have messed with us!' the man bellowed. 'I'm going to fuck you up!'

My aim had been to defuse the situation not ramp it up, but now I was growing irritated. I met his eyes. 'I am having a very bad day,' I said quietly. 'I would like nothing more than to get to my feet right now and bring you to your knees.'

The man opened his mouth to snarl a response but I held up my palm. I dropped the mild façade I usually displayed and gave him my best death stare. It wasn't on a par with He Who Roams Wide's but it wasn't far off. *I'm capable of many terrible things*, I conveyed silently. *If you cross me, you will regret it.*

The man's shoulders dropped an inch and he took a step

backwards as he started to work out that I might not look like much but I was capable of a whole lot. Appearances in Coldstream could often be deceptive; from the man's expression, he'd made a similar error in the past and it had cost him. Perhaps he'd acquired a three-headed dog because he wanted protection from the big nasties in the world. Big nasties like me.

His lip curled briefly in a final show of defiance. 'I'll leave you alone this time,' he said loudly for the benefit of the other passengers, 'because I'm a good guy and I don't want to hurt a woman.' He wagged his fingers. 'But don't you and your damned cat come near me and my dog again.'

He tugged on the leash and dragged away the canine monstrosity to the furthest corner of the tram.

The well-dressed commuter opposite me adjusted his purple tie. 'Impressive,' he murmured. 'Next time I need protection, I'll be sure to get a cat rather than a dog.'

I gave him a polite smile then focused on He Who Roams Wide. 'If only everything were that easy,' I said to him. He was already curling up into a tight ball to snooze away the rest of the journey.

I sighed. 'If only.'

CHAPTER
EIGHT

I wasn't reckless enough to take the tram all the way to the MacTire stronghold. The more time I spent faffing around the more danger Nick faced, but the wrong move could also spell his demise.

I certainly wouldn't do the kid any good if I ended up dead, and alerting the MacTires could easily result in my wolf-gnawed corpse, so I disembarked four stops before my destination. None of the tram passengers looked at me as I left, and the man and his three-headed dog stared resolutely out of the window. That was good enough for me.

As soon as the tram doors closed behind me, I twisted into the nearest alleyway with He Who Roams Wide at my heels. The darkness swallowed us up within a heartbeat.

I waited until the tram's purple sparks were long gone then sidled out of the alleyway and started to march briskly. My feet still ached from my earlier trudge home but I had far greater concerns than sore feet. I maintained a steady pace, taking care not to expel too much energy, and thankfully it was only just after two in the morning when the high walls of the MacTire stronghold came into view.

I found a small nook between an old church and an iron-monger's store and glanced down at He Who Roams Wide. 'It's been a while since we've done this,' I murmured. 'Can you manage?' The cat glared at me, annoyed that I'd even asked the question.

I dropped my bag and checked my equipment. Anything that wasn't touching my bare skin wouldn't survive what I was about to do. Although this was technically reconnaissance, if my investigation proved that Alexander MacTire had abducted his own nephew I had to be prepared to act so I was carrying everything I might need.

Only when I was satisfied with the throwing knife strapped to my bare ankle, the poison taped to my thigh beneath my black trousers, the small bag of herbs with emergency spells positioned near my chest, and the tiny – but often useful – gun at my back did I reach down and pluck a small tuft of black fur from near the cat's hind legs.

'I don't know how long I'll be, but three hours' maximum.' I pointed to the bag that was now hidden in the shadows. 'Make sure that stays there, where nobody can see it.' Then I held my breath, opened my mouth and swallowed the clump of fur.

It tickled as it went down and I choked slightly but there wasn't time to clear my throat. The magic was already taking hold.

It started with a tingle, like electric sparks running through my veins. Goosebumps rose across my skin. As my nose started to twitch and the altered light forced me to shut my eyes, my blood fizzed. It had been too long since I'd felt this rush of power.

My body rose off the ground and I started to spin and tumble. I forced myself to relax; it was far less painful when I simply allowed it to happen. The heat that enveloped me was both welcomingly familiar and disturbingly uncomfortable. I heard my bones crack, and a moment later I was jerked rigid by a searing pain but it was only a brief spasm, over almost as quickly as it had begun.

Then I was back on the ground, albeit on all fours. Everything looked different. I wasn't just a cat lady, I was also a cat-sith. My kind were so rare that I'd never met another.

Miaow.

Viewing the world through cat eyes always took some adjusting to. I rarely shifted into feline form during the day because colours were confusing in daylight, especially reds and oranges, and every colour looked more washed out than usual. Some ultraviolet light seeped through to add to the confusion. Dark colours were easier and my feline night vision was extraordinary, even though it took time to get used to.

When I'd first realised what I could do, I'd spent most of my hours as a cat feeling wobbly and sick. It had taken considerable determination to push past those sensations, and even now I had to use the first moments of every transformation to slowly blink and focus before I moved.

He Who Roams Wide understood this and waited patiently until I was ready before touching his nose to mine. I miaowed in response. Cats don't typically miaow at each other, but despite my temporary body I wasn't really a cat and He Who Roams Wide knew that. He gave a brief purr and settled down by my bag. I knew there was a good chance he'd wander off at some point in pursuit of a shadow, but he'd stay reasonably close to this spot until I returned. It was far more than I had any right to ask for.

I stretched out, tested my feline limbs and made sure everything was in order. My gnawing fear that it had been too long since I'd transformed had vanished; I was a cat once more – and damn, it was good to be back.

Inclining my head to He Who Roams Wide, I padded out of

the alleyway. As soon as I emerged there was the flap of wings and I registered a bat flying overhead. I didn't need to get close to know it was a vampire but she wasn't interested in me, so I wasn't interested in her.

I dropped my gaze and focused on the high wall surrounding the MacTire mansion. It was angled in such a way that it would be difficult for most people to climb over. The biggest threat to any werewolf pack was other werewolves and most of their defences were designed to prevent incursions from competing packs. Although werewolf security took other Preternaturals into consideration we weren't a priority, which was why I'd managed to sneak inside so easily when I'd killed Bruce MacTire. It was why I'd sneak inside so easily now, too. One day werewolves would stop being so inward looking and realise that others posed a real threat, but not today.

After his father's assassination, Alexander MacTire had asked EEL how we'd gained access so that he could plug the holes in his security but I knew that, as per its strict policy, EEL hadn't told him. I could saunter into the MacTire stronghold and nobody would be any the wiser. It was almost too easy.

I examined the wall, checked again that the street was empty and calculated my approach. Eyeing the top, I bunched my muscles and scaled the wall with an ease that would have horrified the architect who'd designed it. It was a great deterrent for werewolves but cats? Not so much.

The top was three inches wide, which was more than enough room for me to pause comfortably and survey the scene below. I couldn't grow over-confident, though; despite my current form, my aim was to remain unseen.

A well-lit courtyard lay in front of me and a gravel path led to the front door of the main building, situated so that it was impossible to avoid. It would be difficult to prevent my paws crunching on those tiny stones but ingress by the door was my only option because all the windows were bound with magic designed to repel intruders. I had to slip in through the front, and that wouldn't be easy given the two guards positioned on either side of the path, but all I really needed was patience.

I walked around the wall towards the eastern side, away from the guards and the front door. There was a narrow gap here between the exterior wall and the side of the mansion and I jumped down easily and landed on all fours in a patch of garden that was choked with weeds. Nettles and thorns scraped irritatingly against my fur and I sprang towards a less-weed strewn corner where I could wait for my chance.

The guards were obviously bored. The one nearest me was turned away so I couldn't see his face, his fingers drumming out a rhythm as he listened to an ear-worm song in his head. The other guard was staring ahead with a vacant expression. People had low attention spans and no guard could stay alert without a break for more than two hours. Very few organisations factored that into their security planning, which had made my old job far easier than it should have been.

The guards' distraction emboldened me and I stepped slowly out from my hiding place. I hugged the walls of the main building, keeping out of the light. Neither of them noticed.

Soon I was in a puddle of darkness less than a foot away from the door. I sat back on my haunches, preparing for another long wait but I was in luck. The courtyard gates opened and Quack and Ribbit strode in.

The two guards snapped to attention. 'Here for your drubbing?' the nearest guard enquired.

Ribbit scowled and stopped, but Quack was more sensible and ignored them in favour of opening the front door and stalking inside. 'We've done nothing wrong,' Ribbit said, taking the guard's bait.

'Oh yeah? I heard you got your arse whupped by a little old

lady who smells of cat pish. By the looks of you two, I heard true.'

I did *not* smell of urine, cat or otherwise, and I wasn't a little old lady but I didn't take umbrage. Instead, while Ribbit bunched his fists and spat out a weak rejoinder, I darted through the front door.

'You weren't there,' I heard Ribbit sneer behind me. 'There were five of them.' It was a pathetic lie even by brawny were-wolf standards and the guards knew it.

'*Five* little old ladies? Oh my!'

I smirked inwardly and took shelter underneath a bureau. It was just as well because Quack turned and snapped at her colleague, 'Stop being a wanker and get over here. We're already late.' Then her nostrils flared and I froze. She'd obviously scented my presence despite the bandages across her nose, which were no doubt the result of our previous encounter. 'And you two ought to do a better job. Some kind of animal is in here.'

'We're not Rentokil, love,' one of the guards laughed.

'Yeah, that'll be your job once the boss is done with you tonight,' the other one chuckled.

Although their words were harsh, their tone was good natured; those bored guards had to get their kicks somehow.

Quack was only mildly irritated but Ribbit stormed through the door in a definite huff. 'Wankers,' he muttered. 'I'd like to see *them* get involved in some action. They'd run a fucking mile.'

'Stop taking everything so personally,' Quack sighed. She turned on her heel and marched into the nearest room, the place where I'd been taken that afternoon.

Ribbit stuck out his tongue like a child but before long his shoulders drooped and he trailed dutifully in her wake. I'd have snorted if I could have done. MacTire's finest. As if.

I didn't need to witness the pair of them receiving their scolding, entertaining as it might have been. Instead I skulked towards a room opposite, a mahogany-lined space that heaved with masculinity and tasteless interior design. I needed to conduct a quick search so I could rule Alexander MacTire either in or out of Nick's abduction, and I didn't want to waste time.

The layout of the building was seared into my mind from Bruce MacTire's assassination; he'd used this room as his office and I was certain that his son did the same. He certainly hadn't changed any of the décor. If there was any evidence, I'd find it in here.

I completed a circuit of the office then padded to the door and nudged it closed with my paw; it would give me a few precious seconds if I had to run and hide. Then I turned and headed for the large desk in the centre of the room. I sprang onto its top and gazed at the neatly arranged papers; most appeared to be bills but I took my time to paw through them, just to be sure. It wasn't an easy task in this body but I didn't want to shift back into my human form unless I had to. It would be too dangerous if I were caught, even though I was prepared for such an eventuality.

Several minutes passed. I did my best to leave the pile of papers looking undisturbed then I checked a large notepad on the far corner of the desk. There were a few scribbled words: *Winstone. Gavin Sitwell, Kit McCafferty.* I grimaced.

There was a creak outside the room. I registered it immediately and leapt off the desk. The heavy velvet curtains were closed and I could hide behind them without being detected but I wanted to see Alexander MacTire's face so I headed for the large bookcase in the corner and scaled it quickly. Once I was on its flat top, I drew back out of sight.

It wasn't the pack alpha who walked into the room, however: it was Quack.

Her sullen expression was heightened by her swollen red nose and the bandage strips carefully pasted over it, and she was carrying a large silver tray holding a plate of sandwiches, cups and a coffee pot. Not only had she probably been bawled out for her and Ribbit's failure to bring me in, but she must also have been assigned scut work as punishment.

I was more interested in the fact that Alexander MacTire was clearly planning a long night than that Quack was having a bad day. Unless it was a full moon, werewolves were diurnal. It was already very late so I could only imagine that he had a lot on his mind. My eyes narrowed at the thought.

Quack lowered the tray to the desk, glared at it then reached forward and opened the lid on the coffee pot. A flicker of amusement rippled through me as she delicately spat into its contents. My, my: she wasn't quite the dedicated MacTire werewolf that she pretended to be. Perhaps she'd preferred Alexander MacTire's father.

When Quack left the lid open and reached into her pocket to withdraw a tiny envelope, my amusement changed to shock. She opened the envelope, dropped the contents – a white powder – into the hot liquid and stirred the contents with a spoon from the tray before wiping it clean and returning it to its place. She closed the lid of the pot and glanced over her shoulder before swivelling and leaving the room.

I stared after her. I hadn't been expecting that. So much for all that vaunted pack loyalty. Alexander MacTire had his father killed and now Quack was trying to kill him.

CHAPTER

NINE

I tried my best to understand what I'd witnessed. There was zero chance that Quack was an EEL employee who'd been hired to assassinate MacTire because the company would never employ a werewolf, let alone a bonded werewolf like Quack whose loyalty to any entity outside their pack could never be absolute. That was why her actions made no sense.

The only vaguely rational explanation was that she'd somehow discovered that Alexander MacTire had ordered his father's death but I didn't see how that was possible. And even if it were, that wasn't information that she would keep to herself.

I gazed at the silver coffee pot. Maybe it wasn't poison, maybe it was … what? Steroids? Some kind of special werewolf enhancement potion? It seemed unlikely. I wondered if this assassination attempt was related to Nick's disappearance but I couldn't connect the dots – and I didn't know what to do next.

I was prevented from making a decision when Alexander MacTire walked into the room with Samantha behind him. He gestured to her and she closed the door. Aha. Whatever conversation they were about to have was not meant for his other furry minions to hear. I straightened up, praying I was about to eavesdrop on something useful.

'You think I was too soft on them?' he asked.

Samantha shrugged. 'Perhaps.'

'They fucked up and they know it. There's no need to rub salt into the wound.'

'You're not your father,' she observed. 'Thank heavens.'

MacTire snorted. 'He would have had them publicly whipped.'

'And then he would have dragged Nicholas home and forced him to say the oath. Are you really going to leave him with that woman?'

My eyes widened and I leaned forward.

'She's already proved her capabilities. He's as safe with her as he is with us.'

Sadness settled in my bones. If only that were true.

'And if he's not?'

'I'll kill her myself.' There was no malice in his tone, Alexander MacTire was simply stating a fact in the same way he might express a preference for beef rather than lamb. 'But she was right. He does need time. I'm confident he'll come to the right decision on his own.'

'You don't want to have him watched?'

'If he spotted any trackers, he'd be off like a shot. Perhaps he does deserve this opportunity to work out what's best for himself. None of the rest of us had that chance.'

Samantha obviously held the position of beta wolf, so MacTire would have no reason to lie to her. He hadn't been responsible for Nick's abduction and that left the field wide open. I'd got the information I'd come for – and a whole lot more besides.

MacTire turned to the desk, lifted the pot and poured two

cups of coffee. My whiskers twitched and Samantha immediately stiffened. 'We're not alone,' she said quietly.

Uh-oh. Suddenly a new problem presented itself. If I were caught here and whatever powder Quack had dropped into the coffee was detected, MacTire would instantly believe I was the one trying to poison him.

I held my breath and watched as he slowly returned the coffee pot to the tray. When he raised his head again, I almost yowled with shock. Half his face had shifted and his lower jaw and nose were no longer humanoid; instead they were wholly wolf.

I'd never know any werewolf managing a transformation apart from during the full-moon period. Alexander MacTire's power was unheard of and I couldn't imagine why he would keep such an ability secret. If the other wolf packs knew what he could do, they'd be terrified into submission.

His nostrils flared as he scented me then his face returned to its original features, albeit with even more of a five-o'clock shadow than before. 'Cat,' he bit out.

Samantha was already in an attack stance. 'Here?'

'In this fucking room.'

With that, my mind had been made up for me. I leapt out from my hiding spot directly for the desk, landing exactly where I'd planned to knock over the poisoned coffee pot, and kicked both cups. As their contents spilled, burning liquid scalded my side.

I sensed rather than saw MacTire lunge towards me but, in a move that might have impressed even She Who Hisses, I sprang away and threw myself towards a heavy cabinet. The space underneath was only four inches but it was enough for me to scoot out of reach.

I was still trapped, and the office door remained tightly shut, but I had a little breathing space to plan my next move;

however, I should have remembered that Samantha had been canny enough to catch She Who Hisses. While MacTire crouched down and thrust his hand underneath the cabinet to try and grab me, she was a step ahead.

'Wait,' she said. 'I've got something.' While I hissed at MacTire's flailing hand, she knelt down and sprinkled something on the floor. As soon as it hit the polished wood, I knew what it was: magically enhanced catnip. No wonder she'd managed to get hold of She Who Hisses.

As everyone knows, catnip is a potent herb that sends many cats into paroxysms of heavenly delight – and magically enhanced catnip is on a whole other level. There wasn't a single feline in the world that could ignore its allure. If I'd been a normal cat, I'd already have been bolting out from underneath the cabinet to roll myself onto it. But I wasn't a normal cat and although the scent was delicious, I was more than capable of resisting its effects. Then again, if I ignored it, Samantha and Alexander MacTire would know that I was more than I appeared. My only hope now was to act like I really was a cat, and I unhappily obliged.

Biting back my next hiss and forcing out a purr, I shuffled out from underneath the cabinet and threw myself at the small pile of dried herbs. I dropped onto my side and started to roll around like an idiot. *Mmm, catnip. Mmm, I'm a cat. Mmm, don't be suspicious of me.*

Two large hands reached out and picked me up. Alexander MacTire. I wriggled and jumped away from him to return to the herbs. 'Where the hell did you get this stuff from?' he asked Samantha.

Good question.

'A black-market seller down by the river.'

Trilby. That arse: I'd kill them the next time I saw them. I rolled around some more and purred again, trying to appear ecstatic. It was beyond humiliating.

MacTire reached for me a second time and this time his grip was more assured. He scooped me up, drew me to his chest and held me firm, despite my wriggling. 'She's a pretty little thing,' he said.

Samantha sniffed. 'She's a cat. There's no such thing as a pretty cat.'

'I know one woman who would disagree with you.'

'Kit McCafferty strikes me as an intelligent, capable woman, but when it comes to cats, she is very wrong.'

Oh, Samantha. Just when I was beginning to warm to you.

There was a sharp knock on the door. MacTire growled and it opened to reveal one of the courtyard guards. 'He's here, boss.'

'Sitwell? About fucking time.'

Sitwell? That had to mean Gavin Sitwell, the name that had been scribbled onto the notepad. Curiosity scratched at me but my need to escape took precedence. As the door opened wider and a nervous-looking man was ushered in, I took my chance.

I opened my jaws and bit down hard on MacTire's finger. He hissed with pain and his hold on me loosened. That was all I needed to wrench free and bolt for the open door. I ran between the legs of the guard to the entrance hall. The outer door was still open a fraction and I headed for it, ignoring the minor commotion behind me.

'Let her go,' I heard MacTire say. 'She's just a cat. Can you fetch us some fresh coffee?'

I released a breath then leapt up the exterior wall and bounded away.

∽

ALTHOUGH MY BAG was in the same place, He Who Roams Wide had disappeared. I gave a small, plaintive miaow to call him back, then tensed and started to cough.

I hated this part but it was necessary. I hacked and spluttered and coughed until, after what felt like an age, I hawked up the hairball. As soon as it was out of my mouth, the painful spasms began again, jerking my bones. Moments later, I was back in my own body with a cold sweat across my forehead.

Nobody was coming after me. I'd made it out scot free.

My black top was damp with dregs of the poisoned coffee that were clinging to it in the same way it had clung to my black fur. I yanked it over my head and folded it to preserve the evidence, then unstrapped my weapons. It was one thing wandering through the streets of Coldstream in the middle of the night in little more than a sports bra, but quite another to display the wares of a professional assassin as I did so.

I returned everything to my bag and slung it over my shoulders. I was shivering a little from the cold but if I moved quickly, I'd warm up soon enough. By the time I'd adjusted the bag straps, He Who Roams Wide was sauntering placidly towards me. There was a tiny smear of blood next to his mouth. It was probably better not to ask.

'Well, he definitely didn't take Nick,' I told him. 'And MacTire doesn't know he's missing.' Yet.

Alexander MacTire had made it perfectly clear what he'd do to me if anything happened to Nick; it was a sobering thought that the entire MacTire clan would set upon me if the boy was dead.

'Unfortunately,' I said aloud, 'I've now got even more questions that need urgent answers. Let's head home and get a few hours' kip. We've got some busy times ahead.'

CHAPTER
TEN

I barely got sixty winks but I knew my body and how to deal with less sleep than I'd grown accustomed to enjoying. There were plenty of hours left before I hit my physical limits, and I wanted to reach Trilby before they opened up their stall for the day. I was on a mission and I didn't have time to arse around in a queue before I could talk to them.

I dropped kibble into bowls for all five cats and reassured them again that I wasn't angry with them for not preventing Nick's abduction. The kid wasn't their responsibility, he was mine. Then I checked on She Who Hisses, who flatly refused to come out from behind the boxes but did miaow to let me know she appreciated the food I was leaving for her and that she was on the mend. Perhaps she was softening towards me.

'This evening,' I promised, 'when we can be sure that your injuries have healed enough. That's when I'll let you go.'

With my immediate tasks completed, I rushed to the river market. A weak dawn had already spread its way across the sky and several of my neighbours were stirring. I waved at them; they'd eyed me with considerable suspicion when I'd first moved in and I'd had to work hard to be accepted.

The presence of a werewolf-driven car the previous day would have diminished my standing in many eyes, so I had some ground to make up. There was no reason not to start now.

Trilby was setting out the last of their wares by the time I arrived at the market. It was surprisingly busy despite the early hour, but the queues were forming by the baker's stall and Natasha's butchery; locals who required Trilby's services would doubtless pitch up later.

I strolled up and eyed the display. It was mostly innocuous: a few love potions that every person in Coldstream with half a brain cell knew would never work; some herbs to enhance perimeter security, and several bottles of dubious moonshine to which the authorities would turn a blind eye. Trilby kept the good stuff out of sight.

'Kit!' They spread their arms wide and beamed as I approached. The eponymous trilby hat perched on their head jiggled slightly. 'You're a sight for sore eyes.'

I didn't smile back. 'Good morning, Trilby.' I folded my arms. There was no point beating around the bush so I didn't waste my breath. 'You've been selling magic catnip without telling me.'

They didn't miss a beat. 'You're not the only cat lady in town, Kit.'

'Since when did werewolves seek out cats?' I enquired.

'Ah.' Trilby nodded. 'I did seek assurances from that particular customer that no felines would be harmed. I believed her. Was I wrong to do so?'

No, but that wasn't the point. I glowered but Trilby only shrugged. 'You could hunt down the werewolf and steal the catnip off her. You'll probably have to kill her first, of course.' They grinned as if the thought that I'd kill anyone, let alone a werewolf, was hilarious. 'If you do that, don't dispose of the body until you've spoken to me. Ground up werewolf bones are excellent for curing cancer.'

I rolled my eyes. Yeah, yeah.

Trilby's smirk grew. 'So I've heard. And apparently werewolf blood can be used to invoke demons.'

I folded my arms. I wasn't in the mood for old wives' tales or Trilby's warped idea of humour, and I certainly wasn't stupid enough to chase after Samantha to steal her damned catnip. I liked my head and my limbs where they were, thank you very much. 'Do you still have some of that catnip in stock?' I'd buy all of it if I could.

'Alas, it was only a small batch, but next time I promise I'll let you know that I've got some.'

I moved on to more pressing matters. 'What about forget-me-not spells? Any of those under that counter?'

Trilby blinked. 'Now why would a lovely lady such as yourself be interested in powerful magic like that?'

I knew they didn't expect an answer; Trilby was one of the few people in Danksville who understood there was far more to me than met the eye. They hadn't been so crass as to ask me directly but I knew they'd asked around about me. I also knew that sooner or later Trilby would find out about my past career, not because people had loose lips but because Trilby was so good at worming out secrets. But I wasn't going to make it easy for them.

After several beats of silence, Trilby sighed and gave in. 'No. I haven't had any forget-me-not spells on my books for a long time. Few people around here can cover those sorts of costs and the ones who can don't need to come to me.'

It was a fair argument and I appreciated Trilby taking the time to make it. 'Fine,' I said.

'Is there anything else? You do appear to be in rather a demanding mood today.' They were still angling for information but they'd need to be a lot more subtle than that if they were going to weasel anything out of me.

As it happened, I did have something else to ask them. I took my carefully folded black top out of my bag. 'An unidentifiable liquid was spilled on this last night. I want to know what it is.'

They made no move to take it from me. 'I take it that it's probably not beer?'

'That would be a fair assumption.'

Interest sparked in Trilby's eyes. 'Is it dangerous?'

'Not to bare skin but I expect that nasty things might happen if you were to ingest it.'

'I see. It will take time to retrieve the answers you require. If you return tomorrow...'

I shook my head. 'That's too long. How about midday?'

They sucked air in through their teeth. 'No can do, Kit.' I waited and Trilby raised their eyes heavenward. 'Fine. But it'll cost you.'

'I can pay.'

'Yes,' they said. 'I do believe you can. I'll do my best.'

I inclined my head and allowed a small smile now that I'd got my way. 'Thank you.'

Trilby doffed their hat. 'Any time, Kit. Any time.'

Several of the other stallholders were watching me, including Natasha; doubtless they were curious about what had happened to me yesterday. I wondered if they'd seen Quack and Ribbit limp out of the alleyway.

I debated the merits of pausing at one of the other stalls to casually mention the encounter and suggest there'd been a third party involved. I didn't want to get a reputation as a hard arse, not here, but the less I said about the matter, the faster the rumours would die away. It wasn't always wise to add fuel to the fire.

With that in mind, I left the market. Although the construction team that had supposedly employed Nick was low on my list of suspects, I couldn't discount it. It would be a good time to check in and make sure its staff were not involved.

ONCE UPON A TIME the area known as the Glebe had been owned by the Christian church, but as the Preternatural community started to grow Coldstream was mostly abandoned by organised religion. Preternaturals were considered to be less than wholesome, and religious figures of all denominations were viewed with equal suspicion.

In recent years there had been a return to some of the older ways. Worshippers of the Masked God, who were considerably better organised than their peers, had been particularly successful in gaining both followers and wealth. As devotees of one of the divine entities benignly associated with death, the members of the Church of the Masked God had accrued a number of legacies – there was nothing quite like impending death to encourage people to make bequests to smooth their path to eternal life.

The more fiscally responsible devotees had taken those legacies and put them to good use, buying up swathes of unused land from the departed Christian church. As in any large group of people there were pockets of corruption but, for the most part, the Masked God's followers were doing good work. The thriving community they were building in the Glebe was evidence of that but there was still a lot of building to be done, which was why there were so many construction crews located in the warehouses on the Glebe's fringes.

Although I hadn't heard of the Crushers until Nick had mentioned them, it didn't take long to track them down. From what I could tell from the outside, they were neither the richest nor the poorest of construction workers; their warehouse was relatively modest but there was a decent bustle in and around the area.

From the materials they were transporting – often by hand as they didn't seem to own any trucks – they were establishing a small docking area for the sole use of the Glebe inhabitants. Anyone who might be resistant to becoming a follower of the Masked God in order to live in the Glebe might be swayed by the convenience and community that was being developed. It wasn't my bag but I had no reason to take umbrage with what they were doing.

If there was one thing I'd learned over the years it was that the majority of people were simply people, regardless of who or what they worshipped, the numbers in their bank account or their proclivities once they were behind closed doors.

I was unclear whether the Crushers were Masked God devotees; Nick hadn't mentioned anything and I didn't know enough to be sure either way. My hour spent watching their activities from across the street didn't shed any light on the matter.

I knew that werewolves were not interested in their religion, although it wasn't beyond the realms of possibility that a few overzealous worshippers might decide that forcing a wolf to join them would be good publicity for their cause. It seemed unlikely, but I had to remain open to all options.

There was too much hustle and bustle for a sneaky incursion so, growing bored with just watching, I drew back my shoulders and walked across the road to talk to the Crushers. A group of burly trolls passed me hefting long planks of wood. Their gritted teeth suggested they weren't in the mood for conversation so I spoke to an older woman sitting outside the warehouse on an upturned bucket. 'Hi there!'

She barely looked up. 'I'm on my break.'

'I'm looking for Tommy.' I gave the name of the foreman Nick had mentioned.

'He's inside.' She jerked her thumb towards the warehouse. 'If you're looking for work, you're in luck. We're so short-handed we'll take on anyone – even the likes of you.'

I didn't take offence; after all, little about my appearance suggested I'd ever worked in construction. I didn't possess bulging muscles and my clothes were those of an unthreatening middle-aged woman. We all judge books by their covers whether we admit it or not.

'Thanks,' I said cheerfully and ambled inside. So far the Crushers were far friendlier than their name suggested.

The warehouse smelled of sawdust and earthy magic. Despite what the woman had said, there were plenty of people inside marching to and fro, lifting equipment, arranging tools and preparing for the day's work. The building projected an atmosphere of focused business and I understood why Nick had been excited about working here. This was a company that, despite its name, took its work seriously.

I spotted the small office on the left-hand side. The foreman, the half-ogre called Tommy, would probably be in there so I made a beeline for it.

The door was ajar so I knocked once, pushed it open without waiting for an answer and strode in. I sat on a dusty chair opposite a burly man wearing a high-vis vest who was muttering to himself as he studied a clipboard. He glanced up when I cleared my throat, swept his eyes up and down my body and turned an interesting shade of pale.

'We're only two days behind,' he said. 'We'll make up the hours before the solstice. As I told your representative yesterday, I can assure you that the tower project will be completed on time. There's no need for concern.'

I didn't say anything.

'I've given my word,' he said stiffly. 'I am well aware of what will happen if we don't meet your targets.'

I remained silent.

He ran a hand over his balding head. 'We're not cowboys. We won't cut corners to meet the deadline either.'

I raised an eyebrow.

'And I'll add a discount to your final bill. Five percent – how does that sound?'

His nostrils flared when I still didn't respond. 'Alright! Ten percent, but I can't do any better than that.'

It was rare to witness an ogre – or even a half-ogre – panicking. A thick blue vein was bulging in his forehead and he was gripping the clipboard with such force that his knuckles were white.

'I'm not who you think I am,' I said gently and held out my hand. 'My name is Kit McCafferty. I want to ask you about a young lad who you employed yesterday.'

Tommy's massive shoulders sagged; his relief was so strong I could almost taste it. 'You're not from the church?'

'No.'

He closed his eyes briefly. 'You should have said that at the start.'

'The Church of the Masked God members aren't usually the ball-breaking sort,' I said, intrigued by his reaction.

'Not usually,' he agreed. 'But they want this project completed by the solstice. They're building a new tower as part of this year's celebrations. We needed the contract so I said we'd get it done by then. I thought we could manage it easily but we're short staffed and we keep coming up against problems...'

His voice trailed off as he realised he'd allowed stress to get the better of him and said too much. Clearly he'd been overoptimistic with his time estimates in order to bag the church gig and now he was regretting the promises he'd made and the contract he'd signed. 'We'll get it done, though. We'll definitely get it done.'

'You've given them your word that you will?' I asked. 'That's a risk, regardless of the situation.'

He pressed his thin lips together. I'd obviously asked one question too many. 'My apologies,' I said briskly. 'I didn't mean to pry.'

He offered me a curt nod and got to his feet. 'We're too busy to take on any new clients. I can recommend the Busters next door.'

There appeared to be a theme to the names that construction crews gave themselves. 'I'm not looking to hire anyone,' I said quickly before he threw me out. 'I'm only here to ask about someone you employed yesterday.'

The ogre's expression cleared. 'You said that already. A young lad? The werewolf kid?'

I nodded again.

'You're not from his pack? You're not a wolf?'

'He's unbound. He's a lone wolf.'

The ogre blinked. 'He told me that. I didn't believe him but...' He gestured helplessly.

'You're desperate for workers.'

'Yeah. I wouldn't usually take on werewolves, unbound or otherwise, but we need all the help we can get.'

I nodded for a third time, to show him that I empathised. I wasn't there to complain about his hiring practices. 'He told me about you. You're Tommy, right?'

The ogre grunted assent. 'Yeah. The kid was supposed to show up first thing this morning but he's not here yet.'

I considered telling him the truth but I couldn't risk the news that Nick had been kidnapped getting back to Alexander

MacTire. 'He's found other work,' I lied smoothly. 'He was too embarrassed to come and tell you himself.'

I watched the foreman's reaction; he was disappointed but not surprised. There was no suggestion that Tommy or any of the other Crushers had anything to do with Nick's disappearance; for a start, they were too busy to focus on one potential employee.

'I appreciate the heads up,' Tommy said, 'but he should have told me himself.'

'Yeah, he should have.' I pulled a face. 'Kids these days, eh?'

Tommy rolled his eyes resignedly while I apologised silently to Nick. If I ever found him – and if he wasn't dead – I would make this right for him.

'Thanks for dropping by,' the foreman said. 'I have to get back to work.'

'Sure.' I moved towards the door. 'By the way, what spell are you using here? Is it a productivity thing that you pump through the warehouse?' He shot me a look. 'Your team are over-worked but nobody out there is complaining,' I continued.

'I pay them good wages.'

Uh-huh.

The ogre lowered his voice. 'And it's not a productivity spell, It's just a simple contentment potion that we add to the coffee urn.'

I knew it. 'I'd be careful with that if I were you,' I told him.

He looked away. 'I know, but I can't afford to lose any more workers right now. It's only a temporary measure.'

I hoped so because those sorts of spells had a way of backfiring. I offered him a half-smile and then I left.

CHAPTER
ELEVEN

Alexander MacTire hadn't abducted Nick and the Crushers had nothing to do with his disappearance. The forget-me-not spell indicated that the kidnapping had been carefully planned; whoever had taken Nick had gone to great expense and trouble, and there had to be a reason why. Was he still alive? The more time that passed, the less chance there was that the boy was alright.

The fury I felt at the unidentified kidnapper more than trumped my fatigue. I wasn't done yet, not by a long shot.

The river market was in full swing when I returned to Trilby's stall. I was early but I reckoned they'd forgive me. I waited in line, sandwiched between a tired-looking witch with several children in tow, whom I vaguely recognised, and a young druid whom I'd never seen before. He appeared to be suffering from a nasty bout of agriwort-induced scabies; he'd been calling on powers beyond his ken.

I refrained from passing comment; we all had our problems and you never knew what someone was going through unless you'd walked a mile in their shoes. I did take care not to brush against him, though; I had no desire to be in the shoes of someone with suppurating boils.

When we shuffled forward, the witch in front of me asked Trilby how much they were charging for a four-leaf clover charged with silver. With a catch in her voice, she asked if they'd be prepared to give her a discount if she bought three of them.

While Trilby hummed and hawed with their usual bargaining skills, I glanced at the trio of children around her skirt and realised where I recognised her from: she lived in the block of flats that had been bombarded by the ban sith's wails the previous night. Somebody in that block was going to die soon and the witch was trying to fix the odds against it being any of her kids. Trilby's special four-leaf clovers would do the trick but they weren't cheap, and from the state of her threadbare clothes, the woman didn't have any money to spare. She wasn't trying to buy a talisman for herself; she was desperate to protect her children.

I pushed myself up onto my tiptoes and caught Trilby's eye. They raised an eyebrow and I nodded. Trilby shrugged. 'It looks like I've more in stock than I realised,' they said to the witch. 'I'll do you a deal. You can have three—' they glanced at me '— make that four, for fifty quid.'

I frowned and shook my head. 'Sorry,' Trilby muttered. 'Did I say fifty? I meant twenty.' One silver-charged four-leafed clover sold for £60 on the open market, so four for £20 was ridiculous. I smiled happily.

'Four for twenty?' the witch asked incredulously.

'I can't get rid of the damned things,' Trilby said. 'They're taking up too much shelf space and their power is already diminishing. In another few days I'll have to throw them away. But it's up to you. If you don't want them—'

The witch interrupted them. 'I'll take them.'

'Thought you might.' Trilby bagged them up, the witch paid and moved to the side so I could take her place at the front of the queue. I passed them £200. They counted it, nodded and tucked the money away. 'Soft touch,' they mouthed at me.

I shrugged. I was hardly perfect; I used to kill people for a living.

'Have you tested the fabric?' I asked. 'Have you got an answer for me?'

'It's only been a few hours, Kit,' Trilby protested. 'And I've got a stall to run. I can't drop everything just for you.'

'Trilby—'

They sniffed. 'Yes, I've got an answer – but it's going to cost you and you're not going to like it.'

No surprises on either count. 'Fine,' I said.

Trilby held up a folded note. 'Eight hundred.'

That was actually cheaper than I'd expected. I counted out the money and passed it over then took the note and opened it. There were only two words: *Death cap*. I stared at them then a moment later I crumpled the paper into a ball.

In its most potent powdered form, death cap would kill someone within twelve hours. Quack really hated her alpha.

'You're welcome,' Trilby said.

I inclined my head in acknowledgment of their work. Trilby was right, though: I didn't like it.

They pointed at the crumpled paper. 'You ought to take care, Kit. I'd hate to lose one of my best customers.' Although their words were light, there was serious concern behind those dark eyes.

'I wasn't the target,' I said.

'I'm glad to hear it.'

I started to step away but they raised a hand. 'Before you

go,' they murmured. 'As you're such a good customer, there's something else I should tell you.'

'Go on.'

'About an hour ago somebody came by the stall and asked me if I had any forget-me-not spells in stock.'

I stiffened. 'Who?'

'A male werewolf. Short red hair, pale skin. I've not seen him around here before so I don't know his name.'

'Which way did he go?' I snarled softly.

'He headed towards Black's, but I lost sight of him pretty quickly.' Trilby waved a hand towards the queue behind me. 'I've had a busy morning.'

I met their eyes. 'Thank you,' I said, meaning it. 'You've helped me a lot.'

They swept a bow. 'Any time, Kit. Any time. Take care out there.'

I wasn't the one who had to take care. I managed to smile through gritted teeth, spun on my heel and jogged towards the coffee shop. If I had to kill that damned ginger werewolf in public while he munched on a cupcake and drank the best coffee in town, then I absolutely would.

I SWUNG OPEN the glass door to Black's with so much force that it threatened to come off its hinges. Every single head turned towards me and the wait staff, who recognised me, glanced over to check that I didn't have any grumpy werewolves on my heels. Chance would be a fine thing. It wasn't Quack and Ribbit whom I wanted to see, it was the mysterious ginger wanker who was dogging my steps and who was surely involved in Nick's abduction.

I marched in and stared hard at every occupied table.

Nobody here was a wolf, not today. I strode towards the toilet and yanked on the door. It was locked. I growled and yanked harder. 'Fuck off!' yelled a very annoyed, very female voice. 'I've got my period!'

I spun around, preparing to head into the kitchen and check that the errant fucker wasn't hiding in there but before I could take a step Black himself blocked my path. 'It's time for you to leave.'

'I'm looking for someone. A werewolf.'

He shook his head. 'There aren't any wolves here.'

'Are you sure about that?'

He met my eyes. 'Yes.'

It was rare that I lost my temper; in my old line of work anger was an emotion that was not permitted. Anyone who killed in anger had no place as an assassin and I'd long since trained myself to tamper down anything beyond mild irritation.

I realised that I was taking Nick's abduction personally. He'd been attacked under my roof and I'd promised Alexander MacTire that he'd be safe, so it wasn't surprising that my blood was boiling. But it wasn't helpful.

I closed my eyes for three beats then opened them again. 'Please accept my apologies, Mr Black. I'm having a difficult day but that is no excuse for my behaviour.'

'It's not a problem. I was concerned about you after your visit yesterday.'

'I'm fine.'

'That is good.'

I relaxed my shoulders. Calm, Kit: be She Who Loves Sunbeams, not She Who Hisses. 'I'm looking for a werewolf. Somebody told me he was heading in this direction.'

Black nodded, as if that were perfectly normal. 'We did have a werewolf customer an hour or so ago. He bought several pastries and took some coffee to go. He didn't linger and I didn't watch which way he went.'

'What did he look like?' I asked. I had to be sure.

Black pursed his lips. 'Short red hair. A fair bit of stubble. He appeared ... unkempt.'

'What do you mean?'

'He didn't look as if he'd enjoyed a hot shower or a proper meal for several days.'

Well, at least that was some information. 'Thank you,' I said.

'We look after our own, Ms McCafferty. You're a part of Danksville now.'

This time I gave him a genuine smile. 'Thank you,' I repeated. It was difficult to judge on a day-to-day basis how much success I'd achieved in becoming part of the community here, so it was good to learn that my efforts hadn't been in vain. I really was putting down roots – and that made what happened to Nick hurt even more.

Black crooked his finger at the young woman behind the counter. 'Liesel, you served the wolf. What was his name?'

I stilled. Of course: anyone ordering a coffee to go would have given their name to make it easier to collect the drink when it was ready. I crossed my fingers tightly, praying that Liesel would come through.

Her brow creased as she tried to remember then her expression cleared. 'Shane. That's what I wrote on his cup.'

Shane, like the mysterious gunslinger in that old Western book. I shivered. It was appropriate. *I'm going to find you, Shane,* I promised silently. Sooner or later.

As soon as I stepped outside the coffee shop, I scanned the busy market. Perhaps Shane was still here, ambling around the stalls. Perhaps he was watching me from a dark corner. Perhaps...

A hesitant voice interrupted my thoughts. 'Hi, there.'

I glanced to my right. It was the harassed mother who'd bought the clover talismans from Trilby. 'Uh, hello,' I said.

She didn't smile. Two of the younger kids, apparently already bored by the market, were kicking clods of dirt at each other. Cats were much, much easier than kids. 'I know that was you that paid for the clover.' Her hands twisted together. 'I'm not usually a charity case. I'm having a hard time right now and there's a ban sith...'

'I know,' I said. I gave her a meaningful look. 'I wasn't taking pity on you. I only wanted to help.'

'I'll pay you back – when I get the money, I mean. I'll make sure you get it all back.'

'You don't have to do that.' I tried to bolster her quiet dignity. 'I live around the corner from you and the last thing I want is a ban sith in the area. If those talismans encourage her to move on, then I win.'

The woman bit her lip. 'Thank you,' she whispered. She nudged the oldest child, a boy who was standing beside her and staring vacantly into the distance. 'Tell her,' she said. 'Tell the lady what you know, Adrian.'

He shook himself into focus. 'Uh ... the man I heard you asking about.'

My eyes widened. 'Yes?'

'He's a werewolf.'

I nodded warily. 'I know.'

The boy shrugged awkwardly. 'He's been sleeping in the old Galbraith building, in a room on the third floor.'

My mouth dropped open and I stared at the boy while his mother filled in the blanks. 'Adrian sneaks in there from time to time, even though he knows he's not supposed to. He knows it's haunted.'

It wasn't, but that wasn't important right now. 'You've seen him in there?'

The boy nodded. 'He gave me some chocolate and told me to stay away for a few days.'

I sucked in a breath then returned my gaze to his mother. 'That information is worth far more than a few talismans.'

'In that case,' she said, 'I'm glad we could help.'

CHAPTER
TWELVE

The Galbraith building was less than ten minutes' walk from my house. It was one of the few unoccupied properties in Danksville; this might be a poor area but it was jammed full of inhabitants. That the Galbraith house remained free of residents – even squatters – was testament to the strength of the rumours about unhappy ghosts roaming its hallways.

My curiosity had led me to investigate it soon after I'd moved into the area but I'd found nothing of note, nothing to worry about: it was just an old building teetering on the verge of rack and ruin. Nobody knew who Galbraith had been and nobody knew who owned the building now. I'd tried to find out but my investigations had come up short; I'd eventually decided that the place was a mystery, and a boring mystery at that.

The windows at the front were boarded up and, as I knew from my previous visit, impossible to see through. Not even a chink of light seeped through the old plywood so at least I didn't have to worry about Ginger Shane seeing me approach. It would go better for me if I could catch him unawares.

Unlike my own less grand but better kept home, there was no front garden so I walked up to the front door from the street. Although the windows were boarded up, bizarrely the door hadn't received the same treatment. All I had to do was duck under a few nailed planks and push it open. No wonder kids broke in here.

In its heyday, the interior must have been glorious but now it was gloomy and full of rubbish. There wasn't a pervasive reek of damp, however; at most, the house smelled a bit fusty.

I paused in the entrance hall, sniffing the air and listening hard, unsure whether the mysterious Ginger Shane was there or not. I had to act as if he were and take my time. Entering a large building in pursuit of a target used to be my bread and butter so I was neither scared nor nervous – but I was determined.

Although I had believed Adrian, I wasn't willing to risk everything on his information that Shane was holed up on the third floor so I checked out the ground-floor rooms first. Next I climbed the stairs to the first floor and did the same. By the time I reached the second floor, I suspected Adrian had been correct; my suspicions were confirmed when I climbed the last flight of stairs and the faint scent of vetiver floated towards me.

I didn't know where the noisiest floorboards were but I knew how to tread lightly, even without shapeshifting into cat form. I slipped off my shoes and moved towards the wall where there would be less chance of loud creaks and pushed my weight onto my rear foot first so that I could judge each step before I committed to it. I was pleased when I reached the third floor without making a sound. I'd not lost all of my skills in the last four years.

Until that point the house had been dark but on the final landing there was a glimmer of sunlight sneaking from a chink in one of the closed doors on the right-hand side. Ah-ha: gotcha, you sneaky bastard.

I started to move forward, lifted one foot and twisted towards the door, then froze abruptly appalled at my lack of due diligence. *Kit. You absolute dick.* I pulled back before crouching down to examine the booby trap that I'd almost tripped: the red-haired wanker was smarter than I'd given him credit for. No wonder he'd bribed Adrian with chocolate to keep him away.

It was a simple trap but the most effective ones usually are. An almost invisible line of thread crossed the hallway at knee height and I'd been within a whisker of colliding with it. I followed the thread with my eyes until I spotted the thumb-sized bag of magical herbs concealed in a gap in the skirting board.

Lowering myself until my nose was almost touching it, I took a long sniff. Passiflora incarnata with a good sprinkling of salt and power thrown in. It wasn't as expensive as a forget-me-not spell, but it wasn't cheap either. It wouldn't have killed me but if I'd tripped the thread I'd have been comatose for the next three hours and had a hell of a hangover afterwards.

Grimacing, I straightened up and stepped carefully over the thread. I needed to be more careful.

I side-stepped along the wall, wary of creaky floorboards and further booby traps. When I reached the closed door, I paused and listened for sounds of life. For several moments all I heard was the gentle thudding of my own heart.

He might still be out, or taking a nap. There might be another trap shielding the doorway. There was only one way to find out.

I carefully slid my favourite dagger from its sheath. It was far too long since it had seen any action. I gripped its handle, held my breath and kicked in the door before leaping back.

Nothing happened: no trap was triggered and no irate

ginger werewolf rushed me. The room was empty – at least of people.

I waited for several beats in case the bastard was hiding somewhere else in the building and was on his way to fend me off, but there was no movement and no sounds. He wasn't home.

I stepped into the room. Black had been right: there was a lingering scent of mothballs and clothing that was long due a good wash, although the smell of vetiver was also stronger here. I took in the neatly rolled sleeping bag, the small hurricane lamp beside it and the battered backpack, then I spotted the small stain by the window. Blood. I was certain of it.

I stopped wasting time and strode towards it. If the blood was fresh enough, there was a chance that I could match it to the blood that had been in Nick's room and I'd have this damned wolf bang to rights. I'd wait for his return and find out what he'd done to Nick – or at least what he'd done with Nick's body.

I peered at the stain. There was no doubt it was blood but its presence wouldn't help me because it was too old. It had dried into the wooden floorboards and, judging by its colour, had been there since before Nick's kidnapping.

Obviously that didn't clear the ginger wolf – if anything, it made me more suspicious. Few people in Coldstream allowed themselves to bleed copiously, and even fewer neglected to clean up their own bloodstains because no substance contained more power than blood.

I already knew that Ginger Shane wasn't stupid, but he was certainly reckless. He probably hadn't expected to be traced back here, which also made him a fool. I was starting to think that my suspicions were correct and I'd found my kidnapper – but there was still no sign of Nick.

I angled my dagger to scrape off a sample of the blood for

testing but I'd barely started when I sensed someone behind me. There was no heavy breathing, no tell-tale creak or footstep, and the smell in the fusty room didn't alter, but there was a shifting of molecules and a feeling deep in my gut born from years of experience.

Ginger Shane was behind me and he was preparing to attack.

I didn't turn around, and I didn't pause or tense. This wasn't my first rodeo; in fact, one of my first assignments back when I'd been a baby killer had been similar. I'd been sent to dispatch a nasty druid to the grave but he'd been aware that several people were targeting him. His home was impregnable and I could have waited months before I had the chance to get him alone so I played on his ego instead.

When he was alone he wouldn't have spat on a kitten if it had been on fire, but in public he liked to pretend that he was a gentleman. I tracked him to Edinburgh where he was meeting with some political bigwigs who he was trying to impress.

I had dressed in my shortest skirt and a see-through top, tottered around on sky-high heels and fallen in a graceless tumble in the street in front of him. He'd come to help me, keen to show his inclination to be of service to helpless young females. As soon as he reached for my sprawled body, I twisted my hand and stabbed him in the gut with a corkscrew blade.

It had been an effective feint and I was up and away before his body hit the pavement and his companions realised what had happened. I'd received a decent bonus for that kill; if I could pull off a similar feat now, the resulting pay-off could be even greater.

As soon as I felt the brush of air against the nape of my neck, indicating that the werewolf was about to make a killing blow, I sprang up and turned in mid-air. I caught a glimpse of a shocked face and an iron crowbar as I adjusted my blade and slashed at the hand holding it. Ginger Shane had no choice but to stop his attack, but unfortunately he didn't drop the weapon and he recovered from my defence far quicker than I'd anticipated.

He grunted then kicked with his left foot before swinging the crowbar with his right hand. I managed to dodge and stay upright, but his foot caught my calf and there was a flash of searing pain in my leg.

I jabbed my dagger at his neck. I didn't want to kill the bastard or knock him out, more's the pity; I needed him to talk so I needed to be more careful than usual. The tip of my dagger scraped his skin and his nostrils flared.

I knew exactly what he was thinking. 'Yeah,' I told him. 'It's coated with poison.'

He snarled and swung the crowbar again, this time catching my shoulder. It hurt like bejesus but I wouldn't give him the satisfaction of seeing me wince. I'd had plenty of practice at swallowing pain and I could pretend to be unhurt, at least for long enough to bring him to his knees.

'It won't kill you,' I told him, 'but it will attack your limbs and weaken you.'

I scored his cheek so that blood welled up to dribble down his skin and mingle with his coarse stubble. The dagger wasn't really poisoned – too much could go wrong with a poisoned blade and only the inexperienced bothered with such idiocies. That was why I had suspected Quack's blade was poisoned; I knew of more people who'd inadvertently killed themselves using them than had killed their targets. No, I was banking on the power of suggestion.

Ginger Shane danced to my left and bared his teeth. 'I guess that I'm immune because I feel absolutely fine,' he said in a Scottish burr. He proved his point by hefting the crowbar towards my head. I ducked but the iron tip still caught the back of my skull. Agonising pain jarred through me.

I gritted my teeth and fought on. Switching the dagger to my left hand, I twisted it towards his forearm and sliced expertly through his flesh. He hissed with pain and pulled away but he didn't withdraw. Instead he moved his crowbar from his right to his left hand. I wasn't the only ambidextrous one, then.

He smashed its tip into my shoulder. As I staggered back, I met his eyes and nodded to acknowledge his skill. Ginger Shane grinned then came at me again but this time his body language telegraphed his plans.

Before he could slam it into my stomach, I dropped my dagger and grabbed the crowbar, pulling it out of his hands. He stooped, obviously planning to reach for my fallen blade, but I kicked it away and used the crowbar to whack him hard between his shoulder blades. He collapsed at my feet.

'Shit,' he wheezed – then he lifted his head and bit my ankle.

This time I was surprised and pained enough to yell aloud. 'What the fuck?' I kicked, more from reflex than design. I could have killed him with that move but at the last beat I pulled my foot back to avoid serious damage.

I was pissed off, though, seriously pissed off. 'I know you have an animal's soul, Shane, but biting is bad. Didn't your mother teach you that?'

He mumbled something and I cupped a hand to my ear. 'What was that?'

Ginger Shane raised his head and sent me an angry glare. He spat a globule of blood onto the wooden floorboards, adding to the existing bloodstains. 'I said,' he repeated with considerable malice, 'who the hell is Shane?'

I stared at him. 'You.'

He returned my stare. 'My name is Thane,' he bit out.

Oh. Damned coffee-shop name scribblers. 'Thane? What kind of name is that?'

He didn't miss a beat. 'What kind of name is Shane?'

I shrugged. So much for the lone gunslinger vibe, then, but I didn't give a cat's arse what he was called. 'Shane. Thane. Bird-brain. Whatever. Tell me where Nick is.'

Suddenly he became very still and his eyes, which I belatedly realised were an astonishing shade of bright green, narrowed. Uh-oh.

'What do you mean?' he asked slowly. 'He's staying with you. You're the one who should know where he is. I haven't seen him since yesterday morning.' There was an appalling ring of truth to his words.

I hunkered down until we were face to face and searched his expression. I scanned every inch of his pale, stubble-laden face, and my stomach tightened with every second that passed. Eventually I stood up, shoved my hands into my pockets and turned away. 'Fuck.' The expletive bore repeating. '*Fuck.*'

I took several deep breaths before swivelling back to the werewolf. He was starting to get to his feet but I shook my head in warning. 'No. Stay where you are.'

His expression flickered as he debated whether to obey or ignore me. Fortunately for both of us, he chose the former. 'What happened to him?' His voice was low and calm.

'He was kidnapped yesterday afternoon while I was out.'

His eyes narrowed even more. 'Fuck,' he muttered, echoing my own sentiment. 'When you went to the MacTire mansion?'

I nodded.

Thane's fists tightened. When he spoke again, his voice was still measured but he couldn't disguise the rage that clouded his face. 'Why did you think I took Nick? I'm good but not even I can be in two places at once, and you knew I was following you yesterday.'

He'd only followed me on my way *back* from the MacTires; he'd have had plenty of time to nab Nick before then. I folded my arms defensively. 'You're not *that* good.' I indicated his position on the floor. 'I thought you'd dealt with Nick then come for me.'

Thane's lip curled. 'I don't care about you, I care about Nick.'

'Then why did you follow me?'

'You took Nick in,' he snapped. 'Then you went to the damned MacTires.'

'They didn't give me much choice in the matter.'

'I think you've just proved that you're capable of standing up for yourself. You didn't have to go. Besides, I needed to know what your intentions were.'

'I'm a cat lady,' I said. 'I can't do shit against a pack of werewolves, especially when those werewolves are MacTire. My intention is to live a quiet life.'

'You're much more than a fucking cat lady, and if you wanted to live a quiet life you wouldn't have taken Nick in. And you wouldn't be standing here now.'

He had a point but I needed more convincing. 'You spoke to Trilby about getting a forget-me-not spell.'

'Trilby? The market-stall dealer with the hat? That's not true.' Thane sighed. 'I spoke to them to find out if anyone had *tried to buy* a forget-me-not spell recently. I didn't want one for myself.'

I hesitated; that wasn't what Trilby had told me.

He appeared to register my doubts. 'I didn't stroll up and demand to know who their recent customers were. I don't know Trilby and they obviously deal in black-market goods, so they'd have no reason to tell me the truth. I was trying to find out if forget-me-not spells were something they normally sold.

When I found out they hadn't had any in stock for more than six months, I knew I was barking up the wrong tree.'

'You didn't know Nick had been abducted until all of two minutes ago so why did you care about forget-me-not spells?'

Thane's expression hardened further and he nodded as if I'd just confirmed something. 'What?' I asked.

'I wanted to know about forget-me-not spells because I've been targeted twice recently by similar magic.'

I sucked in a breath. 'You're sure?'

'Yes,' he growled.

'Similar magic? Or an actual forget-me-not spell?'

'I don't know,' he snapped. 'I can't remember.' He tapped his skull. 'There are blanks where there shouldn't be any.'

'Do you drink a lot?'

His eyes flashed. 'You mean do I regularly get so blind drunk that I can't remember my own name? No, and I don't take drugs either. Do you?'

I didn't bother answering.

'I take it that whoever abducted Nick used a forget-me-not spell,' he ground out.

I nodded reluctantly. 'On every single one of my neighbours.'

Thane ran a hand across his skull. I watched him; I still had far too many unanswered questions. 'Why do you care so much about one teenage werewolf?' I asked.

'He's a good kid.'

I sniffed. 'And you're a lone wolf.' I was certain that Thane had to be the 'friend' Nick had mentioned. 'Despite his uncle, Nick isn't bound to any pack. There are plenty of reasons why you might be interested in him.'

'I'm not trying to create my own little fiefdom, darling. I like being alone. I was trying to *help* Nick, not recruit him.' This time he ignored my scowl and stood up. He towered over me, but if he thought I'd be intimidated by his height he hadn't been paying attention.

I raised a sceptical eyebrow. 'Really?'

'Really. Nick won't do well as a lone wolf and I wanted to show him that he ought to bind himself to the MacTires. His uncle cares for him and that boy needs a pack by his side.' He looked away and lowered his voice. 'Needed a pack by his side.'

'He's not dead,' I said. Probably not dead.

His gaze flashed back to me. 'How do you know?'

'Whoever kidnapped him could have killed him then and there. It would have been smarter and easier to slit his throat than to snatch him.'

A muscle jerked in Thane's jaw. 'How many hours has it been since he was taken?'

'Seventeen.'

'It will be a miracle if he's still alive.'

I didn't want to think about that so I tilted back my head and examined his face. 'Why are you here?' I asked softly. 'Why were you following me, and why are you staying so close to my house? You could take an interest in Nick's wellbeing without stalking the poor kid and bothering me.'

'I told you already. I wanted to check you out to make sure you wouldn't harm him.'

I lowered my voice further, trying to coax out the truth. 'Why would I harm him? Why would anyone harm him?'

Thane didn't answer. I abandoned my gentle attitude; it wasn't getting me anywhere. I bared my teeth, tapped my foot and growled. I was good at growling. 'Tell me.'

He sighed. 'Six months ago there were four lone werewolves living in Coldstream. If you don't include Nick, now there are only two.'

'Where are the others?'

'Dead.' He met my eyes. 'Neither as a result of natural causes.'

I didn't react. 'There's a reason werewolves usually live in packs. It's dangerous being a wolf on your own.'

'Somebody attacked the third lone wolf four months ago. She barely escaped with her life.'

I waited.

'And not long after Nick and his parents came to Cold-stream, somebody attacked me.' He jerked his head towards the dried bloodstains. 'And then again two nights ago.'

'That's when the forget-me-not spells were used on you?' I guessed.

He nodded. 'During both attacks. Lorna, the lone wolf who's still alive, had a similar experience. She knows she was attacked but she can't remember a thing about it.'

Nothing about this was good and Thane hadn't finished. 'Five days after the second attack on me, Nick's parents were killed.'

'That was an accident,' I said. Supposedly.

Thane snorted. 'Sure it was. You know they completed the unbinding ritual before Nick was born, right? They had each other so they weren't true lone werewolves, but they didn't have a proper pack, either. They weren't considered MacTire.'

'You think somebody is targeting lone werewolves.'

'I don't think that,' he said with absolute certainty. 'I know it.'

CHAPTER

THIRTEEN

Taking Thane home with me seemed the most prudent course of action: for one thing, he already knew where I lived and I'd proved I could take him in a fight if I needed to; for another, he was in dire need of a hot shower and clean clothes.

I reckoned that once he was clean and had some decent food inside him, I'd be able to winkle more information out of him. Anyway, I didn't want to let him out of my sight for long; I wasn't going to be swayed from my mission to find Nick and Thane was the only person I'd met who seemed to have any real information about him. He certainly seemed to know far more than Nick's own blood uncle, Alexander MacTire.

Before we left the old Galbraith house I made Thane wrench up the bloodstained floorboards and dismantle his booby trap. He might be prepared to take reckless chances with his own body fluids but I wasn't that stupid. 'What would you have done if a nosy kid had set off the trap by accident?' I enquired.

Thane looked considerably more relaxed and cheerful now that I wasn't trying to render him unconscious. 'I've dealt with the local children. I told them not to come around for a few days. They promised to stay away.'

'You've not spent much time around kids, have you?' I asked drily.

He frowned and didn't answer.

He Who Crunches Bird Bones was curled up asleep on the garden path when I pushed open the gate. Or at least he was pretending to be asleep; as soon as I set foot in the garden, his tail twitched and he opened one yellow eye to squint at me. She Who Loves Sunbeams also slunk into view from around the corner.

'It's okay,' I told them softly. 'You can stand down.' Whoever had taken Nick had already got what they wanted and I doubted they'd be back. There was no need for the cats to stand guard.

Behind me, Thane grunted, 'Huh?'

'Not you,' I said. 'The cats.' I looked over my shoulder at him. 'I did tell you that I'm a cat lady.'

He snorted. 'Yeah, yeah. You know, I tried to persuade Nick to stay away from Danksville by telling him that people here ate cats.'

'That was you?'

He grinned suddenly and I shook my head in disgust. 'You're going to need to watch that mouth. You're on my territory now.' I gestured to the cats. 'And theirs.'

His smirk didn't diminish. 'You mean you could kill me with your thumbs and then your cats will eat what remains of my body?'

'Something like that.' I gave him a long look because yes, if I wanted to I could definitely kill him with my thumbs.

Dave strolled out of his house with his hands in his pockets, whistling off-tune and making a show of staring in our direction. Some nosy neighbours watched from behind their lace curtains but others displayed their curiosity with unabashed glee. 'Another damned wolf. Who the fuck is this one?' he asked.

'His name is Thane,' I said.

'What kind of name is Thane?'

It was my turn to smirk.

Thane moved to my side, presented Dave with a disarming smile and stuck out his hand. 'It's wonderful to meet you.'

Dave gazed at him as if he were mad – actually, so did I. This was not the same man who'd been trying to kick my arse to kingdom come less than an hour ago. Now he wouldn't have looked out of place at a royal garden party; somehow even his clothes looked less grubby and crumpled. How had he done that?

Dave's gaze started to morph into a glare but Thane didn't appear to notice; he simply held out his hand and continued to smile.

A shaft of sunlight had emerged from the clouds overhead, illuminating him as if he were some sort of angel. It glinted off his coppery red hair and, as I watched him, I realised that he was better looking than I'd initially registered. Charisma was oozing out of him as if he'd turned it on with a tap. Then I noticed She Who Loves Sunbeams padding towards his feet, blinking slowly with pure feline adoration.

'She's not brought a man here before,' grunted my curmudgeonly neighbour whose company I used to enjoy until about ten seconds ago. 'Three years and no sex.' He shook his head. 'None. And now she's plumped for a damned werewolf?' He looked at me. 'What will the cats say?'

I didn't know whether to be astonished, affronted or amused.

Dave clicked his tongue, snapped his hand forward and

gave Thane's a perfunctory shake, then went back inside his house without another word.

'Three years, huh?' Thane murmured.

My eyes narrowed. A visibly active sex life didn't suit my cat-lady persona but just because I didn't bring anyone home didn't mean I didn't get my kicks when I needed to. I was about to say that in a sniffy tone of voice before I remembered it was none of his business. Or Dave's.

I tilted my chin. 'Actually,' I said, 'I'm a virgin.' Thane blinked. Ha.

'I'm waiting for Mr Right to come along. I won't accept anything beyond marriage before my precious hymen is broken. I want thunderbolts, fluttering heartbeats, kisses that make me weak at the knees and,' I smacked my lips for emphasis, 'a binding contract and a joint bank account. Only then will I bestow the gift of my virginity on a very, very lucky man.'

'What about the cats?' he asked. 'Where do they fit in?'

'They don't want my virginity,' I told him. 'Trust me.'

He sighed. 'Finally.' I watched in astonishment as he raised his right hand and placed it over his chest. 'I've been waiting for someone like you all my life. Somebody pure, untouched. Somebody who knows not only what it means to be a life partner but also how to stab me in the heart. Literally. And I've finally found you. I knew from the moment you tried to kill me that you were the one for me. I'm also a virgin and I'm the knight in shining armour you've been waiting for.'

I met his eyes. 'Great,' I said flatly.

He grinned again.

～

WHILE THANE TOOK A QUICK SHOWER, I checked on She Who Hisses. She screeched from behind one of the cardboard boxes, indicating her continued displeasure at both her confinement and my presence. I tried to get closer but she refused to let me so much as glance at her wound to check it was healing so I left her in peace and headed into the kitchen to heat some stew.

I had a lot of information to sift through and a lot of potential leads. I was going to have to prioritise my next moves very carefully if I was going to help Nick.

'We're going to have to prioritise what we do next,' Thane said, wandering into the kitchen with damp hair and cleaner clothes. The cloud of vetiver that seemed to continually envelop him was stronger than ever.

My eyes narrowed. 'We?'

He gave an easy shrug. 'You came looking for me for a reason, right? You want to save Nick. So do I. It makes sense that we work together.' He eyed me. 'Two heads are better than one. We should team up and both search for him and the fucker who took him.'

I let out a frustrated hiss of breath. 'I don't play well with others.'

'I'm a lone wolf,' he reminded me. 'Neither do I.' He continued to watch me calmly. 'But Nick is worth the effort.'

I couldn't argue with that.

'I didn't kidnap him,' Thane said. 'And neither did you. We're on the same side, Kit.'

I hadn't told him my name so he'd clearly been researching me. My thoughts must have shown on my face. 'So what are you really?' he asked. 'You're obviously not just a cat lady.'

As if on cue, He Who Crunches Bird Bones padded into the kitchen and gave me a questioning look. 'I *am* just a cat lady,' I said. My insistence sounded pathetic even to my ears.

'A cat lady and what?' Thane enquired. 'You're not a witch or a druid, but you have some magic. I can smell it. And you possess skills beyond that magic.' He rubbed the back of his head ruefully. 'You kicked *my* arse.'

I snorted. 'That wasn't hard.'

'It wasn't easy, either.' He stepped closer and stared at my face. He Who Crunches Bird Bones growled a faint warning but didn't move towards him. 'You're a loner like me,' he said softly. 'You're not a gang member or a team player. You like to go solo but you...' He paused.

I ought to have shut him down while I had the chance but I was too fascinated by his thought process. 'But I what?'

Thane stepped back. 'You're a killer.' He said it quietly, with no fear or awe in his voice. 'You don't kill for fun – you don't have that gleeful, psychotic edge – but you do have the skills. You're trained.' He raised his eyebrows. 'EEL. Betcha.'

I did my best to maintain a blank expression but I couldn't deny my shock. Nobody had ever guessed what I used to do for a living; even Trilby, with all their street smarts and insider knowledge, hadn't come close. And yet within an hour this solitary werewolf had worked it out.

I didn't bother trying to deny it; I was a great assassin but I wasn't a good liar. 'If you breathe a word to another living soul —' I began.

'You'll kill me?'

'In a heartbeat.' I meant it; my continued existence depended on as few people as possible knowing who I used to be. Nick MacTire's safety depended on our mutual silence. Thane, however, remained an unknown quantity.

'If people know what you are, they'll come after you. They'll want revenge, even if you weren't the assassin responsible for their loved ones' deaths. Or,' he added, 'they'll see you as a challenge. They'll want to prove they could take out an EEL assassin.'

'Ex-assassin. I'm retired.'

For the first time, I'd surprised him. 'By choice?'

'All EEL employees have to retire after twenty years' service. The organisation don't want us to become too used to killing, and their research has indicated that older killers' abilities grow less sharp. You have to be top of your game to be EEL.'

'So I've heard.' Something shifted in Thane's bright-green eyes and I waited for whatever was coming next. Finally he said, 'I'd love some of that stew.' He grinned easily. 'If that's alright.'

He Who Crunches Bird Bones chirruped then flopped by Thane's feet with a light thump. The moment had passed. If the white cat had decided there was no threat then I had to trust Thane. At least for now.

WE ATE. I needed to fuel my body as much as Thane did, and we both shovelled down the stew without speaking. He only paused for one moment to carefully pick out a cat hair that had somehow found its way onto his plate. I didn't apologise; cat hair was an occupational hazard as far as I was concerned. It was fortunate that I had to swallow a large tuft of it to start my shapeshifting process rather than a single hair or I'd have been transforming into a feline in a far more regular and uncontrolled manner. No magic spell or cleaning method could rid a five-cat home of loose fur.

Once we'd finished, Thane scooped up the plates and started washing up. 'So,' he said, 'talk to me about the blood.'

I told him what I knew. It didn't take long.

His expression darkened, returning to the same snarling fury I'd encountered when we'd fought in Galbraith House, so I gave him a moment or two to absorb the information and calm down. I was surprised at his level of emotion because a lone wolf wasn't supposed to care what happened to anyone else. It wasn't as if he had any allegiance to Nick; they weren't in a pack together.

During the last couple of days I'd learned a lot of new information about werewolves that had made me revise much of what I'd already known. I hoped some of that learning could be put to good use.

'I'm going to want to see that blood for myself,' Thane said eventually.

I'd expected as much. 'I'll take you upstairs – but *I'm* going to want to talk to this other lone werewolf you mentioned. Lorna? The most likely culprit is another wolf who wants to piss off the MacTires or gain control of a vulnerable werewolf who's fresh for the taking. I can't think of any packs that would risk invoking war, but a lone werewolf is a different prospect.'

'She didn't take Nick,' he snapped. 'A lone wolf did not do this.'

I didn't waste my time arguing. Another beat passed before he gave an unwilling nod. He spoke more calmly. 'I'll take you to her, but Lorna definitely didn't do this.'

His shoulders dropped as he relaxed slightly. 'It has to be Alexander MacTire – that's why Nick wasn't killed at the scene. His uncle wants him alive. He's a fucking idiot because this isn't the way to gain the boy's trust. I thought he'd know better but at least MacTire won't hurt him so maybe this isn't as bad as I thought initially.'

I shook my head. No, it was exactly that bad. 'Alexander MacTire doesn't know that Nick has been abducted.'

Thane scoffed. 'You're right that no other werewolves would kidnap the boy and risk war with the MacTires, so that means Alexander took Nick or ordered one of his pack members to do it. No MacTire wolf would act without their alpha's knowledge.'

I licked my lips but said nothing.

'What?' Thane asked.

'That's not necessarily true. If it's not Lorna—'

'It's not.'

I inclined my head. 'Then there is another MacTire suspect.' I told him about Quack and her attempted poisoning without explaining how I'd got into the MacTire stronghold.

'Bullshit. You can't begin to fathom how hard it is to murder your own alpha.'

I flicked him a glance. There was an odd note in his voice although his expression remained blank. I thought about Alexander MacTire and his father as Thane stared at me.

Finally he exhaled heavily. 'Well, damn,' he whispered.

CHAPTER
FOURTEEN

I changed out my casual clothes into a fuzzy jumper with a loud geometric design, a long flowing skirt and sensible shoes. I was tying my laces when I heard a loud feline yowl followed by a canine howl. I sprang up and pounded out of my bedroom down the hallway.

Thane was clutching his face – and the door to the back room where I'd confined She Who Hisses was lying open. 'Whoever said curiosity killed the cat,' I spat, 'hadn't experienced the nosiness of your average werewolf!'

Thane pulled his hand from his face to reveal a nasty scratch down his cheek. 'There was a strange noise,' he said stiffly. 'It seemed prudent to investigate under the current circumstances.' He straightened his shoulders. 'And I am not your average werewolf.'

Yeah, yeah. 'You're just not like the other boys?' I said in a faintly mocking tone.

Thane held his ground and sent me a challenging look. 'Exactly.'

I sighed, abandoned the conversation and ducked into the room. I didn't need to search behind the cardboard boxes to know that She Who Hisses had gone. Hopefully her wound had healed enough; the most I could do now was hope she was alright. At least she was a survivor who could defend herself. She'd probably be fine.

I tidied up the food and water bowls then turned around. Thane was staring at me with a strange expression on his face. 'If you're looking for sympathy for that scratch,' I said, 'then don't look at me.'

'I'm not bothered by it.' His voice suggested mildly wounded pride. 'Although I apologise for opening the door and letting that cat out.'

As he should do. I sniffed. He was still staring at me. 'What then?'

He waved a hand up and down my body. 'What on earth are you wearing?'

I knew what he meant but my lingering irritation about She Who Hisses made my answer cranky. 'You're commenting on *my* fashion choices? You? The man who's been living out of a backpack?'

Thane waited. I rolled my eyes and explained. 'It helps to present myself as a harmless, middle-aged woman. People judge by appearances. Folk are more willing to yield their secrets to a cat lady than a hard-arse assassin.'

He nodded, conceding the point. 'Which side of you did Nick see?'

'Cat lady, of course.' I paused. 'With a touch of hard arse.' And then, to prove that I was both, I made him wait while I ambled around and spoke to each cat in turn.

It was at least another twenty minutes before we left the house. At my insistence, we sought out Lorna first. I was inclined to believe Thane when he said that she couldn't have been involved, but I wanted to rule her out for certain before we confronted Quack. For one thing, Lorna would be easier to track down; for another, taking on Quack might antagonise the entire MacTire pack. I didn't want the most powerful werewolf clan in the country baying for my blood unless it was absolutely necessary.

Thane huffed some more about my lack of trust in his judgment but yielded quickly enough, suggesting that he wasn't any keener to piss off the MacTires than I was. I also suspected he was hoping that I'd agree with his assessment once I'd met Lorna because he wanted to prove himself to me. Strangely, that thought warmed me to him – despite what had happened with She Who Hisses.

Thane called ahead to confirm Lorna was at home and would see us before we jumped on the tram and headed off. We ended up in a surprisingly nice part of the city. I'd half-expected to find her hanging around one of Coldstream's homeless shelters or squatting in an empty building like Thane had been doing, but her flat was in an expensive-looking, low-rise building in one of the gentrified areas. Perhaps being a lone werewolf wasn't so bad after all.

Thane sensed my thoughts and smirked. 'Yeah,' he said. 'She's done well for herself.' There was a touch of pride in his voice as if her success reflected on him. Perhaps it did.

'Is this where she was attacked?' I asked. I wondered about the security and eyed the small red graffiti tag etched onto the corner of the building. It was a circle with a slash through it and it had been sprayed with precision, as if the artist had been preparing his artwork for an exhibition rather than being worried about getting caught in the act.

Thane's mouth flattened. 'No. They came for her when she was out.' He gestured upwards. 'She'll tell you herself.'

We were buzzed in quickly and took the lift up to the third floor. A woman was standing by the front door of one of the flats. Much like this building, Lorna wasn't what I'd expected.

She looked to be in her early fifties and was stunningly beautiful. Her ash-blonde hair was immaculately coiffed in an elaborate chignon, her skin was clear enough to be used in any number of beauty cream advertisements and her clothes were an understated but obviously expensive shade of beige.

'You two are friends?' I asked Thane dubiously in an undertone.

'Great friends,' the woman responded. Damned werewolf hearing. She held out her hand. 'I'm Lorna Minton. It's a pleasure to meet you.'

I plastered on a friendly smile. 'I'm Kit. Thank you for agreeing to talk to me.'

'Anything for the great Thane Barrow,' she said.

I glanced sideways at Thane. Barrow? That was a small detail he'd failed to mention. I didn't get any chance to comment, though, because Lorna was already ushering us into her flat.

The décor matched both the woman and the building. There was very little clutter, only a few artful objects placed in carefully painted alcoves and a neat array of glossy magazines splayed out on the stylish coffee table. I eyed the most visible title: *Cat Care Monthly*. I raised an eyebrow. 'You like cats?'

Thane snorted.

'I love them,' Lorna declared, ignoring him completely. 'Unfortunately pets aren't allowed in this building so I have to content myself with magazines instead of the real thing.' She smiled. 'Would you like something to drink? A cheeky afternoon gin and tonic, perhaps?'

I declined, keen to get down to business. Now that I'd met her in person, I had the sense that my befuddled cat-lady routine would be useless so I got straight to the point. 'Tell me about the attack,' I said without preamble.

Lorna moved away from the elaborate drinks trolley she'd

been hovering over and perched on the sofa opposite Thane and me. 'She doesn't waste any time, does she?' she asked Thane, who simply shrugged.

She folded her hands in her lap and looked down, then raised her head and gazed at me with cool blue eyes. 'There's not a vast amount to tell,' she replied. 'I don't remember it.'

I waited. Successful feline hunters are well-versed in the art of patience. You don't catch a mouse by leaping in without hesitation, and assassinations are also a waiting game. You need the right moment before you act and I was prepared to wait for Lorna's real story if it meant I'd get to the truth.

For several moments none of us spoke. Finally Thane cleared his throat and broke the silence. 'Lorna,' he growled, 'just tell her so we can get out of here.'

She raised a plucked eyebrow. 'You never change, do you, darling?'

I glanced between them. Ah, there was some sort of intimate history here. I wouldn't have put them together as a couple but I guessed that anything was possible. No wonder his trust in Lorna was absolute.

'It was a long time ago,' Lorna said and I knew she wasn't talking about the attack. 'We were different people then.' A ghost of a smile crossed her face. 'Well,' she amended, '*I* was different. Sweet Thane here is the same as ever.'

Sweet? That wasn't the adjective I'd have used to describe him. He was far more like He Who Crunches Bird Bones than She Who Loves Sunbeams.

'Sweet,' Thane growled again and Lorna got to the point. 'Fine,' she sighed. 'I was attacked about four months ago.'

I needed specifics. '*About* four months?'

'January 26th.'

That was better. I nodded.

'It was a Friday. I always go to a Pilates class at the gym up the road on Fridays. I left home just after eight in the morning. That's the last thing I remember until that afternoon.'

I leaned forward. 'You were attacked on your way to the gym?'

'No.' Her eyes remained clear. 'I spoke to several people who'd been at the class and I checked the gym records. I signed in and completed the class as usual. I just don't remember being there.'

Whatever version of the forget-me-not spell had been used on her had been backdated so she'd probably been followed to the gym by her attacker. There was no other rational reason for why her memory had been wiped so significantly.

'Do you always take the same route to and from the gym?' I asked.

Lorna nodded. 'It's not far from here so there's only one logical route.'

I tapped my mouth thoughtfully. A regular appointment and a regular route were an assassin's dream because they made any planned attack far, far easier. But if she'd been followed on her way to the gym, her attacker had either been stupid and not scoped her out in advance, or it had been an unplanned attack. Assuming, of course, that Lorna was telling the truth. So far I believed her.

'Okay. Then what?' I asked.

She shrugged. 'The next thing I remember I was lying on my bed with lacerations to my face and hands. And my right arm was broken,' she said matter-of-factly. 'There was a trail of my blood leading from the front door of the building into my bedroom and no signs of any disturbance in here.'

Which was why she believed she'd been attacked on her way back from the gym. 'Any witnesses?'

'I asked around. Nobody saw anything.'

I considered that then asked, 'Who's the better fighter? You or Thane?'

Lorna looked amused but Thane was pissed off, which was answer enough in itself. 'Why is that relevant?' he asked.

'He's the better fighter,' Lorna replied, surprising me. At my reaction, she gave a small, musical laugh. 'You're not asking the right question.'

I gazed at her askance.

'I don't see what our abilities have to do with anything,' Thane objected.

'She was attacked once,' I responded calmly. 'You were attacked twice. Nick was attacked once and abducted.'

He drummed his long fingers on his leg. 'So?'

'If the same person is responsible for all four attacks, it seems likely that abduction was their goal. It's easier to kill someone outright than to snatch them away.'

'Should I ask how you know that?' Lorna enquired.

'No.' I smiled; I could also be sweet when the situation called for it. 'But they only attacked you once and they went after Thane twice. That suggests they thought they had a better chance of defeating Thane rather than you.' I gave him a side-long look. 'At least until Nick came along. An inexperienced teenager would be easier to grab than either of you.'

Thane's nostrils flared. 'Whoever is behind this wants an unbounded werewolf. Alive.'

'That's my theory,' I said.

'Why would anyone want a lone werewolf?'

I had no answer for that. Yet. There were several seconds of silence before Lorna spoke again. 'I'm faster and stronger than I look, and I fight dirty. I might not remember what happened but I know I'd have fought tooth and nail against anyone who came for me. Thane is far stronger than me and more skilled, but he'd have held back.'

I looked at him again. 'Because you're *that* Barrow were-wolf,' I said softly, finally understanding. No wonder he'd seemed so certain about how difficult it was to murder your own alpha. Thane Barrow hadn't done that, but he *had* killed the beta werewolf of the Barrow pack – and he'd only been a kid when he'd done it.

'He's *that* Barrow werewolf,' Lorna answered. 'The one who flew into a rage, killed his uncle by accident and was thrown out of his pack as a result.'

'That was twenty-odd years ago,' I said, morbidly fasci-nated. 'I thought that boy was dead.'

'Twenty-seven years ago,' Lorna said. 'He was fifteen at the time and has reined in his temper – and his natural abilities – ever since.'

'And I'm definitely not dead,' Thane added.

No wonder he'd been so keen for Nick to join the MacTire pack and swear allegiance to them. Thane hadn't had a choice; he'd been summarily thrown out of his pack at a similar age. He might not have wanted me to know but that information certainly filled in a lot of gaps. It wasn't the sort of thing that happened often with the wolves; truthfully, I didn't know of any other werewolves who'd suffered a similar fate.

I stood up. 'Thanks for your time, Lorna,' I said briskly.

'My interrogation is over?' She looked amused. 'You've cleared me as a suspect?'

I nodded, but then I pointed at the cat magazine. 'You don't really like cats, do you?'

'I can't stand the little bastards.' She shrugged. 'But Thane told me about you and I thought it might be wise to ingratiate myself. I've survived this long on my own for a reason.'

Given my strategy in dressing the way I had, I couldn't blame her. I wondered what her story was and why she was alone, but it was none of my business and it wasn't relevant to

Nick's kidnapping. 'What else did Thane tell you about me?' I asked with narrowed eyes.

'Nothing,' he muttered tightly.

'All he said was that you liked cats.'

They both seemed to be telling the truth. Just as well. 'We'll take our leave,' I murmured, relaxing slightly. 'We've got other wolves to talk to.'

'Come back for that G&T anytime.' Lorna's tone was warm.

I smiled. I reckoned I might take her up on that.

FIFTEEN

Thane and I walked towards the nearest tram stop. 'You were right,' I said, conceding the point. 'Lorna doesn't seem to be the kidnapper.'

He didn't reply, not even a snarky 'I told you so'. 'Go on then,' he said instead. 'What do you want to ask me?' His voice was dark.

I paused and turned towards him. 'I don't care who you are or what you've done, Thane. All I care about is that you're not responsible for what happened to Nick.'

As his green eyes roved across my face, I wondered how many people knew his true identity. Were Lorna and I the only ones? 'I'm hardly in a position to judge anyone for their past actions,' I told him. 'And whatever happened back then, you were a kid.'

His jaw tightened and he looked away.

'Were you holding back when we fought at the Galbraith house?' I asked.

'A little,' he answered shortly.

Translation: a lot. Oh well. Some of the biggest battles were psychological and the fight he appeared to be having with himself – and losing – was far greater than the one he'd had with me.

'Good to know,' I said cheerfully. I started walking again. 'Come on, it's time for us to track down Quack MacTire. Nick still needs us and I reckon she can help, whether she wants to or not.' And with that, the subject was closed.

I'D PLANNED to head back to the same dark nook where I'd been with He Who Roams Wide the previous night to spy on the MacTire mansion and locate Quack without being noticed. Thane, however, had a different plan and veered off course without a by-your-leave.

'Hey,' I protested. 'There's a great spot back that way. We should head there.'

'My spot is better,' he said, without glancing at me.

'You don't know that.'

'Unless your spot has a full view of the MacTire mansion and its inner courtyard plus a clear line of sight through several interior windows, my spot is better.'

I didn't respond and he snorted mildly. 'Thought so.'

I refrained from passing further judgement until I saw for myself whether his spot was indeed a better vantage point. We wound away from the main street, down a narrow alley and through a tiny vegetable patch on the edge of an allotment before scaling a three-metre-high wall that led to an open sash window on the second floor of an old tenement block.

'Ladies first.' Thane gestured towards the gap.

Suspicion curled in the pit of my belly. Had I been wrong about him? Was he leading me into a trap? I glanced through the grimy window and saw nothing except a narrow hallway and several closed doors. There was no whiff of barrier magic around the window frame and nothing that suggested danger, but I was still prepared for the worst as I squeezed through the gap and into the building.

Nothing happened. As Thane followed me through the window, I looked around and registered the numbered doorways. I tried to place the building in relation to the MacTire stronghold. We were three streets away, although the distance as the crow flies was probably less.

Thane grinned, suggesting he knew exactly what I'd been thinking. 'This way.' He pointed towards the end of the corridor. 'We have to go up another flight of stairs. I'll take the lead, if you wish.'

'Age before beauty,' I murmured.

He grinned again. 'Ain't that the truth.' Then he took off, loping ahead of me while I blinked after him in surprise.

I could hear the soft buzz of life from behind several of the doors, and a couple of them were adorned with autumnal wreaths; they were the cheap sort that offered more in the way of decoration than magic but they suggested that the residents took care of their homes. Somebody below us appeared to be in the middle of making a curry. Children's laughter drifted over from somewhere to the right.

The stairway at the far end was clean; although it was a communal area there was no lingering scent of urine and no sign of trodden-in dirt. The people who lived here looked after their space. Some graffiti etched into one of the walls had been scrubbed until it was barely legible; it seemed out of keeping with the rest of the building but I didn't pause to examine it because Thane was already on the flight of stairs above me.

The third floor was quieter. Thane headed for the last door on the right and opened it without a key. I held back for a moment, nonplussed. 'It's alright,' he called. 'This flat is unoccupied.'

He certainly seemed to know an awful lot about this building and my concern ratcheted up again. It couldn't be a coincidence, not given the proximity of the MacTires. I double-checked my concealed weapons – knife, gun, poison – then I followed him again.

The flat was bare apart from a single chair. The walls were whitewashed and the floorboards were clean, although I spotted another small piece of graffiti carved into them in one corner.

Thane was already squeezing out of the window on the far side. 'Almost there! It's an easy climb from here!'

'Right behind you.' I raised my voice slightly then I veered away from the window towards the carving. It wasn't fresh: from the smoothed-over lines and worn surface, it had obviously been there for some time. Two letters had been crudely etched into the wood: TB. No prizes for guessing what they stood for.

'Kit?' Thane's voice drifted towards me. I jogged to the window and peered out. He was already on the roof above me. 'You can use the drainpipe to clamber up. If it's secure enough to hold my weight, you'll be fine.' He stretched down a hand. 'I can help you if you're worried.'

As if. Ignoring him, I stepped out and made short work of scaling the last few metres until I joined him on a small section of flat roof. I glanced around. Huh. He'd been right about the view.

We were hidden from the MacTire mansion's sight by a row of Victorian chimney stacks but by stepping to the edge of the last one, we could see into the stronghold.

I swallowed my pride and offered Thane a grudging nod. I was impressed; I'd scoped out this area thoroughly when I'd been tasked with assassinating Bruce MacTire, and I rated myself and my skills, but I'd never noticed this place. It wasn't accessible from other rooftops and there was no obvious route to it, but my lack of awareness still rankled. There again, I didn't have Thane's history.

'How old were you when you started coming here?' I asked.

His body stiffened. 'I was seventeen the first time,' he said. 'At first I didn't realise how close it was to the MacTires. Barrow wolves were on reasonably good terms with the MacTire pack back then, but we certainly didn't visit each other's homes.' He sighed and stared into the distance. 'An old homeless druid told me about this place. It was pretty much derelict back then, but there was a good group of squatters of all creeds who used it. It was January when I...' he paused, choosing his words carefully '...left my pack. It was cold. I needed somewhere to stay and this place worked for a time. I used to climb up here and watch the stars at night.'

'And spy on the MacTires?'

'Not for the reasons you think,' Thane said quietly.

I reckoned it was exactly for the reasons I was thinking but I didn't say anything. This was his story.

'I'd been in a pack all my life and I didn't know how to be alone – I didn't *want* to be alone. I met good people on the streets and in places like this but they weren't werewolves. They weren't like me. I was young and scared, and naïve enough to think that another pack might take me in despite what I'd done.'

He gazed down at the MacTire mansion. 'At least I was smart enough to scope them out before I tried to approach them. When I realised who lived down there, I spent a month watching them.' His mouth twisted. 'I knew within a day that I'd never ask if I could join them. Bruce MacTire was a fucking bastard.'

My response was soft. 'So I've heard.' I waited for a beat. 'This building isn't used by squatters now.'

'No.'

'But that flat, the one that gives access up here – nobody lives there?'

'I own the building now,' Thane told me. 'I let the rooms out for a peppercorn rent to anyone who needs somewhere to stay for however long they need it. Sometimes I still come here and watch the MacTires. I'm long past the point where I want to join a pack but I like to check in and see what I'm missing about pack life, if anything. It's how I learned about Nick. It's why I approached him.'

A lot of things about Thane Barrow were falling into place. 'Why do you watch the MacTires?' I asked. 'Why not the Barrow pack?'

'Some things and some people are too close to my heart and too painful to see.'

I could believe that. I raised a hand to reach for him.

'If you're going to pat my arm in sympathy and tell me that I'm a survivor or that you feel my pain,' Thane growled, 'I'll take your pity and ram it down your throat.'

'That's not what I was planning to do,' I said and grabbed his arm anyway. 'Look down there, in the courtyard at the woman who's just come out of the front door. That's her,' I said. 'That's Quack. And it looks like she's about to head out to the street.'

CHAPTER
SIXTEEN

We watched her until we were sure. Quack paused and spoke to the guards, both of whom were different werewolves to the ones I'd seen last night. She seemed to be on better terms with these two and chatted for several moments, at one point throwing her head back with what sounded like genuine laughter.

Even from this distance it was obvious that her nose was still bruised and swollen though she'd removed the bandages and done her best to disguise it with make-up. Quack wanted to appear tough; she would already have lost considerable respect by allowing herself to be bested by a little old cat lady. From the way she was acting, she was doing her best to butter up the guards and keep them on side. Doubtless she had a lot of ground to make up.

'Could she have tried to poison Alexander MacTire because she wants to make her own bid for alpha?' Thane sounded unsure. 'She'd be opening herself up to a world of agony if she tried that. Believe me, I know what it feels like – and it wasn't even the Barrow alpha that I killed. I recognise her face. She's never appeared particularly ambitious or capable. I've not seen her look so ... schmoozy until now.'

'Schmoozy? Is that even a word?'

He waved a hand. 'You know what I mean. There's no need for the grammar police,'

I grinned: he was right about Quack's manner and I'd take the rest under advisement. But we were only seeing part of the picture. 'Do you know who Samantha MacTire is?' I asked.

'I've seen her around and Nick mentioned her from time to time. He said she's a scary bitch. She's the blonde, the MacTire beta wolf, right?'

'Yep. And Nick was right, she's definitely scary. She's also intelligent, strong and about a million times more capable than Quack.' I shook my head. 'There's no way Quack would make an alpha run with someone like Samantha in the mix.'

However, if I hadn't intervened both Alexander MacTire *and* Samantha would have been poisoned. There was a slim chance that Samantha had been the main target but surely if Quack wanted Samantha out of the way, she wouldn't have risked taking Alexander down too. Either he'd been the target or they had both been.

I conceded Thane's point. 'It's possible she was the target. I don't know where Quack ranks in terms of the MacTires' pack but she's not as good as she thinks she is. Maybe the MacTires are weaker as a whole than they pretend to be. I'm not convinced about that, especially given the timing, but we can't rule it out.'

Thane scratched his chin. 'That's what I thought.'

We stayed where we were while Quack waved goodbye to the guards and went through the main gate. She paused on the street and glanced in both directions, almost as if she were expecting to be approached, then put her hands in her pockets and turned right, moving briskly with her dark brown ponytail swinging behind her.

Thane and I didn't need to speak. He clambered down the drainpipe to the ground. I followed hot on his heels, then we were both running in Quack's direction.

We picked up her trail quickly and fell in behind her as she marched along the old, cobbled street. If I'd been on my own, I might have been tempted to hold back and see where she was heading before I went for her, but I could tell from Thane's brisk steps and stiff spine that his patience had almost run out. He wanted answers – and so did I. I was still no closer to finding Nick and the sensation that his time was running out was growing stronger. Sometimes there was no choice but to act.

Quack turned left, abandoning the busier thoroughfare for a narrower side street. It was devoid of people and I knew this was our chance. I nudged Thane and pointed to the parallel street. Thankfully he understood and took off, sprinting away so he could curve around and block Quack from the front while I approached her from behind.

It was a classic pincer move that reminded me there were occasional benefits to working with a partner. It didn't mean I'd be signing up for a permanent double act any time soon, though, and I suspected Thane felt the same, but it was nice to know I had reliable backup even if it was only temporary.

I held back for several breaths, allowing him time to run around the block and reach the other end of the street, then I started in Quack's wake. I'd gone less than ten metres when I saw her back stiffen and her head rise a fraction. She didn't immediately turn around but I knew she'd scented me; we'd spent enough time together that she'd recognised my smell.

She continued walking, albeit more slowly, whilst I did the opposite and picked up speed. She knew I was behind her so there was no longer any reason to be circumspect. I watched her fists clench and unclench: Quack was preparing for a fight. That was good because so was I.

'Hi there!' I called out in my most cheerful voice. 'Fancy meeting you here!'

She stopped walking but didn't turn around. Her body was rigid and I knew she was scared. That pleased me even more.

'Can we have a wee chat?' My voice echoed around the narrow street, making it louder than I'd intended. A flicker of movement snagged my eye and I glimpsed a skinny tabby cat peering over the edge of a building to my right. He yawned, displaying a fine set of sharp teeth; doubtless he'd been snoozing up there and my shout had disturbed his nap.

I raised my hand, half in acknowledgment and half in apology, and he blinked at me but continued to stare. I guessed he was hoping for a show. I shrugged and returned my attention to Quack, who had finally turned to face me.

I drew closer until the gap between us was only a few metres and grinned; unsurprisingly, she didn't smile back. 'You've been following me,' she said with a soft snarl.

I didn't bother to deny it. 'We need to talk.'

'My orders are to leave you alone.'

'For your own safety, I imagine,' I nodded towards her swollen nose.

Her eyes narrowed. 'You're looking for round two?'

'I'm looking for a chat.'

She folded her arms. 'I'm busy.'

'It won't take long.'

'I'm *very* busy.' Her gaze was hard and I matched it with my own stare. Her nose twitched then she spun around and started to sprint away. I guessed I'd won the staring contest.

I stayed where I was. Quack didn't get very far; she hurtled fifteen metres down the street to where Thane was already waiting. He reached out and snagged her arm.

Quack exploded. 'What the fuck?' She tried to wrench away but he held her fast. She kicked and lashed out with her fists, twice landing blows that would have sent a weaker man flying, but Thane was stronger than he looked. He tightened his hold on her then raised his head and smirked at me.

As he started hauling her back to me, Quack fought him every inch of the way. 'You don't know who you're messing with,' she spat. 'One word from me and the entire MacTire pack will be after you. You're dead meat. I know who you are, loner, and I know who she is. You're going to regret the day you laid eyes on me.' She kicked him again. 'Let me go.' Her voice rose. 'Let me go, you fucker!'

She was making an incredible amount of noise. We weren't so far off the beaten track that her yells wouldn't attract attention and that was the last thing we needed. 'Be quiet!' I commanded.

She looked at me. 'Fuck you!'

I lifted my hand and smacked her on the side of the head. It was little more than a glancing blow but even so she howled. I cursed. Goddamnit, I wanted her to be quiet, not raise more hell. 'Shut your trap!' I commanded.

She struggled against Thane. 'The fuck I will. My alpha is going to bleed you dry for this.' She opened her mouth and gathered her breath, clearly preparing to scream.

I jumped in before she brought half of Coldstream to her side. 'You mean the alpha who you tried to poison two nights ago? Alexander MacTire? That alpha?'

With that, the fight was over; Quack's scream died in her mouth and she stared at me mutely.

'Oh yeah,' I said. 'I know all about that.'

Her eyes darted from left to right; now she was wondering if Alexander MacTire himself had put me up to this.

'He doesn't know,' Thane murmured.

'*Yet*,' I added menacingly.

He rolled his eyes at me. 'We won't go running to him if you tell us what you've done with Nick,' he whispered to Quack.

Her expression slackened with astonishment and my stomach sank. She didn't know; she didn't know about Nick's abduction. From his position behind her, Thane couldn't see her face. 'Tell us where he is and we might forgive your involvement,' he said.

Quack stopped struggling and looked at me. 'Nicholas is with you.' She paused. 'Isn't he?'

When I didn't answer, she started to laugh. 'Oh, you're so screwed! It doesn't matter what *I've* done. When Alexander MacTire hears you've lost his last remaining blood family member, you'll be dead meat.' She laughed again. 'Is he actually dead?' she asked. 'Or only missing?'

Something sparked in Thane's green eyes and he opened his mouth to speak. I shook my head; we didn't need to provide her with any more ammunition against us. And she still had questions to answer.

'Why did you try to kill your own alpha?' I demanded.

Quack paled.

'Answer me.'

'I didn't try to kill him, you stupid bitch.' She hawked up a ball of phlegm and I raised my hand, preparing to smack her again. Fortunately she saw the light and swallowed it.

'Last time I checked,' I said conversationally, 'death-cap mushrooms induce death.'

Quack squinted. 'What are you talking about?'

Thane gave her a shake. 'You know exactly what she's talking about.'

I nodded. 'You dropped powdered death cap into Alexander MacTire's coffee pot.'

'No, I didn't.'

'You did.'

'I didn't.'

'You—' I sighed. This could go on forever. 'I saw you do it.'

Quack was shaking her head, alarm lighting her eyes. 'I spiked his coffee, but not with fucking death cap! I don't want him dead! He's my alpha! Why would I want to hurt him?'

'Why do you think I'm asking you that question?' I returned, but doubt was creeping in. 'I had the liquid tested. It was death cap.'

'No, no, no! It was maca and gingko with a sprinkling of extra magic. That's all.'

'Maca and gingko?' I asked disbelievingly.

'Aphrodisiac herbs. Designed to increase virility and desire,' Thane said.

Quack nodded vigorously. 'He's single, he has no children and he's getting older. We need him to start living up to his responsibilities and establish a proper dynasty.'

The corner of Thane's mouth lifted. 'With you?'

'With anyone!'

'But you hoped it would be you.'

Quack muttered something under her breath, but she didn't deny it.

'Let me get this straight,' I said. 'You decided to spike his coffee so he would mate?'

'Yes!'

I pressed on. 'Who gave you the idea to do that?

'A friend.' She bared her teeth. I wasn't impressed. She'd need to do more than show me her pearly lupine whites if she wanted to intimidate me.

'Did this *friend* also give you these supposed aphrodisiac herbs?'

She nodded. Thane and I exchanged glances. 'Who?' I asked. 'Who was it?'

'It was just maca and gingko!' she protested. 'It wouldn't have hurt him!'

'I can assure you it was not maca and gingko that you dropped into his coffee,' I told her firmly. 'Not to mention that you spat in the pot first.'

Quack swallowed. 'I shouldn't have done that. I was pissed off that he'd bawled me out and I wasn't thinking straight. But I definitely didn't try to poison him. I wouldn't – I couldn't!'

My voice was flat. 'You did.' There was nothing concrete to link this apparent poisoning with Nick's abduction, but the two events could easily be related. 'Who gave you the powder?'

She stared at me. 'It was really death cap?' she whispered.

'Yes.'

I hadn't thought it was possible for Quack to go even paler but she did. 'Oh shit.' And then some.

Thane shook her. 'We need a name.'

Quack finally found the words. 'I met him in a pub a few weeks ago. We got on well. He listened to me, paid me attention. He...' Her expression altered and her voice dropped, as well as the proverbial penny. 'Bastard. He manipulated me from the beginning. It was a set up.'

Yeah, yeah. I was growing irritated even though she'd finally seen the light. 'Who is he?' I demanded.

She looked defeated now. 'A druid,' she said. 'His name is—'

A sharp crack rang out and Quack's body went rigid. Her jaw worked, she blinked twice, then her knees buckled and she collapsed in Thane's arms as bright red blossomed across her chest.

SEVENTEEN

It took me a fraction of a second to react. I lurched towards Thane and knocked him to the ground as another shot rang out. Fortunately this one hit the wall rather than our far more vulnerable bodies.

I rolled. I had more than enough experience to know the trajectory of the bullet that had hit Quack: the shooter, whoever they were, was situated up to the right, probably less than fifty metres away.

As soon as I knew I was shielded from any further hits, I reached for Thane and yanked him next to me. His nostrils flared and I felt the thud of his heart, but other than that he displayed no signs of panic.

He stretched out his hand to grab Quack but I shook my head. 'She's already dead,' I said grimly. I didn't need to check her pulse to know that because the bullet had struck her directly in the heart. Even if it weren't silver, she had already passed out of this life. Not even a werewolf could escape such a hit.

Thane's jaw tightened but he nodded. He pointed upwards

and raised an eyebrow. I indicated agreement; we couldn't allow whoever had fired that shot to get away.

He knelt and made a foothold for me with his cupped hands, then lifted me so I could scale the wall and reach the rooftop. I paused for a moment, taking the time to look around and double-check we weren't about to be shot again.

When I saw the back of a black-clad figure sprinting over the nearby rooftops, I reached down and extended a hand to Thane to help him up. As soon as he saw the shooter, he took off in pursuit.

I started to follow but stopped when the killer sailed across a wide gap that no normal person could cross. It might have been a temporary magic spell or naturally enchanted ability, but either way we wouldn't catch the assassin without a little enhancement of our own.

I turned back and spotted the tabby, still in the same position and still with the same frank curiosity in his gaze. The shot had startled him but he was brave enough to hold his ground.

'Sorry about this, mate,' I said. I strode over and plucked a tuft of fur from his side. He gave a startled miaow and blinked at me. 'I appreciate it,' I told him. 'Come visit me in Danksville and I'll repay you.' The cat emitted a brief purr.

There was no time to waste. Both Thane and Quack's killer were already some distance away so I swallowed the clump of fur and waited for the painful magic to take hold. Mercifully, the transformation was swift and within seconds, now in feline form, I was springing forward in their wake. I was quite some distance behind them but in this body I could catch them up; I might be small, but I had the power and the ability to jump a long way without fear of falling. I could do this.

My claws skittered across the roof tiles and I leapt to the next building. I veered around a narrow chimney stack and startled a bird pecking at something in a gutter. I paid it no attention as it squawked in surprise but maintained my momentum, flashing forward with far more grace and poise than I could ever produce in my human body.

Thankfully I was soon nipping at Thane's heels on the flat roof of what appeared to be a supermarket. He was breathing hard and leaving a vetiver-scented cloud behind him – but then he came to a stuttering halt.

The fleeing assassin was closer now but the gap between this roof and the next one was vast.

I miaowed. Thane jerked and stared down, his brow furrowing as he gazed at me. His features appeared different as I looked at him through cat eyes. I hadn't told him *how* I'd witnessed Quack's attempt at poisoning Alexander MacTire or that I possessed this special ability but now he understood.

'Interesting,' he murmured as he recovered from his surprise. 'Can you make that jump?'

Unable to smile, I blinked instead. *Watch me.* Then I took off, sailing easily across the gap and leaving Thane behind me. I put him out of my mind: I had to reach that killer. Feline endurance was not limitless and if I was going to catch up, I had to do it soon.

I gathered more speed and strength and powered ahead. The rooftops here were trickier to traverse, many of them dotted with cemented shards of broken glass designed to deter would-be thieves, skulking vampires or parkour runners. Such elaborate forms of discouragement would slow my quarry but they caused me few problems.

I danced through the jagged glass, jumped to the next rooftop and scaled the angled tiles. With each building, I was moving upwards – and the next rooftop was four storeys high.

I heard a loud oomph as the assassin only just cleared the distance and scrambled for purchase. Then he turned, revealing his face: not a werewolf but quite possibly a druid judging from the blue tattoo on his left cheekbone. Was this the same druid 'friend' who'd given Quack the poison? I'd find out soon enough.

He smiled as he registered how far behind Thane was but he didn't notice me. In that instant I knew I had him, even though he turned and quickly disappeared from my view.

I bunched my muscles and jumped again, this time landing on a narrow windowsill below where I wanted to be. I took a breath, warier of this next leap – one wrong paw and I'd tumble to the street below. I'd survive the fall but Quack's killer would get away and I was determined that wouldn't happen.

I eyed the side of the building. With just the right amount of power and well-placed steps, I'd do it. I gulped in air then launched myself upwards, bouncing twice against the stone on my way up. Two seconds later, my four paws were safely on the solid roof.

The assassin was only ten feet away. I padded forward, taking care not to make any sudden movements. He checked over his shoulder, yet again glancing towards Thane who was still trapped on the rooftop far behind us. He could have dropped to the ground to track the man from the ground but Thane was smart; he was doing everything he could to lull the shooter into a false sense of security and give me the space and time I needed.

The assassin chuckled and muttered, 'Stupid wolf wanker.' He turned left and I realised he was planning to switch direction to make it even harder for Thane to follow him. If he crossed the next gap, he'd be out of sight and could head anywhere he wanted. Thane had never gotten close enough to get a decent whiff of the man's scent so he'd lose him for good in minutes. But I was here and I was ready.

I braced myself and started to hawk up the hairball. It wasn't a quiet process and I knew I'd alert my target; I just had to hope that he wasn't switched on enough to work out what was happening until it was too late.

I spat out the hairball and felt the familiar twist and crack as I reverted to human form. As I sprang up, I glimpsed the assassin's gaping mouth and shocked eyes. I slid out the sharp blade that had been strapped against my skin and had therefore made the transformation with me, and I smiled slowly.

The man reached inside his jacket, doubtless for the gun with which he'd killed Quack. I ran at him, grabbed hold of his wrist and wrenched it hard. He gave a high-pitched moan and dropped his weapon. I kicked it away and smiled again. Sometimes all you needed was to appear confident that you were stronger, faster and better and your target would cave. I was banking on that happening now.

His expression twisted and the blue tattoo scrunched up. The way his muscles bunched and his body leaned forward broadcast his plans almost as if he'd shouted them on a loudspeaker: he was going to make another run for it.

I moved to block his path and he stared at me empty-eyed before twisting and jumping off the roof. He didn't try and land on the next rooftop. He plummeted straight to the ground.

I blinked. I hadn't been expecting *that*. I darted to the edge of the roof and peered after him. He was lying on his back, his leg at an angle that suggested it had been broken in at least two different places.

He looked up at me and reached into his jacket again. I expected him to aim another gun at me, but he pulled out a little glass vial. He raised it in my direction as if toasting me and I realised what he was intending to do. I shouted, my voice bouncing uselessly down to him, as he used his teeth to extricate the cork stopper and gulped down the vial's contents.

He blinked up at me and smiled beatifically. 'I shall be

rewarded in the next life,' he said. 'My sacrifice will not be forgotten.'

Whatever he'd taken, it was fast acting; he'd barely finished speaking when his body started to convulse. Thane, who had realised that the assassin was on the ground, was by his side in seconds but he was too late.

Whatever secrets the assassin had, and whatever his dealings had been with Quack, he was taking them to his grave.

I TOOK my time returning to the ground. By the time I reached Thane and the dead assassin, he had already rummaged through the man's pockets. 'Nothing. No ID. No wallet. No written orders.'

I wasn't surprised; anyone who was prepared to kill themselves rather than get caught wasn't going to make the rookie error of leaving tell-tale information on their corpse. I hunkered down by the man's ankles, before pulling off his right shoe and sock.

'What are you doing?' Thane demanded.

'Checking.' I peered at a large and somewhat hairy big toe. 'EEL assassins are marked discreetly so they can be identified if they're killed during the course of a job. Everyone, without exception, has a temporary magicked tattoo on a hidden part of their body.'

'Their toe?'

I flipped the body over, lifted up the man's shirt and yanked down his trousers. 'Sometimes the buttocks or small of the back. This guy is clean – he's not EEL.'

I gave him a little dignity and returned his clothes to where they'd been then stared at his hands. His fingertips were stained with something red: it wasn't blood but paint, perhaps.

I frowned, then I spotted the gold watch around his wrist. I gave it a closer look then undid the clasp and slid it off. The dead assassin wasn't as clever as he thought he'd been.

'So we know who he isn't,' Thane said. 'But we're no closer to knowing who he is. In fact, all we've succeeded in doing is causing the deaths of two people. We haven't gained any new information at all.'

That was where he was wrong. 'This guy is a druid, or at least he appears to be. He voluntarily went to his death muttering something about a sacrifice that would be rewarded, which suggests some sort of warped religion or cult.'

'That doesn't narrow things down. Not in this city.'

'Perhaps not. But we can still learn more from him. He's got very small feet, which don't match the imprints left in the rug in Nick's living room. This isn't the person who took Nick but that doesn't mean he wasn't involved.' I held up the watch. 'They're not separate crimes because the last time I saw this it was around Nick's wrist.'

Thane sucked in a breath and stared at it. 'You're sure?'

'Yep.' I pocketed it. 'Our killer definitely had something to do with what's happened to Nick. If it weren't for the attacks on you and Lorna, I'd assume that the MacTires are the main target but we need to look at these crimes from a different angle.'

'Go on.'

I stood up. 'Nick is the target because he's a lone wolf like you. The people who wanted Alexander MacTire dead – and by extension Quack – are the people who kidnapped Nick. We both know that if MacTire discovers his nephew has been abducted, he'll turn this city upside down to find him and the whole of Coldstream will suffer as a result. Somebody wants to stop that from happening by killing MacTire first and sending his pack into disarray. Everyone would forget about Nick in the chaos.'

I paused. 'We're looking for a team of people, not a lone

predator who saw Nick as an easy target. This team think he is important enough to risk provoking the anger of the most powerful werewolf pack in the city and their recent actions suggest they'll do almost anything to ensure Nick isn't found. Which strongly suggests that he is still alive.'

Thane's eyes widened. 'In that case, it begs the question of whether we go to MacTire and tell him what's happened. He's going to find out eventually – that's his dead werewolf back there.' He nodded towards the place where Quack had died. 'He's going to miss her sooner or later.'

I didn't see how Alexander MacTire could help us at this stage and I was sure we'd have more chance of finding Nick if we sneaked around on our own. Thane and I could keep our investigation clandestine but Alexander MacTire didn't do sneaking; I didn't have to read the man's secret diary to know that much about him.

'I think we should give it another twenty-four hours,' I suggested. 'If we've not found Nick by then we'll have to tell MacTire, but let's hold off for now and continue with our own investigation. There's something else we can try first.'

Thane raised an eyebrow. 'What?'

I met his gaze. 'Nick's dead parents. You said that you don't believe it's a coincidence that they died last month. If we seek them out, maybe they can help us pinpoint who's taken Nick.'

This was the first time I'd genuinely shocked him. He took a step back and held up his hands. 'Seek them out? I want to save Nick and find answers as much as you do, Kit, but necromancy is a step too far. I can't go there and neither should you.'

'I'm not talking about necromancy,' I said. 'I have another plan. It's a long shot but it might work. Let's get these bodies out of the way so nobody finds them for a day or two, then we need to go back to my house.'

For this, I was going to require the services of She Who Loves Sunbeams.

EIGHTEEN

We broke into a house nearby that looked as if it hadn't been lived in for several decades. Nick carried the assassin's body inside while I used a fireman's lift to bring in Quack's corpse. I was sorry about her death; she'd been stupid and naïve, but those weren't reasons to die. I laid her gently down on the dusty floor and mumbled a brief prayer; it invoked no god, but at least it wished her a peaceful afterlife.

'You won't be here for long,' I told her. 'We'll get you to a proper resting place soon.'

Thane joined me. 'I'm not sure we could have done anything differently. Even if we'd not chased her down, he might still have killed her.'

I didn't blame myself for her death but that didn't mean I wasn't angry about it. 'I don't even know her real name,' I said quietly.

He reached for my hand and squeezed it; his warm touch was oddly reassuring.

I allowed myself another moment with poor Quack then we left her where she was.

'So you're a cat,' Thane said, when we were finally seated on the tram and heading for home.

I glanced around to make sure nobody was in earshot. 'A cat sith,' I corrected him. 'And if you're planning on any pussy jokes, I won't be impressed.'

'I wouldn't dream of it,' he protested. I eyed him. 'I mean it!' He grinned faintly. 'I've never met anyone who could do that before.'

'There's not many of us around – but it's a useful trait.' Very useful. I didn't miss the gleam of fascination in his eyes.

'Do you have nine lives?' he asked.

'I'm a cat *sith*,' I said primly. 'Not an actual cat.'

'Do you like being stroked?'

I gave him a hard look. 'Do you?'

He didn't miss a beat. 'Absolutely.'

I should have expected that. Fortunately, he decided to abandon his weak attempt at lightening the mood in favour of something more sensible. 'You can transform at will?'

'It's a little more complicated than that.' I explained the process to him.

He rubbed his chin. 'It sounds painful.'

'It is.'

Thane nodded as if in understanding, although I knew that werewolves had a far easier time even if their shapeshifting was governed by the moon. He changed the subject. 'Do you really think Nick's still alive?'

'I certainly hope so.' I eyed him. 'You really can't think of any reason why someone would want a lone werewolf?'

Thane sighed. 'None that makes any sense.'

I grimaced and we lapsed into silence for the rest of the journey.

~

MY OLD DARLING was stretched out in the garden, ignoring the tickle from some late-season daisies that were brushing her pale-pink nose. There wasn't much sunlight for her to enjoy but she was doing her best and seemed to have located the only remaining bright patch. I glanced up at the sky. The clouds were drifting in the wrong direction; in another five minutes even this spot would be shady.

I knelt down beside her while Thane waited several metres away, sensible enough to give us some distance. 'Hey.'

She Who Loves Sunbeams opened an eye. The tip of her tail twitched, suggesting that she already had an idea about why I was disturbing her.

'I'm sorry,' I said quietly. 'I wouldn't do this if I had an alternative.'

Her tail twitched again and her ears started to flatten. I stroked her head and tickled her chin. 'It's to help find Nick.'

She Who Loves Sunbeams expelled a long sigh then rolled, heaved herself up to her feet and stretched before offering me a long-suffering miaow.

'Thank you.' I gathered her up in my arms and stood up. 'Much like you werewolves,' I explained to Thane, 'different cats have different affinities.' I scratched She Who Loves Sunbeams behind her ears. 'Some are strong hunters, some are better at hiding and sneaking through shadows. And some, like this lovely one here, are good at sensing the spirit world.'

Thane watched me, unblinking.

'I take on a lot of the same characteristics of whichever cat's fur I swallow,' I said. 'And the closer I am to the cat once I'm transformed, the stronger those characteristics are.' I adjusted She Who Loves Sunbeams in my arms, making sure she was as comfortable as possible. 'She'll have to come with us.' I raised my eyebrows. 'Do you know how Nick's parents were killed?'

He shook his head. 'Only that it was supposedly a tragic accident.' His mouth flattened. 'I'm inclined now to think there might have been more to it.'

Indeed. 'Do you know where it happened?'

'Somewhere close to Henderson Market. From what Nick told me, they weren't the only ones who died. But Kit, even if they were murdered by the same people who took Nick, how does that help us?'

'Quite often when someone dies unexpectedly, their soul lingers before departing this world for good.'

'Ghosts?'

It was a bit more complicated than that. 'Sort of. Regardless of the number of people making a living through exorcism and the like, these spirits are rarely malevolent and don't do much beyond re-live their own deaths over and over again until they come to terms with their passing. They're far less than a non-corporeal version of their living selves – they're obsessed with themselves and pay little attention to the living. I'm not sure they think or feel anything. They're less ghosts and more...' My voice trailed off as I struggled to find the right words.

'An echo of what was?'

I met his eyes. 'Yes,' I said. He got it. 'An echo, exactly that. If there's an echo of Nick's mum and dad in the place where they died and we can find out exactly what killed them, we might get closer to finding who else was involved and why.'

'And when we know that,' Thane said, 'we'll find Nick.'

I licked my lips. 'Here's hoping.'

HENDERSON MARKET WAS a far grander affair than the small riverside market I usually frequented. It was at least five times the size and probably ten times louder. Hawkers and market sellers bawled out discounts, slogans and enticing details of their wares; the whole area was a maelstrom of noise, bright colours and strong smells.

For any normal person it was overwhelming – and for She Who Loves Sunbeams it was a nightmare. She burrowed her head into my chest until Thane, with surprising thoughtful-ness, shrugged off his jacket, placed it over my shoulders and zipped it up so that the cat could enjoy some respite.

'I was feeling too hot in this crowd anyway,' he said when I nodded gratefully.

We passed along the main walkway. I was momentarily tempted to stop at a fishmonger's, who seemed to have a better choice of fish than the stall I normally used closer to home, but there was a long queue of people waiting to be served. I suspected that She Who Loves Sunbeams would happily forgo a fishy treat if we could get this operation done and dusted.

'I need somewhere to transform, ideally out of sight of people,' I told Thane.

'I have the perfect place. I know someone who has a small shop over on the western side. She owes me a favour.'

I frowned. 'A werewolf?'

Thane shook his head. 'No.' He lowered his voice. 'A squib.'

I was surprised that anyone, let alone a squib who possessed no preternatural powers or magic, would be in debt to a lone werewolf like Thane but I tamped down my curiosity. No doubt all would be revealed soon.

He led the way, turning left at a candlemaker's stall towards a small pub on a corner behind a large witchery stall. He pushed open the frosted glass door to reveal a bustling bar. It was standing room only and certainly not the sort of quiet spot I'd had in mind, but before I could protest he swivelled to a door marked private and went through it without knocking.

There was nothing beyond the door other than a small,

framed map of Coldstream with seemingly random coloured dots pressed onto it and a narrow wooden staircase. Thane started to climb the stairs, which creaked loudly under his weight. I followed him, my misgivings growing.

There was another unmarked door at the top of the stairs. Thane knocked sharply on it then waited. The landing was tiny and I was forced to squash against him to stand upright. Underneath the jacket, She Who Loves Sunbeams gave a chirrup of annoyance.

Before I could apologise to her, the door opened and a dishevelled woman with frizzy hair of an indeterminate shade of brown gazed out at us. She didn't look upset at the interruption; if anything, she appeared delighted to see us – both of us.

'Thane Barrow,' she beamed. Her smile was sunny and welcoming and I instantly relaxed. She was remarkably petite, looked to be in her mid-thirties and appeared totally unthreatening. 'And a companion. To what do I owe this pleasure?'

Thane raised a hand. 'Hi, Mallory. It's been a while.'

'Ten weeks and three days, to be exact.' She smiled some more. 'But who's counting?'

Hmm: clearly *she* was counting, although Thane didn't appear bothered by her words. 'I need to call in that favour,' he said. 'Right now. Time is a factor.'

Mallory didn't appear surprised. 'Then I suppose you'd better come in.'

We followed her into a small flat. Although the bar was directly below us, no sound drifted upwards. The place was nothing like the grand apartment where Lorna lived but its cheerful atmosphere seemed to match its occupant. Every corner was cluttered but it was very clean and, despite the bright colours and myriad items from crockery to artwork to random objects that seemed to have no purpose at all, it felt warm and inviting. Even She Who Loves Sunbeams caught a whiff of the welcoming air and poked her head out from underneath the jacket to look around.

'A cat!' Mallory clapped her hands with delight and pointed to a squashy armchair draped in a lurid purple throw where a large ginger tomcat was curled up and snoring gently. 'Bert, look who's come to visit!'

Bert clearly wasn't his real name, and he didn't bother to open his eyes, but I knew from the faint twitch of his ears that he was aware there were visitors and one of them was another cat.

'He's new,' Thane said. 'I didn't realise you were a cat person, Mal.'

'I'm a cat person, a dog person and a person person, Thane,' she said, gently chiding. 'But Bert is only a temporary addition.'

Thane stilled and his voice altered. 'A favour?'

'Yes.' Mallory linked her fingers together and smiled benevolently. At my curious glance, she said, 'I'm a broker.'

I was willing to bet the contents of my bank account that she didn't mean a stockbroker.

'I broker secrets,' she said. 'And favours.'

My back straightened. Now that was interesting.

She gestured to Bert. 'This is an easy one. I've agreed to look after this fellow while his owner recovers in hospital from a nasty accident. In return, I will receive a favour to be delivered at the time and in the manner of my choosing. It's a simple transaction – some of my deals are considerably more complex.'

I stared at her, fascinated.

'It's a living.' Mallory gave a relaxed shrug. 'Although I have to admit it's rare for me to owe someone like Thane a favour – usually it's the other way around. I'll be glad to get this off my books. What do you need?'

Thane didn't beat around the bush. 'Your flat.' He glanced at me. 'For ... four hours?'

That was more than enough time. 'Three will be fine.' If I couldn't locate the lingering spirits of Nick's mum and dad in that time, they weren't going to be found.

Mallory glanced at Thane; it was obvious that whatever Thane had done for her she was getting the better end of the deal. 'You want me to leave?'

'Yes.'

'Can Bert stay?'

Thane looked at me and I nodded.

'Very well,' she said. 'Give me a few minutes to grab my things and the place is all yours.' She went into the next room.

I leaned towards Thane. 'What did you do for her?' I whispered.

'I saved her life.' He said the words without any trace of pride or ego; he was simply stating a fact.

'And this is what you're asking for in return?'

His response was ambivalent. 'This is what we need. What else would I ask for?'

Fair question, but something about Mallory's capable aura suggested that she could offer Thane a great deal more than the use of her flat for a few hours. However, the deal was already done and I wasn't going to argue.

A moment later she returned with a bag over her shoulder. 'The place is yours for three hours,' she said. She curtsied and walked out, leaving us alone: no questions, no caveats, no trouble. My fascination with both Mallory and the bargaining process hadn't diminished in the slightest.

'There is always something new to learn about Coldstream and its inhabitants,' I murmured.

I unzipped the jacket to allow She Who Loves Sunbeams to

hop out. Mallory was more than interesting, but she wasn't my priority.

The cat jumped onto the burnished coffee table and sniffed, then circled the room to inspect every inch of it. I reached out to Bert and offered him some attention. He opened his eyes, raised his head and let me stroke him; he seemed content enough and even gave me a brief purr. He was entirely unfazed by She Who Loves Sunbeams.

Satisfied for now, I prepared for my transformation. It felt strange to complete the process while Thane was watching. His gaze wasn't judgmental, merely curious, but I turned my back on him, suddenly shy.

'I can wait in the other room,' he said, sensing my discomfort.

'No, it's okay. I'm not used to an audience but it doesn't really matter.' I bent down to She Who Loves Sunbeams. 'Are you ready?' I asked her.

Her whiskers quivered, which I took as a yes. I calmed myself and plucked the fur I needed from her body. 'Thank you,' I told the cat. 'I appreciate your help more than you know.' Then I swallowed it down and opened myself up to the change. Thankfully, it happened quickly.

Bert was as fascinated by me as I had been by Mallory. Once I was on all fours and stretching out to become accustomed to my feline body, he jumped off the armchair and came towards me. With a surprising burst of speed, She Who Loves Sunbeams inserted herself between us and hissed in warning. I nudged her gently and crooked my head up towards Thane.

'Don't worry,' he said, 'I'll make sure they behave themselves while you're gone.' He paused. 'Unless you want me to come outside with you?'

No: this would be easier if I were alone. I managed to shake my head to convey that, and he seemed to understand. He walked to the door of Mallory's flat and opened it so I could sidle out. 'Take care,' he said. 'Watch out for dogs.'

Yeah, yeah. I padded down the stairs just as an inebriated punter from the pub lurched for the front door and opened it, allowing me to escape into the outside world. It was time to find some ghosts.

CHAPTER
NINETEEN

Crossing the busy market as a cat was far different to walking around as a human – for one thing I could move faster by weaving in and out of people's legs. But I was also more aware of rats on the hunt for scraps of discarded food, and I had to tamp down some deep feline instinct to chase them.

There were other issues, too. I was at the mercy of people's kindness – or lack of it. I had to skitter away three times to avoid being kicked by irritated passers-by who obviously thought that their right to walk these paths was greater than mine. They weren't as annoying as the supposedly friendly hands that stretched towards me, usually from children who wanted to grab my fur. Honestly, if I'd been a full-time cat I'd have done everything I could to stay away from places like the market, even if there was a good chance of nabbing some food.

Thane had told me that Nick's parents were killed in the far northern corner just beyond the last few stalls; he only knew that much because Nick had wanted to visit the area and asked him for directions. I headed straight there, hoping my plan would work though there was no guarantee that there would be anything to find; in fact, there was every chance that the souls of Nick's mum and dad had already moved on despite their untimely deaths.

I edged around a muddy puddle and wiggled underneath a bookseller's stall near the intersection I'd been looking for. It wasn't as busy as the rest of Henderson Market; this would be easier with fewer people around.

I scanned around for a vantage point and spotted a disused water fountain with a flat section on top. However, with the characteristics of She Who Loves Sunbeams rather than He Who Roams or the skinny rooftop cat, it was harder than I'd expected to leap onto it. I felt my bones creak and it was an effort to haul myself up. No wonder my old girl preferred to lie around in the sunshine; leaping around wasn't for everyone.

Once I'd recovered, I sat back on my haunches and licked a paw. In my experience it was easier to spot spirits when they didn't know you were looking for them so I focused on grooming and used my peripheral vision for the telltale shadowy flickers of the recently departed.

Several minutes passed but I remained patient. I ignored the dribble of rain that started to fall and the pigeon who was looking annoyed, as if I'd nabbed his favourite spot. Thankfully my patience was soon rewarded, probably because of the darkening sky: ghostly spirits were far easier to see when the light was dim, especially with cat eyes.

Perhaps it was a testament to their strong relationship, or perhaps Nick's mum and dad hadn't yet realised they were dead, but they had stayed together. Their souls were flitting through the streets less than thirty metres away from me. I continued to groom the same spot on my paw as I watched them. They weren't the only spirits haunting this place: two others looked as if they'd been caught in the same accident – if it had been an accident.

Although they were more shadows than people, their lupine heritage was obvious. Nick's dad looked very much like his son, with the same long nose and curling hair. He reached the intersection and prepared to cross the street, his hand clasped with a woman whom I took to be Nick's mum.

The other two spirits didn't appear to know each other or Nick's parents. One approached from the right and one from the left; both, as far as I could tell, were witches. The one on the right had a battered satchel over his shoulder, but neither of them were holding weapons or displaying any interest in the werewolf couple.

Nick's dad bent his head and his lips moved as he spoke to his wife. She glanced up and for a moment I thought she was looking directly at me, then I realised she was staring at something that I couldn't see.

I leaned forward as the four spirits paused and then converged on the same spot in the centre of the road across from the last line of market stalls. At the same time, a chubby arm waved in front of my face and I almost fell off the fountain top.

'Kitty! Cute kitty!'

Bloody kids. I hissed loudly, hoping to scare him off because he was blocking my view. A woman snatched him away. 'Frederick! Leave that mangy cat alone!'

I hissed indignantly this time: I was pleased the kid was being removed but I most definitely wasn't mangy. I glared after them then returned my attention to the four spirits. I'd missed the action so I'd have to wait for them to repeat it.

It didn't take long. Nick's mum and dad approached the intersection and his dad said something to his mum who stared at the same blank spot. One witch came from the right, the other from the left and there was a momentary pause. Now, with my view uninterrupted, I watched the finale.

The left witch brushed past Nick's parents and the right witch started to frown. A split second later they all froze, their expressions displaying a rictus of confusion and shock, then their shadows blurred away at the same time.

Hmm. Whatever had taken place had happened in the blink of a cat's eye.

I waited and watched again. Nothing changed. I watched them for a third time and a fourth. Once I was certain that there was nothing new to be learned from where I was sitting, I jumped down from the fountain, ignored the jarring of my bones and headed towards the spot where the action had happened.

All four spirits were repeating what they'd done in the lead up to their deaths and they would probably continue to do so until they came to terms with the event and their lack of physical existence. Only then could they depart to whatever lay beyond.

There was nothing obvious to indicate why the four had died: they hadn't been hit by anything, their bodies didn't writhe or collapse, they didn't choke, they simply ceased to be at the same time. The likeliest explanation was some sort of explosion but there was nothing in the middle of the street that could explode. I needed a closer look.

I reached the spot and stayed there despite the living, breathing cyclist who was bearing down on me. Determined to scare me out of his way, he rang his bell but I ignored him. With a curse, he wheeled around me. 'Fucking moggy!'

Stupid cyclist. I sniffed and focused on the ground.

It was several weeks since Nick's parents had died; if there'd been any odour to indicate an explosion, it had long since dissipated. There was a faint mark on the old cobbles but it might have been there for years. I was beginning to think that I could watch the ghosts re-live the moment of their deaths a thousand times and still be none the wiser.

I raised my head and my fur bristled as the spirits drew closer. This time, because I was so close, I could feel the chill emanating from them. One witch came from the left, one witch came from the right. Nick's mum and dad walked towards me hand in hand. I held my breath, waiting for the moment when they vanished – but then there was a lull in the action.

Nick's mother turned her head not to look at the same blank spot as before but to stare at me. Her ghostly figure wavered.

Her husband tugged on her hand as if trying to encourage her to relive the moment of her death once again but she resisted. Her lips formed words I couldn't read and couldn't hear: she was trying to tell me something but I didn't know what it was.

The two witches had also stopped their grim charade and were watching Nick's mum with frustration. Suddenly the witch to my right circled my feline body before aiming a kick at my haunches. I flinched, even though I knew his ghostly form couldn't connect with my live one.

It was unusual for a spirit to be so aware of the physical world so I reckoned that was a good thing: it probably meant that he was on his way out of here. So too was Nick's mum, even if her husband was some way behind her.

As she stamped the ground, her foot hit the cobbles with an eerie silence. She flounced over to a lamppost and punched it. I blinked: I hadn't expected such anger. She raised both arms heavenward – and a second later she vanished, followed by the other three ghosts.

Then they were back, repeating their macabre re-enactment yet again.

I waited for several more rounds but whatever Nick's mum

had been trying to convey, I was obviously not going to witness it again. When I was certain nothing new was forthcoming, I stretched and twisted. I didn't understand what I'd seen, but with Thane's help maybe I could decipher it.

By the time I got back to the small flat above the pub, there were only twenty minutes left before Mallory returned. I changed back into human form and explained to Thane what I'd seen. His ginger eyebrows drew together. 'Let's have a look together, shall we?'

I gathered up She Who Loves Sunbeams and bade farewell to Bert. He blinked slowly and looked away, which was good enough for me. We left Mallory's flat again and returned to the scene; although the four ghosts doubtless remained in situ, I could no longer see them. Not with human eyes.

'They were right here?' Thane asked, pointing to a spot on the cobbles.

'Slightly to your right,' I said. He side-stepped and I nodded. 'Whatever happened took place right where you're standing.'

He lowered himself to the ground until his nose was almost pressed against it. Several passersby who were leaving the market stared at him but we paid them no attention.

I doubted even his werewolf nose would scent anything so I walked over to the lamppost that Nick's mum had punched. There was a tattered sheet of paper pinned to it that I'd not noticed from the ground when I was a cat. I squinted at it, expecting to see yet another advertisement for some winter solstice shindig, but it was nothing of the sort.

The lettering was faded and the ink had bled as a result of the recent weather but I could read enough of it; it was an appeal for witnesses to an incident that had killed four people, posted by an officer of the MET, the Magical Enforcement Team that was the closest equivalent to the police in Coldstream.

I smiled grimly. Captain Wilberforce Montgomery: finally we had the name of somebody useful to talk to. I bowed in the direction of the street. *Thank you*, I projected silently to Nick's dead mother. *We owe you one.*

TWENTY

We dropped She Who Loves Sunbeams back at my house and I made sure all the cats, including the feral strays who popped by on a regular basis, were fed and watered then we high-tailed it directly to the MET office.

Captain Montgomery was a harassed man. He had reluctantly agreed to meet us, although he gave the impression of someone who had no time and even less inclination to talk to members of the public.

I wasn't sure why he felt under so much pressure because most criminal activities were taken care of in-house in Coldstream: the witches' council took care of the witches; individual werewolf packs and alphas covered their own shapeshifters; the druids had a board of governors, and the assassins – well, they'd have to be caught before they got into trouble.

MET officials only mopped the leftovers and dealt mostly with petty crime and public disorder issues that couldn't be taken care of elsewhere. Perhaps there had been a spate of such problems recently or maybe the MET was woefully understaffed; either way, Montgomery was eyeing us with a weary expression and barely contained irritation.

'If you don't have any new information for me and you didn't witness the accident, I don't know why you're here.' He gave a disparaging sniff.

I gave him my best dotty cat-lady routine; I even injected a slight tremor into my voice that I was particularly proud of to give the impression that I was both vulnerable and still grieving. I needed to get Captain Montgomery on my side; he wouldn't give us any useful information if he took against us.

'We're friends of the family.' I dabbed my nose with an embroidered handkerchief then took Thane's hand. 'Very good friends.'

Thane immediately understood what I was doing. He patted my hand and leaned into my ear. 'It's alright, darling. It's alright.' He lifted his head. 'Captain, we're here for young Nicholas. He wanted to come in person to find out how the investigation is progressing but he still feels too raw.'

Montgomery didn't show any signs of softening. 'You mean Nicholas, the son of Andrea and Thomas, both deceased? Nicholas, the MacTire werewolf? The same MacTire werewolves who told me they'd investigate the incident and didn't need my interference?'

Ah. 'His uncle, Alexander MacTire, is rather overbearing. Nicholas is not officially a MacTire wolf – he is unbound. His uncle has not been forthcoming with information, which is why we are here on Nicholas's behalf.

Thane nodded. 'He's an orphan now. He just wants to know what happened to his parents.'

'I sent a copy of my findings to the MacTires,' Montgomery said stiffly. 'Even though they asked me not to look into the matter, there were four deaths. It wasn't only werewolves who were killed.'

I was starting to realise that the captain's attitude was more the result of wounded pride than anything else. 'That man,' I muttered. 'That bloody MacTire. Why wouldn't he tell us? Why wouldn't he tell Nick?'

Thane hugged me. 'I don't know, darling.'

Montgomery's eyes flicked between us and his expression lightened a little. We had him; if Alexander MacTire didn't want us to know anything, he suddenly wanted to tell us everything.

'Look,' he said, with a heavy sigh as if this were a great imposition but he was prepared to make an exception in our case, 'I can tell you that it was a tragic accident. The explosion that killed all four victims resulted from the incorrect handling of materials.'

This time I didn't have to fake my confusion. 'What do you mean?'

'Ernest Smith, one of the witches who died, was carrying a small amount of dragon's beard. We believe some of it leaked from his bag. Unfortunately he was also carrying some old gypsum with him, which can be used as a fertiliser. Given the volatile nature of dragon's beard, it was an accident waiting to happen. Mr Smith should have known better – there's a reason why dragon's beard is highly regulated and should only be transported in sealed glass containers.'

My mouth had dropped open. 'That's it?'

Thane leaned forward. 'Four people died because some idiot couldn't screw on a lid properly?'

'Essentially, yes.' Montgomery gave a small smile. 'If only stupidity and laziness could be classed as crimes.'

The last possible clue as to who had taken Nick was slipping away. I was so used to death being the result of murder that I was astonished that these had been nothing more than an accident.

'This Smith fellow. You're sure about him?' I demanded. 'You looked into him?'

The captain raised an eyebrow. 'You think he created a magical suicide bomb? If that were the case, why didn't he release it inside Henderson Market to cause more damage and make more of an impact?'

'Maybe that's what he intended but his plans went wrong,' I said. But I knew that wasn't right. I had watched Smith's spirit; he hadn't expected to die and he hadn't yet accepted his death. It couldn't have been suicide.

Montgomery opened his mouth but before he could speak there was a knock on the door. 'One moment.' He went to open it while Thane and I exchanged defeated looks.

'Apologies for the interruption, sir,' said a young fresh-faced officer. 'But we're getting reports of a problem at a warehouse in the Glebe. Some outfit called the Crushers.'

I stiffened.

'What is it?' Montgomery asked him.

'Some spell seems to have gone awry and a lot of the employees appear to be experiencing mania and, uh, violence. The entire warehouse is ablaze.'

That damned contentment spell to encourage productivity; I should have done more to warn Tommy about it when I'd spoken to him about Nick.

Montgomery hissed an expletive and turned to us. 'I'm afraid I have to cut short our meeting. You can find your own way out?'

Thane and I nodded, thanked the captain and left the building.

❧

Our return journey was slow. Yes, I was physically tired, but it was the weariness in my heart that was causing most of the problem. From the tightness of Thane's body next to mine, his own heart was experiencing red-hot fury. By the time we turned onto my street he was huffing and muttering, barely able to keep himself in check.

I stopped walking and turned to him. 'This isn't over, Thane. We'll keep searching and find whoever took Nick.'

'He's been gone for days,' he bit out. 'What are the chances that he's still alive?'

'We don't know why he was taken,' I pointed out. 'Whoever did it might not want him dead.'

'Even if that's true, we don't have any more leads. We don't have Nick's scent.' He ground his teeth. 'We don't have *anything.*'

'There are still things we can try.' I chewed the inside of my cheek. 'For a start, we can look for anyone who sells forget-me-not spells. We might track down the kidnappers that way.'

'And if *they* made the spells?' Thane asked. 'It would make more sense that they did, given how many times they've used them.'

'Then we search for anyone who sells the ingredients. We are *not* done, Thane. We're *not* giving up on Nick.'

He eyed me. 'Are you trying to convince me or yourself?'

I wasn't sure. I sighed and pushed back my hair. Maybe it was finally time to involve the MacTires, though I couldn't see how invoking Alexander MacTire's wrath was going to help Nick. There was no scent trail to follow and no suggestion that he'd been taken by another werewolf pack.

We were missing something, I was sure of it. 'Let's rest for a few hours then re-group,' I said, 'We're both tired, and tired minds make mistakes. Let's come at it fresh.'

Thane's jaw clenched but he nodded. 'Fine.'

We covered the last section of road in silence. There was a faint miaow about fifty metres away from my house, and He Who Crunches Bird Bones emerged from underneath a hedge. He didn't usually roam at that hour; his presence suggested my cats were as worried and unsettled as I was.

I scooped him up in my arms and he nuzzled my shoulder, his warm body offering comfort. Unfortunately that brief respite only made me think of Nick again. If he were still alive, was there anyone nearby to comfort him? I hoped that he wasn't completely alone.

'We'll find him,' I whispered, as much to myself as to Thane. 'We have to.'

I SLEPT like the dead for six hours surrounded by furry, purring bodies. When I woke up the crescent moon was high in the sky and I knew instinctively that it was hours before dawn.

I debated rolling over and snatching a few more hours of blessed kip but my mind was already churning with worry about Nick, so I hauled myself out of bed and pulled on some clothes. All five cats were delighted at the prospect of breakfast several hours earlier than usual but I ignored their plaintive miaows and told them they'd have to wait. I shrugged off their disdainful glances; I was more than used to being judged and found wanting by my motley crew of felines.

I made a cup of coffee and headed into the garden. The sky was free from clouds, allowing the stars to shine unimpeded. I gazed upwards for several moments before casting my gaze closer to home. The lights were off in all of my neighbours' houses; in fact the only artificial light was coming from the direction of the Glebe. I suspected the flickering orange glow was emanating from the Crushers' warehouse. Whatever had happened there had clearly been disastrous if the building was still on fire.

Swallowing the dregs of my coffee, I padded upstairs to check on Thane; if he was awake, he'd be chewing over Nick's abduction. Maybe he'd come up with a new theory during the night and there was another line of enquiry we could pursue.

The door to the upstairs flat was ajar and for a horrified second I thought that Thane had been attacked in the same way as Nick. Then I realised I was being daft: the door was already broken and there'd been no time to fix it. Thane wouldn't have bothered to close it.

Just to fully reassure myself, however, I pushed it open gently so I could sidle inside. I wanted to see him with my own eyes to be sure he was alright.

Perhaps the thought of sleeping in Nick's bed was too painful, but Thane was fast asleep on the living-room floor. There would have been more than enough space for him on the sofa but he'd chosen the hard floor; maybe that was what he preferred after spending years of his life squatting in rundown buildings. This strange ginger werewolf with his dark history, troubled intelligence and fascinating acquaintances had experienced a tough life.

I watched him for several seconds. He was lying on his side, one arm flung upwards as if he were reaching for something. He hadn't closed the curtains and moonlight dappled his bare skin.

It was the first time I'd seen him in anything other than baggy clothing and, as I'd suspected, his body was taut with sinewy muscles that indicated his innate physical strength. There were several faint silvery lines stretching across his back and I bit back a gasp: they were scars. They were old, perhaps even decades old, but they told a story of hideous pain and punishment.

My heart went out to him. I might have been an experienced assassin used to the art of killing, but I wouldn't brook any form of torture – and there was no doubt that Thane had been tortured.

I dragged my eyes upwards to his face. He looked different in sleep and his features were softer somehow. I gazed at the rough stubble on his jaw and the line of his cheekbone, as well as his surprisingly long eyelashes...

He emitted a brief snore and I jerked. I was being a voyeur: I had no right to come in here and watch him like this. I left quickly, feeling guilty for spying on him even as the curve of his muscled shoulder and the way the moonlight illuminated his skin filled my mind.

The dim glow from the Glebe caught my eye when I returned outside. I stared at it and then, for lack of anything else to do to ease my restless thoughts, I slipped out of my garden gate and headed towards it.

CHAPTER
TWENTY-ONE

I didn't have a plan, I simply needed a distraction. I was also curious as to how bad the Crushers' situation was because if things had been different Nick could have been caught up in it. Maybe I could help in some way; I still wanted to maintain a reputation as a good citizen, even if Alexander MacTire was about to chop off my pretty little head for allowing such terrible harm to come to his nephew. And I'd liked Tommy; he'd struck me as a good guy who was doing his best under difficult circumstances.

When I turned the corner and crossed the invisible line that led to the Glebe, the level of devastation became obvious. Very little of the existing warehouse remained; only one wall was standing and the rest had collapsed in heaps, several of which were still aflame. A few water witches were in attendance, however, suggesting that the fires were under control and they were waiting for the last of them to burn out.

It was no surprise that there wasn't any sign of Captain Montgomery or any other MET officers. Whatever had happened was over now and it was still the middle of the night.

They'd probably return when dawn broke to continue their investigation – although it was possible I was giving Montgomery too much credit.

I cast a dispassionate eye over the scene. I wasn't a huge fan of fire. Several of my fellow assassins used it to cleanse murder scenes of annoying scraps of evidence that could lead their way, but in my experience its effects were too unpredictable. Besides, the best assassins didn't leave any evidence behind.

A group of people were huddling at the edge of what had once been the perimeter of the warehouse. From the hulking size of the figure at the end, one of them was Tommy, the foreman. I walked towards him, hoping for their sakes that there'd been few casualties.

Tommy was still standing, though he must have been exhausted. When I'd met him earlier it had been obvious he had worries but he'd been managing them; now his shoulders were hunched, his head was drooping and he seemed to have collapsed in on himself. It was hardly surprising; all his hard work and hours of toil had gone up in flames and he'd probably lost everything.

I sidled around the group, most of whom appeared to be employees who were lingering out of loyalty, and approached Tommy, trying to appear sympathetic without being pitying. 'Hello again,' I said softly.

He swung his head slowly towards me and blinked as if trying to place me. He was a shadow of the man I'd met. 'I'm so sorry about what's happened,' I said.

He ran a hand over his head and shook himself. I wasn't sure if he recognised me or cared who I was. 'It's all gone,' he said desolately. 'All of it. There's nothing left.'

'Was anybody hurt?'

'A couple of the guys were taken to hospital with burns and

minor injuries but they'll be alright, thank goodness.' He paused. 'And there are a few more who need to have their stomachs pumped, but I've been told they'll recover.' His voice cracked. 'This is all my fault.'

'The contentment potion,' I murmured. 'In the coffee urn.'

Tommy's head drooped. 'We told them not to drink too much of the coffee, but with all the overtime...'

Uh-huh. 'What happened?'

'Several of my workers overdosed and went crazy. I didn't notice anything was wrong at first – they were a bit louder than usual but I didn't think anything of it. I only noticed when the shouting progressed to throwing things around. When I went to intervene, two of them took off to a different corner of the warehouse and decided to have some fun with fire.' He swallowed hard. 'Because they thought the flames were pretty.'

That was pretty much what I'd expected; there was such a thing as too much happiness. 'You know it's not their fault,' I said, not unkindly.

He sagged even further. 'I know,' he muttered. 'But the deadline...' His voice drifted away. 'The only reason I'm still here is because one of the church deacons is on his way to talk to me.'

'Now? In the middle of the night?'

He nodded dully. Damn: he really was in the shit. 'What can I do to help?'

'Nothing. There's nothing anyone can do.' He turned away.

Even so, I stuck around. Given what I'd seen of Thane he'd sleep for hours, and I was strangely reluctant to waltz off and renew the hunt for Nick on my own. Besides, if we decided to focus on anyone who might sell forget-me-not spells, we'd have to wait until daylight to talk to them. I could spare an hour or two to help Tommy with the clean-up.

Tommy was a good guy who'd made bad decisions and in

an odd way he reminded me of Quack – and nothing I'd done had helped her. Sifting through the burnt remains of a warehouse for an hour or two for anything that could be salvaged didn't make up for her death, but something about the mindless physical work eased my tension – even though I was quickly covered in a layer of black soot.

Although most of the warehouse had been destroyed, it was surprising what had survived. I found a cache of tools covered in ash; if Tommy couldn't get the Crushers up and running again at least he might be able to sell them and claw back a bit of money. Equipment like this could be costly and it was worth retrieving.

Some small fires were still burning and others had only recently been doused so the metal was too hot to touch. I brushed away as much of the ash as I could, then went over to a man who was working at a similar task. From his clothes, I surmised he was one of Tommy's employees. 'You're not a coffee drinker, then?' I said when I drew near.

He gave me a wan smile. 'I've been avoiding caffeine since the summer. Wife's orders. She thought I was drinking too much of the stuff so I promised I'd try and cut back. It's probably one of the smartest things she's ever made me do.'

I grimaced in sympathy. 'I've found some tools back there. They're in pretty good nick all things considered, but I can't pick them up yet.'

He brightened slightly. 'Great. Show me where they are and I'll—'

He didn't get to finish his sentence because the shouting had already started where Tommy was. It didn't take a genius to work out that one of the deacons for the Church of the Masked God had finally shown up to make his displeasure known.

I turned to watch. So did everyone else.

Although it was close to four o'clock in the morning, the deacon was dressed in full church regalia and didn't have a hair out of place. I gazed at his moss-green cassock, the pristine white-lace collar around his neck, his bouncy brown hair and his upright figure; for a man who appeared to be in his fifties, he was the picture of rude health – until you took a closer look. I could have been mistaken but the little red bumps on his neck didn't appear to be the result of a vigorous shaving routine: they were hives. The deacon was under far more stress than first impressions suggested.

'You promised us completion by the solstice,' he bellowed, as if the volume of his voice would encourage Tommy to snap out a salute and rush off to continue working despite having no materials, tools or energy. 'We expect you to fulfil that promise or there will be consequences! There are six days to go and the tower isn't finished. We need it done!'

The deacon was upset about something that was essentially little more than a cherry on top of a public-holiday cake. Why did it matter so much? It was out of character for the Church of the Masked God – and that made me uneasy.

'We can't finish it,' Tommy said. 'Everything has gone.' He waved towards the smoking ruins. 'All the materials we had to finish the job have burned.'

'Buy more!'

'There are no more. I already spoke to our supplier – if we want more wood to finish the tower, we'll have to wait until after Christmas. There's nothing I can do.'

'You gave us your word! You know what you'll forfeit if you don't complete the project.' The deacon's tone was ominous enough to send a shudder through everyone watching.

'I know,' Tommy whispered. 'But that doesn't change the outcome.' Horrifyingly, he lowered himself to his knees in an act of submission. 'I am sorry.'

Enough was enough; while it could be argued that he'd brought this on himself, there was no need for public humiliation. Any respect I'd had for the Church of the Masked God had well and truly dissolved.

I marched up to the deacon, my arms swinging and my fists clenched. 'Why is this necessary?' I demanded. 'Why are you acting this way when you can see for yourself what's happened here?'

'Unless you work for this pathetic loser, this has nothing to do with you,' he sneered.

I sucked in a breath and prepared to snap back, then I paused. My goal here was to make things better for Tommy, not worse, and I wouldn't achieve anything by matching the deacon shout for shout.

'I live nearby and I'm a part of the local community. I know how hard Tommy and the Crushers have been working to complete your project. It's terrible that this has happened and he can't finish on time, but is that really so bad? There'll always be another solstice. I thought better of the Church of the Masked God than this.'

The deacon's head jerked. 'You're one of our devotees?'

'No, but I don't need to be one of your followers to know that this sort of approach won't endear you to anyone.'

'Then fuck off,' he muttered. 'We don't need some middle-aged Karen getting involved.'

A faint gasp rippled through the watchers and the deacon realised belatedly that he'd gone too far. 'I apologise,' he said stiffly. There was a flicker of regret in his dark eyes, although I wasn't sure whether that was because he regretted the sentiment or saying it aloud.

He turned away but I wasn't finished. I grabbed his elbow and forced him to swing back in my direction. 'What's this really about?' I asked softly. My gaze drifted to the hives. 'Why are you so upset about an unavoidable delay?'

The deacon's chest was rising and falling rapidly and a vein was bulging in his forehead. He stared at me and then at the small crowd of onlookers before reaching into his pocket and pulling out a crumpled flyer. 'This,' he spat, and threw it at me. 'This is what it's about.'

I smoothed out the flyer and started to read. *Life in the doldrums? Failed by your faith and their old routines? Why not do something different this solstice and join us at Crackendon Square at noon for a new beginning?*

'Demon worshippers,' the deacon hissed. 'They're luring away our followers. They've said they're doing something big for the solstice. Half my flock are planning to go and see what they're up to instead of coming to the Masked God celebrations. We've had to make big promises to keep our followers engaged with us instead of with them.'

Like building a brand-new tower. It seemed like little more than a dick-waving contest. The Church of the Masked God shouldn't have been afraid of competition – but then I remembered what Quack's dying assassin had murmured about sacrifice. Perhaps there was more to this competitive spat than I'd realised.

'Demon worshippers?' asked somebody in the crowd with a derisive snort. 'Really?'

'You don't understand,' the deacon returned. 'These are not good people.'

Others in the crowd were gaining confidence. 'When was the last time anyone saw a demon?' another person called out mockingly.

There was a ripple of amused snickers. I didn't join in; instead I turned over the flyer and looked at the other side. There was a hand-drawn symbol of a bright red circle with a slash through it. I'd seen it before, spray painted onto the side of Lorna's apartment building. And the assassin who'd taken Quack's life had red paint staining his fingertips.

'This is them?' I asked the deacon, my voice dangerously quiet. 'Who are they?'

'They call themselves Umbra.' His mouth thinned. 'Like their name, they stick to the shadows. We don't know who their leaders are, but we've seen enough to know that they have tried to invoke several demons in the past.' He looked at the small crowd. 'Just because no one in Coldstream has seen a demon for two hundred years doesn't mean they no longer exist.'

'You think this Umbra outfit is run by a *demon*?' I asked, horror beginning to supplant my disbelief. The deacon's suspicions suddenly felt very real.

'No, but we think they're trying to conjure one into existence. And if that happens, the Masked God help us all. If Umbra gain enough followers, they will succeed.'

Ice-cold prickles ran down my spine.

Tommy, who had remained on his knees, staggered to his feet and stared over my shoulder at the flyer. 'I've seen that symbol before,' he muttered. 'Somebody graffitied it onto the side of the warehouse. I thought it was kids but...' His voice trailed off.

I raised my eyebrows at the deacon. 'Maybe it wasn't a contentment spell that caused the warehouse to burn down.' I held up the flyer. 'Maybe these people had a hand in what happened.'

The deacon hesitated, then wrinkled his nose. 'You should all go home,' he said finally. 'There's nothing more that can be done here.' He turned to Tommy. 'Get some rest. We'll talk about what can be salvaged for the tower later.' He nodded briefly to me then he marched away with considerably less energy than when he'd arrived.

Tommy was staring at me wide-eyed. 'Do you really think it was arson and not the contentment spell?'

'Oh, it was definitely the contentment spell,' I said. I started walking away. 'Do what the deacon said,' I called out. 'Go home and get some rest.'

And I broke into a run.

CHAPTER
TWENTY-TWO

I returned home in a fraction of the time it had taken me to get to the Glebe, my mind working overtime with all that I'd learned.

It was too early to get hold of Trilby and ask what they'd meant the other day about werewolf blood being used to conjure demons. I'd thought it was a throwaway line at the time but now I wasn't so sure. I didn't know where Trilby lived and even the riverside market traders wouldn't be setting up their stalls at this hour.

But there were still things I could do. I darted through the garden and swung into my little kitchen, startling all five cats who were still hovering there desperately hoping for an early breakfast. I ignored their plaintive miaows and the cupboard containing their food; instead I upended the bin in one swift motion and scattered the rubbish across the floor. It didn't take long to find the flyer I'd received with the rest of my junk mail and so casually discarded without a second glance.

It was an exact copy of the one the deacon had given me. *Life in the doldrums? Failed by your faith and their old routines?*

Why not do something different this solstice and join us at Crackendon Square at noon for a new beginning?

For fuck's sake; I'd had the answer all along, I just hadn't recognised it because I hadn't given the junk mail any attention. I turned over the flyer and traced the red symbol, then another thought occurred to me. I dropped the flyer onto the floor and headed back outside.

Dawn was still at least three hours away. The darkness didn't make it easy but I scanned the walls of my house carefully. There was nothing on the front or side walls so I moved back through the garden until I was standing in the middle of the potholed street staring at my home.

She Without An Ear followed me, her head tilted with curiosity. I glanced down at her. 'I'm looking for graffiti,' I told her. 'Have you seen any around here?'

She sat back on her haunches and gazed at me, unblinking. I stared back. 'I could really do with some help here,' I said.

She Without An Ear merely sniffed.

'Show me,' I said. 'And then I'll feed you. I promise.'

Unfortunately she was cannier than that. She stayed where she was and started to delicately wash her face with her paw. I ground my teeth.

I knew when I was beaten. 'If I feed you first, then you'll show me?' I asked. She paused mid-lick. I sighed. 'Alright then. Come on.'

I returned to the kitchen and put out kibble for the baying brood. As they munched, I shifted my weight impatiently from foot to foot. Finally She Without An Ear offered me a tiny miaow and returned to the garden, although she sauntered with a maddening lack of speed.

She wandered out of the garden gate to the left then nudged my aluminium bin, which was still outside after Maggie the wirry cow's visit. I stared at it, then stared at She Without An

Ear before darting to the bin and twisting it around. *There.* Splattered on its side in bright red paint was a circle with a slash through it. It was far cruder and messier than the version on the side of Lorna's apartment or the one on the flyer but it was undoubtedly the same.

'Go to the flat upstairs,' I told She Without An Ear. 'Wake up Thane.'

There was no immediate reaction. When I turned to repeat my request, I saw that her ears were pinned back and her teeth were bared. She hissed and spat – then something smacked into the back of my head sending a sharp pain spiralling through my body.

I started to turn but I was hit a second time – and this time darkness descended before I could do anything.

THE FIRST THING I was aware of was the throbbing pain in my skull. I was reasonably hard-headed and I'd received my fair share of serious injuries in my old line of work, but it was rare for anything to hurt this badly.

I gritted my teeth against the agony and tried to raise my hand to touch my head but I was bound tightly to a chair. There was a blindfold across my eyes and a gag stuffed in my mouth: in short, I was screwed.

I'd finally worked out who had taken Nick and I had a working theory as to why, but they'd nabbed me before I could do anything about it.

I grimaced and then, as I fought against the waves of pain emanating from my head, I realised I must be wrong. If this was Umbra, I'd already be dead. The fact that I was here, trussed up like a chicken but still breathing, meant that my attacker was someone else.

The last time somebody had managed to sneak up behind me, I'd been a baby assassin barely out of training. My target had been a rich witch visiting from Russia and his bodyguard had attacked me after I'd dispatched his boss.

I'd been lucky to walk away from that one, but I wasn't so sure I'd walk away from this because now I was older and rustier. And if it wasn't Umbra who'd captured me, there was only one other person who could have done it. I wasn't naïve enough to think that Alexander MacTire would let me talk my way out of this predicament, though I'd give it my best shot.

Although I was obviously in danger the risk wasn't immediate so I zoned out and used an old meditation technique to force my physical pain to subside. It wasn't easy, but after several minutes of trying it was at a level that allowed me to think more clearly and pay attention to my surroundings.

I couldn't see, I couldn't move and I couldn't speak – but I could still use my ears and my nose. All was not lost.

It took me a few moments to separate the several competing smells. The strongest ones were of darkness and deep earthiness. Anyone who doesn't believe that darkness possesses its own distinct odour had never spent any time in a cat's body: darkness definitely smells, although it isn't unpleasant or scary. Instead it has a perfume, subtle but which speaks of peppery spices and musky amber. That smell, combined with the scent of earth, made me certain that I was being held underground.

I doubted this was the MacTire mansion because it would have been too troublesome to cart my unconscious body all that distance; however, they probably had other properties that were closer and were making use of one of them. All the easier to dispose of my corpse afterwards, I supposed.

There were other scents: the faint iron tang of blood, likely my own, and the tickle of bleach. Underlying them all was a whisper of vetiver.

As soon as I registered that particular smell, I held my breath and strained my ears. Beyond the incessant drip of water, a faint, rasping breath that told me I wasn't alone. Thane was in here with me.

Shit. It had been too much to hope that Alexander MacTire or Samantha wouldn't have realised he was staying with me and left him in peace. My stomach clenched. Nothing about this was good.

I concentrated on my breathing, inhaling and exhaling until I was fully centred and calm, then I focused on my first priority: freeing my hands. When I could move properly, I could deal with my other problems.

I wiggled my fingers. From the rough chafing against my wrists, I'd been bound with rope. The good thing was that it was possible to escape from almost any binding given skill, patience and dexterity; the bad thing was that it often took time and patience, neither of which I possessed in abundance.

I flexed my arms, rubbed them together then stretched them as far apart as they would go to create some slack in the rope. Even an inch would help. Once I had some leeway, I could use my fingertips to find the knots and start to unpick them.

Unfortunately for me, whoever had tied me to the chair knew what they were doing. After several minutes, I still hadn't managed to magick up any slack. That was annoying.

I changed tactics and tapped my right foot against the chair to make sure it was made out of wood and not metal then shuffled backwards inch by inch. Alexander MacTire had missed a trick by not bolting the chair to the floor.

I kept moving for what felt like an age, sweat pouring down my forehead and dripping onto the tight blindfold until it was moist from my efforts. I inched back, ignoring the noise of the chair scraping against what sounded like concrete, until I was rewarded for my trouble when I finally hit a wall.

I heaved in a breath; I couldn't afford to waste any more time. Rather than gathering my energy by resting, I tipped the chair to an angle. Every muscle in my legs complained at the unnatural strain but a beat later I was slamming the chair into the solid wall. The sound reverberated around the room.

I gritted my teeth and repeated the movement again and again and again.

On my ninth attempt I finally had some success. I'd shifted my weight to try a different angle and the chair was already weakening. As I connected with the wall, there was a satisfying splintering. I crashed against the wall again and there were more rewarding cracks. Almost there. A couple more hits and the chair would be destroyed enough for me to wriggle free. I smiled beneath my gag.

There was the sound of a door opening and a loud tut. Goddamnit. 'I'll give you this, Ms McCafferty,' Alexander MacTire drawled, although there was no doubting the anger in his voice, 'you don't surrender easily.'

I tried to move faster, inhaled and shoved myself backwards against the wall with all the force I could muster, but it wasn't enough. I'd barely released the air in my lungs when hands reached for my shoulders and dragged me forward.

'You've ruined my chair,' he murmured in my ear then he pulled off my blindfold.

I blinked several times to adjust my vision. MacTire was standing right in front of me as if he expected that I'd somehow make a dash to escape. That was hardly likely since I was still tied to the damned chair that now felt as though it would collapse at any moment.

The room was what I'd surmised: a dark underground basement with a concrete floor and whitewashed walls. There was a single lightbulb overhead. To my right, Thane was also tied to a chair, his head drooping against his chest. He was neither gagged nor blindfolded, likely because he was still unconscious. Behind him was a long glittering mirror.

I gazed at it. Oh.

'Yeah,' MacTire said. 'It's a two-way mirror. I've been watching you trying to free yourself for some time. You're certainly determined.' He smiled coldly. 'I've not been in this room – or even this building – for a long time. My father used it a lot. I'm sure you can guess what for.'

Unfortunately I could.

MacTire stretched his hand towards my face and I flinched. As I jerked backwards there was a loud creak and the wooden chair finally gave way. I fell to the floor. Although the rope was still loose around my wrists, I was free of the tightest of the bindings – not that it would do me much good now.

Alexander MacTire reached down, grabbed the front of my jumper and hauled me upright, dark fire glittering in his eyes. 'What happened to Nick?' he growled.

I sighed inwardly. Thane gave a brief groan – he was coming around. That was good because at least he could confirm my words.

MacTire yanked the gag roughly away from my mouth. 'Where the fuck,' he spat, 'is my nephew?'

CHAPTER

TWENTY-THREE

I didn't answer immediately; I wasn't trying to piss him off but to find a way to reply that wouldn't result in immediate violence. I drew a complete blank.

'I heard Nicholas had gotten himself a job at the Crushers' outfit in the Glebe, then it was burned to the ground,' Alexander said. 'I went to your place to speak to my nephew and make sure he was alright. There was no sign of him and his scent was days old. So where the fuck is he?'

I gave up and simply told him the truth. 'He was abducted.'

The werewolf stared at me; this clearly wasn't the answer he'd been expecting. 'Abducted?' he snarled.

'I'm afraid so.' I licked my lips. 'Though I think he's still alive.'

His hands tightened and he shook me until my teeth rattled – I wasn't sure he was even aware of what he was doing. I could have defended myself and kicked at his groin, but my only real way out of this situation was to defuse it.

'You think?' he bellowed, his voice raising to a roar.

'Oy!'

MacTire and I both turned to stare at Thane.

'Stop that, you wanker! You're not your damned father! There's no need for violence!'

MacTire stopped shaking me but I sensed that his fury was still growing. 'You'd know all about violence, wouldn't you, Barrow?'

Thane's blue eyes narrowed but he held his temper. 'Shaking a poor defenceless woman to death isn't going to get you any answers.'

'Poor defenceless woman? You're a lot of things, Barrow, but I never thought you were a fool.'

I gazed at him primly. 'I'll tell you everything you need to know, Mr MacTire, but first you need to calm down and take your hands off me.'

His eyes shone yellow and his teeth had already sharpened into fangs; he was shifting in front of my eyes in a way that no werewolf should be capable of.

The door opened again and Samantha walked in. Was this good or the absolute worst that could happen? The traffic lights in my head weren't just on red, they were screaming scarlet warnings and telling me to run for my life. Would that I could have done.

'Boss.' Her voice was calm.

MacTire froze and within three seconds his features had smoothed back to normal again. He even released his hold on me. I fiddled with the ropes around my wrists until I'd loosened them and they'd dropped to the floor, but I didn't dare move my feet.

'Go on, Ms McCafferty,' MacTire's tone was calmer but no less dangerous. 'Tell me what happened.'

I smoothed my hands down the front of my jeans. 'Somebody broke into the house, attacked Nick and took him.'

MacTire's nostrils flared. 'You said he'd be fine. You said you'd look after him.'

'Yes, I did say that, but I wasn't at home when he was kidnapped.'

'Where the fuck were you, then?'

I gave him a straight answer. 'I was with you. When you dragged me to your mansion, Nick's kidnapper made their move.'

He looked fit to explode. 'That was three days ago.'

'Yes.'

'Why didn't you come to me as soon as he was taken?'

Now it was Thane's turn to snort. 'Because you're taking the news so well now?' he asked sarcastically.

Without a flicker in her expression, Samantha walked over and gazed down at him. She didn't speak and she didn't raise a hand but Thane averted his eyes. He was smarter than he looked.

I wet my lips. 'At first I thought you'd taken him yourself,' I said.

'Kidnapped my own nephew?'

'You wanted him back.'

'Not like that.'

I conceded the point. 'Then I started working with Thane to find Nick, and we thought that maybe one of your werewolves was responsible.'

MacTire bit back his rage but only barely. 'One of *my* wolves?'

This was awkward. 'Logic suggested it was a werewolf who'd broken into my house and attacked Nick to take advantage of his vulnerability.'

'So you immediately assumed it was a MacTire wolf? That's impossible.'

Samantha stared at me. 'Who?' she asked quietly.

I returned her look but I didn't need to say anything; Samantha already knew. 'Rebecca,' she muttered. 'I knew something was up with her.'

'Is Rebecca the female wolf you sent after me the first time?' I asked.

'She is.'

'Then, yeah. Her.'

MacTire turned on his heel and marched to the door. 'I'll get Joseph to bring her down.'

I pulled a face. 'I wouldn't bother.'

Samantha was still staring at me. 'Why?'

I sighed again, then explained what Thane and I had learned from Quack aka Rebecca. Then I told them where they'd find her body. Unsurprisingly, that revelation didn't improve MacTire's mood. 'You were there?' he demanded of Thane.

'I was. Everything she says is true.'

'It does make a sick sort of sense,' Samantha said softly. 'It's practically the only topic of conversation amongst the entire pack. Everyone wants you to mate, Alex.'

He rolled his eyes in irritation and returned his attention to me. 'How did you know?' he barked. 'How did you know that she spiked my coffee with magical Viagra?' As I hesitated, he bared his teeth and answered for me. 'The cat.' He raised his eyes heavenward. 'The damned cat. That was *you*.'

I kept my gaze level. 'I'm a cat sith,' I admitted.

'That's how you—' He broke off and glanced at Samantha. She raised an eyebrow and waited for him to finish his sentence, but there were some things even his right-hand woman couldn't be allowed to know. He changed the subject. 'Rebecca didn't take Nick, so who did?'

Thane sat a little straighter in his chair. 'Kit,' he breathed. 'What have you found out?'

I told them everything I'd learned from Tommy and the deacon from the Church of the Masked God. I even told them about the junk mail flyer I'd received and the dying assassin's muttered words.

'A demon-worshipping cult called Umbra has abducted Nicholas? Seriously?' MacTire's incredulity was palpable.

I nodded. 'It appears that way.'

'I've had that flyer,' Samantha said slowly.

'I think Umbra have been delivering them all over the city. They're planning some sort of solstice event in Crackendon Square. If what the deacon told me is correct, they're going to try and invoke a demon.' I paused. 'And somehow they'll use Nick to help them.'

MacTire stared at me. 'A cult is all very well, but a demon hasn't been seen in this country for...'

'Two hundred and three years,' Thane finished for him. 'My mother, God rest her soul, used the word as a threat to try and keep me in line – behave or the demons will get you.' He shrugged. 'I was a contrary child and I didn't believe her, so I asked one of my teachers and he said no demon has come to Britain from the netherworld since 1822.'

Samantha folded her arms, her scepticism clear. 'What exactly is a demon?'

'A chaotic creature with nothing but destruction on its wish list,' MacTire answered grimly. He glanced at me. 'According to the old stories, anyway. But this can't be true. Even if Umbra exists, nobody would be stupid enough to call upon a demon and bring them into this world. They answer to no-one and they can't be controlled. Umbra must know that. And what on earth would Nick have to do with any of this?'

'Somebody mentioned something recently.' I hedged my words. 'They suggested that a demon can be invoked through the blood of a werewolf.'

MacTire's eyes blazed. 'Who?' he demanded. 'Who said that?'

'It was a throwaway comment. They're not part of Umbra.'

'You're positive about that?'

'Well, no, but—'

'Then who the fuck are you talking about?'

I didn't want to drag Trilby into this mess; they had nothing to do with it and didn't deserve to be involved. But Nick didn't deserve this either, and I didn't know anyone else who might have any answers.

My shoulders sagged. 'A black-market seller at the riverside market,' I whispered. I looked at Samantha. 'The one who sold you the magicked catnip.'

It took a lot of arguing on my part before MacTire agreed to let me go to the market rather than send several burly werewolves to haul Trilby kicking and screaming back to this hellhole of a hideout.

'You catch more flies with honey than vinegar,' I'd repeated over and over again until he yielded simply to shut me up. But he insisted on accompanying me and instructed a posse of muscle-bound wolves to join us. He left Thane behind in the torture basement with Samantha, but at least allowed her to untie him.

Before I left, Thane sent me a long look and a clear warning. 'Watch yourself,' he said. 'And make sure you come back safe.' I had absolutely no intention of doing otherwise.

As soon as we were outside, with Alexander MacTire sticking so closely to my side that he could have been mistaken for a needy kitten looking for a new home, the werewolf alpha glanced at me. 'I've never seen Thane Barrow interested in anyone's welfare before.'

He obviously didn't know Thane very well. 'He's been

worried about Nick from day one.' I refrained from mentioning the building with the viewing platform into the MacTire stronghold and the flats that Thane rented out at a pittance. I doubted it was information that he'd want me to reveal.

MacTire grunted. 'He's a lone wolf. His interest in Nicholas is simply to encourage a malleable young boy into following in his footsteps.'

I frowned. 'That's not true.'

He chuckled.

'What?' I demanded.

'I thought that Thane Barrow was sweet on you,' he said. 'Now I'm beginning to think it's the other way around.'

My mouth dropped open. Hang on a minute.

MacTire leaned towards me. 'Maybe you're not the committed cat lady you think you are.'

'Piss off.'

'That's your best comeback? Piss off?'

'At least everyone I know isn't conniving behind my back because I've decided to live like a monk.'

His mocking smile vanished. 'I don't live like a monk. I'm not celibate, I'm just choosy about who should become the mother of my children.'

'I hope that the future Mrs MacTire will have a say in the matter, too.'

He glared. 'I'm not a tyrant, Ms McCafferty. And I'm not a murderer either.'

I crossed my arms. 'I think that I'm done talking to you now,' I said icily.

I marched on ahead towards the market. I'd already lost more than enough time talking to him; I wasn't going waste any more.

THE RIVERSIDE MARKET was in full swing by the time we arrived. MacTire grasped my elbow as if he were afraid I'd make a run for it. I wrenched away from him. 'Stay close if you want,' I hissed. 'But don't push your luck.'

I strode up to Trilby's stall and stood behind a shifty-looking witch who was purchasing something dubious. MacTire, however, had no plans to wait patiently in a queue; he elbowed the witch out of the way and marched us to the front. 'What?' he asked at my annoyed look. 'That witch shouldn't be trying to buy a curse of that magnitude. I probably saved his sorry arse from having it blow up in his face.'

The witch in question glowered but was obviously too intimidated by the MacTire alpha to argue. He picked up his long billowing cloak and scurried off.

Trilby wasn't like the terrified witch and they gave Alexander MacTire a look that was icy enough to freeze a bottle of whisky – but that was nothing compared to the glare they gave me. 'Have I not done enough for you, Kit? Why the fuck are you scaring my customers away?'

'I'm sorry,' I said, meaning it wholeheartedly. 'But we have to talk to you, Trilby. It's important.'

'Don't blame her,' MacTire intervened, surprising me. 'I'm the one you should blame. But she's right, we do have to talk to you. Now.'

Trilby folded their arms. 'Then talk,' they said, not softening a jot.

MacTire gestured to me and I cleared my throat, feeling awkward. I prayed that Trilby wouldn't simply laugh in my face for making such a big deal out of one single casual comment. 'Okay,' I said. 'The other day you said something about werewolves.'

Trilby's face cracked, then they looked at Alexander MacTire and smirked widely. 'I did. I told you that if you grind werewolf bones into dust, you can cure cancer. I assume that the MacTire alpha here is volunteering in the name of medical science?'

I wasn't surprised that they knew who Alexander MacTire was. 'Not that,' I said.

Trilby tutted. 'Shame.'

I hesitated. 'Is it true?'

Trilby laughed loudly. 'What do you think? Of course, it's not true, Kit.' They reached across the stall and chucked me under the chin as if I were a child. 'But it's cute that you asked.'

MacTire shifted impatiently from foot to foot. I kept my expression calm. 'I'm asking,' I said, 'because you mentioned something else about werewolves. You said that a werewolf's blood could be used to invoke a demon. Is *that* true?'

Trilby's amusement vanished in an instant. 'Ah. Yes. Unfortunately, I believe that little rumour is true.' They gazed at MacTire and me then straightened up and waved to Natasha. 'Hey, Tash! I have to shut up for a few hours. Can you keep an eye on the stall for me?'

Natasha, who had been openly staring at Alexander MacTire as if she'd never seen a werewolf before, nodded quickly. 'Sure, Trilby.'

'Thanks.' Trilby waved at her in thanks and turned back to us. 'You'd better come with me. I can show you what I know.'

I swallowed hard; I didn't know whether to feel relief or horror that we were finally on the right track. And then the three of us trooped out of the market.

CHAPTER
TWENTY-FOUR

Trilby led us to a narrow house as close to the river's edge as it was possible to get. The building stood on its own, canting to one side in the higgledy-piggledy fashion of very old houses. 'I don't usually bring visitors here,' they said. 'I like my privacy. You'll understand that, Kit.'

I nodded. I absolutely did.

'But *you* won't understand that, MacTire.' Trilby was right: Alexander MacTire was squinting as if the concept of privacy was a brand-new idea that had just been presented to him.

'We won't come here again,' I said quietly. 'Unless we're invited to do so.'

'Thank you.' Trilby smiled. 'I appreciate that.'

They looked across at MacTire, who shrugged. 'Sure,' he said. 'You don't have to worry about me.'

'So said the spider to the fly,' Trilby murmured.

'I'm walking into your web,' MacTire pointed out. 'Not the other way around.'

'He's got a point,' I added.

'Perhaps,' Trilby replied. 'But you two came to me, remember?'

'Maybe we should just get this over and done with as quickly as possible,' I said hastily.

Trilby tipped their hat in response. 'In that case, in you come.'

The door had been painted bright orange for reasons that escaped me but which put me in mind of Mallory and her colourful flat. It creaked open seemingly of its own accord. Trilby said something under their breath before walking inside and I frowned as I followed them in. 'What was that?'

'Nothing you needed to hear,' they told me.

'They thanked the house,' MacTire told me. Unsurprisingly, his hearing was better than mine.

I wasn't taken aback by MacTire's werewolf hearing skills but the possibility that Trilby's house was sentient. Such a thing was rare indeed, but I knew better than to comment. I was now inside the house and it would be wise not to annoy it.

As if it heard my thoughts, the front door swung shut as soon as MacTire had crossed the threshold. He didn't visibly react but I reckoned he was as surprised – and as nervous – as I suddenly was.

'There's more than one reason why it's not wise to show up here without an invitation,' Trilby told us.

Uh-huh.

We trailed through a series of twisting hallways and I craned my neck so I could catch glimpses of the rooms on either side. Most of them appeared to be crammed full of objects, suggesting this was as much a warehouse as a home.

When we'd made three turns, it occurred to me that this house was far bigger on the inside than on the outside. I stopped trying to sneak glances into the rooms and started paying attention to the layout; it would be all too easy to get lost for hours – perhaps even for days.

We walked in a straight line for fifty metres or so then

turned left and walked for another thirty metres. We turned left again and then again. 'Are we walking in circles?' MacTire demanded. There was a loud creak as if the house itself were answering.

'Be quiet,' I hissed.

Trilby chuckled. 'You always did strike me as a smart kid, Kit.'

Kid? How old *was* Trilby? I opened my mouth to ask, decided it would be better to take my own advice and keep my questions to myself and closed it again.

Still we walked on. I should have brought some breadcrumbs so I could create a trail.

After about fifteen minutes, Trilby stopped in front of a closed door. It was made out of oak and unremarkable in appearance. They bowed their head for a moment as if in prayer, then reached forward and twisted the knob. The door opened to reveal a large room – or at least I supposed it was large. Darkness curled around the edges making it impossible to judge where the walls were. Interesting.

Only the centre of the room was illuminated, though there was no bulb overhead and no candles so the only explanation was magic. Whatever powered the light clearly existed for one reason alone: to provide light for the single piece of furniture.

I stared at the lectern. Although it was simple in design, it appeared to be made out of solid gold that was glinting against the light. I gaped at Trilby; with wealth like that, I couldn't think of a reason why they needed to wake up at the crack of dawn every day to run a small market stall.

Trilby must have felt my stare but they didn't react; they simply bustled towards the lectern.

On top of it was a closed book; it looked ancient, with a cracked black leather cover and a fae rune etched on the surface. Was Trilby one of the fae? Full fae? I watched agog as they reached out and gently caressed the book's surface then they looked up, their clever, dark eyes crinkling at the corners at my expression.

'Don't ask questions to which you do not need the answers,' they said. I inclined my head in understanding; knowledge could be very dangerous indeed.

Alexander MacTire didn't appear to give a flying fuck about the strange house or Trilby's heritage. He folded his arms and growled, 'Let's get on with it. My nephew has been captive for far too long.'

'You'll get your answers,' Trilby told him and stroked the book again. 'This isn't a grimoire and it doesn't contain magical spells. Think of it as an encyclopaedia of knowledge.' They paused. 'Ancient knowledge that this modern world often forgets.'

They dipped their head and their lips moved. I couldn't hear what they were saying so I glanced at MacTire, but he had pursed his lips; apparently this time he couldn't hear what Trilby was murmuring either.

After several seconds, Trilby stepped back, their eyes glowing golden. Without any help, the book juddered and the pages flipped while motes of old dust flew up into the air. Even from the doorway I could smell the ancient parchment. The book rose an inch, hung suspended for a breath then fell open back onto the lectern.

'Cool, huh?' Trilby grinned and beckoned to us. 'Come and see.'

My feet stumbled forward as if of their own accord until I was standing by their left shoulder. MacTire moved to their right and all three of us leaned forward to gaze at the open page.

Words danced across the yellowing paper before settling

into legible paragraphs. There was a single heading, *Demons*. A shiver ran through me.

MacTire read the words aloud. '*Beware of demons. They cometh from the netherworld and they art not to be trusted. Hunters art they, first and foremost: natural predators equipped with sharp claws, keen senses and a most terrifying agility. They are highly adaptable and can thrive in many a clime, yet make no mistake: a demon is a killer and may murder up to three thousand souls within its own lifespan. This predator is capable of conscious manipulation and can twist unwary mortals into subservient stations whereupon the demon's will alone doth become law. However, anyone who canst bind and command a demon shall wield power most formidable, far beyond the ken of mortal men. Such mastery over the infernal arts doth grant dominion over forces unseen, and with it the might to shape the very world to their will.*'

Great. I ran a hand through my hair. 'I think we can be certain we don't want to meet any damned demons,' I said. 'And we don't want anyone to gain authority over one.'

Out of the corner of my eye, I saw Trilby's mouth twitch oddly. 'Go on, MacTire,' they said. 'Keep reading.'

MacTire did as he was told. '*There be many ways to bring demons forth from the netherworld. In times long past, oft there would be a simple rent in the fabric that held the netherworld at bay. Through this rent, demons couldst and wouldst sneak. In time the breach was sealed, yet this doth not mean that demons are wholly contained. They can yet be invoked into existence through diverse foul means.*'

I licked my lips. Here we go.

'*On the seventh night of the seventh month at the seventh hour, mayhap seven witches shall gather and chant the seven scriptures with seven tongues. 'Tis said that in so doing they may invoke a demon and bring it forth into this world.*'

MacTire paused and looked at Trilby. 'The seven scriptures?'

They waved a hand. 'Nothing to worry about, they've been lost for generations. Besides, the seven tongues include three languages that haven't been heard for more than a thousand years.'

MacTire grunted then continued. *''Tis also believed that demons may be brought forth by harnessing the power of the werewolf.'* He sucked in a sharp breath.

'Keep going,' Trilby said. 'Keep going! We don't have all day.'

The werewolf stiffened but he did as Trilby demanded, though his voice was tighter, darker. *'If thirteen pints of fresh blood, newly harvested from a werewolf with no kin, be scattered upon sacred ground on the day of the solstice, then mayhap a demon shall emerge.'*

Trilby snapped their fingers. 'There we go. That's what you wanted, right? That's the information you were looking for?'

I half-closed my eyes. Shit. Sadly, it was.

MacTire raised his head. 'How many pints of blood would the average teenage werewolf hold inside their body?'

I used to be an assassin and I knew the answer. 'An adult werewolf typically has around ten to twelve pints,' I said dully. 'A teenager would likely have slightly less – between nine and ten. But they've had Nick for several days and they could have drawn several pints of blood already. He'll still be alive and generating more. Umbra have already advertised their presence at Crackendon Square. There's an old church on the western corner – I guess that counts as sacred ground.'

A muscle throbbed in MacTire's cheek. 'I guess so.'

The words on the page started to move. I stared at them, unsure at first if I was imagining things, but then they coalesced into a black shadow that expanded until it covered the whole page. 'Watch,' Trilby whispered.

The page altered again, only this time there weren't words. Staring at us from the cloud of blank ink were two elongated eyes, the pupils narrow vertical slits. The eyes blinked and I gasped, while MacTire reached out and slammed the book closed.

Trilby appeared unperturbed but my heart was hammering. I'd seen a lot of weird shit in my lifetime but I'd never seen anything like that.

'Well, my work here is done.' Trilby dusted off their hands. 'We should head back. My regular customers will be getting impatient.' They looked between MacTire and me. 'It seems to me that you two have rather a lot to do as well. Do take care of yourselves. The solstice is almost upon us.'

CHAPTER
TWENTY-FIVE

We returned to the MacTire hellhole; it wasn't my preferred choice of venue but it was convenient. When we arrived, there were far more werewolves inside the building than before; Samantha must have called in the troops.

Despite his supposed status as a prisoner, Thane had been making himself at home and was regaling a large group of muscly MacTire werewolves with tales of his time as a lone wolf. Samantha was watching him darkly from the corner but she needn't have worried that he was trying to persuade them they'd be better off on their own. From what I heard, he was being both self-deprecating and self-mocking, making no attempt to glamourise his lifestyle.

'And that was when the vampire threw a stick,' he said to his fascinated audience. 'I couldn't help myself. I didn't have back-up or anyone to tell me to keep focused. My instincts kicked in.'

'And?' A particularly burly wolf leaned in. 'What happened?'

'What do you think happened?' Thane said. 'I chased after the damned stick.'

Everyone in the room burst out laughing and even Samantha cracked a smile. Thane grinned easily, happy to be the butt of the joke. Good for him; it is a hell of a lot harder to torture and kill someone whom you've had a laugh with. He was definitely a canny ginger bastard.

His eyes fell on me and his grin vanished as he raised his eyebrows in question. I nodded. Yes, Trilby had confirmed the theory about Nick's blood being harvested to raise a demon. No, we still didn't know where Nick or Umbra were.

Alexander MacTire strode to the centre of the room; although he didn't clear his throat or ask for silence, silence was what he received. The power he held over his pack was obvious. 'Clear the room,' he said quietly.

Within ten seconds everyone had gone and only Samantha, Thane, MacTire and I remained. He repeated what we'd learned in short, clipped syllables that didn't do very much to disguise his rage.

'So they might have already drained his blood,' Samantha said when he'd finished. 'Nicholas might already be dead.'

I didn't think so. 'Umbra need thirteen pints to invoke a demon. Even if they took every single drop from Nick's body, they wouldn't have enough. Plus,' I added, 'the book said that the blood has to be fresh. I reckon they've probably taken some from him but they have to allow him time to recover. They'll be waiting until the last minute before they drain him dry.'

'We can't wait until the last minute,' Thane objected. 'His life is still in the balance.'

MacTire frowned. 'Exactly. Our priority is finding Umbra. We don't know how many of them there are or where they are hiding, but we *have* to find them.'

'And how will we manage that?' I asked.

Samantha smiled grimly. 'This is one of those many times when it pays to be part of a pack.' She gave Thane a pointed look. 'Most of the MacTire wolves who are not in this building are already out searching. While you were gone and Thane was courting his fans, I also called in favours from several of our allies. The Stewarts, the Fergusons and the MacGregors have agreed to help. And thanks to you, we have a scent marker to search for.'

'The assassin,' I breathed.

She nodded. 'We couldn't catch his trail from where Rebecca was killed – there was more than one reason why he was using the rooftops to get around. The higher up you go, the fresher the air is.'

'And the stronger the wind,' Thane agreed. 'That's why I didn't waste time searching for his scent trail at the time. There'd have been little left to follow and too much chance of his scent getting mixed with others.'

Samantha went on. 'With hundreds of us searching and a scent anchor to seek, we can cover every street in Coldstream. The Fergusons in particular are known for their good noses. If any hint of the assassin lingers anywhere in this city, it will be found. If he sat in a pub or ate dinner in a restaurant, passed a few minutes on a park bench or blew his nose and dropped the tissue in a public bin, the trail *will* be found.'

Alexander MacTire shoved his hands in his pockets. 'But will it be found in time?' He wasn't expressing doubt about what Samantha had said or the other werewolves' skills; his question reflected his anxiety for Nick.

There was a sharp knock at the door and Samantha answered it. When she returned, there was a scrap of paper in her hand and a wide, unpleasant smile on her face. 'I can categorically state that it will be found in time.' She held up the piece of paper. 'The Fergusons have come through – they are certain they've located Umbra.'

Barely an hour later, I was standing across the street from a nondescript building with more werewolves than I'd ever seen assembled in one place. It wasn't only the Ferguson, Stewart and MacGregor packs who'd come to help, there were other werewolves, too. It was genuinely astonishing.

'I didn't realise the MacTires were so popular,' I murmured to Thane, who was next to me and managing to appear relaxed despite the frank stares he was garnering from the other werewolves.

'They're not,' he told me. 'It's purely political.'

That made more sense. 'You mean nobody wants to risk suggesting that their pack was involved in Nick's abduction? Nobody wants to risk conflict with the MacTires?'

Thane nodded. 'If Nick is dead, the MacTires will be out for blood. They'll attack first and ask questions later.' He waved a hand. 'By being here, these werewolves are asserting their innocence even though some will secretly be celebrating the MacTires' weakness in losing one of their own.'

'Nick isn't theirs.'

'He is to all intents and purposes. You know that.'

I did, though I merely grunted in response. 'Some won't be celebrating. They'll be terrified that if this could happen to Nick it could happen to them.'

'Everyone has a weak point,' he agreed. 'Even old Bruce MacTire had one when he collapsed and died of a heart attack.'

I felt Thane's eyes on me and wondered if he'd picked up on an atmosphere between Alexander and me that suggested that I'd induced Bruce MacTire's coronary. I would never confirm it, not to anyone.

Fortunately Thane moved on to a more immediate matter. 'What the fuck are we waiting for?' he muttered. 'Whoever is in that building knows we're here and the jig is up.' He glanced around with undisguised impatience. 'The longer we wait, the more chance there is that the demon-worshipping bastards will kill Nick. We should get in there before that happens.'

I was inclined to agree. This scenario was exactly why I'd wanted to keep Alexander MacTire out of it: too many people were involved, and too many people meant too many variables. I hated situations that I couldn't control.

'There is a reason why we haven't made a move yet,' Samantha said from directly behind us.

I jumped; I hadn't realised she was there although Thane obviously had, and had probably voiced his complaint so that she would hear it.

She pointed to the building. 'I'd have thought that you'd already have noticed, Barrow. Why don't you go closer and see for yourself?'

Thane frowned then walked stiffly across the road. Since we'd arrived, nobody had attempted to get that close to the grey concrete building. I suspected I knew why, but I wanted to see if Thane's approach encouraged any sign of life at the eight windows that looked out from the two-storey façade.

There was nothing. 'You're sure this is where Umbra is holed up?' I asked Samantha in an undertone.

'Oh, yes.' She was gazing at Thane with glee. 'It absolutely reeks of that bastard assassin. His scent is all over this place.'

Thane jerked to a halt and started choking, then his knees gave way and he collapsed. 'Plus,' she said, with an arch grin, 'it's ringed with concentrated wolfsbane. I can't think of any reason why anyone would go to that sort of expense unless they were expecting an army of werewolves to show up at their door.'

Well, shit. I darted forward to Thane, hooked him beneath his armpits and dragged him back across the road with his feet trailing behind him. There was a chorus of snide laughs from the watching werewolves. I wasn't surprised that a lot of them were inclined to take against Thane – a lone wolf went against everything they stood for – but they didn't need to be so obvious about it.

'How does it feel to be rescued by a cat lady, Barrow?' somebody shouted.

My eyes narrowed. Clearly my reputation had preceded me. Usually I'd have been quite happy about that – after all, it was the persona I cultivated – but I was annoyed on Thane's behalf. None of those other werewolves had dared to get close to the damned wolfsbane.

Thane coughed and wheezed, his eyes red and streaming with tears. 'Fuck!' he spat. 'That's strong stuff.'

'You must have known what it was before you got close to it,' I told him. 'Why did you keep going?'

'I wanted to see how potent it was.' In other words, he'd wanted to see if he could play hero in front of the schoolyard bullies and push past the barrier. Idiot.

'I guess that now you know.'

'I guess I do.' He coughed again.

My eyes landed on Alexander MacTire, who didn't appear even faintly amused. His arms were folded and his expression was tight. I assumed he had a plan; doubtless he was waiting for a group of expensive – albeit highly trained – witches to cast a web of spells to nullify the wolfsbane. That would take hours, and I wasn't sure he was seeing the bigger picture.

I dropped Thane, leaving him to recover, and stalked towards the MacTire alpha. Before I got close, two of his minions stepped in my path. 'He's not talking to you,' one of them growled.

I rolled my eyes but MacTire was already beckoning me forward. 'Your boyfriend is a fool for getting so close,' he said.

I didn't bother to rise to the bait. 'If Umbra are prepared to scatter that amount of wolfsbane around that house, they'll be prepared for you to eventually break through. They'll be armed with silver – I can almost guarantee it.'

He scratched his chin. 'That's a risk I'm willing to take.'

I sighed. I didn't need to tell Alexander MacTire that silver in its purest form was lethal to every werewolf on the planet. 'How many lives are you willing to risk?' I countered. 'How many other lives is one teenager worth?'

MacTire bared his teeth and two patches of fur appeared on his cheekbones. There was a shocked murmur amongst the werewolves from the other packs; I wasn't the only one who hadn't known just how powerful the MacTire alpha was. 'You're giving yourself away,' I said.

He dipped his head and raised his hands, not to threaten me but to show everyone what he was capable of. When his fingers twisted and sharp claws emerged, there was another collective gasp. 'Nicholas is my nephew,' he said. 'He is one of mine. I would do the same for anyone in my pack.'

I held my ground. 'Nick isn't in your pack.'

MacTire snarled and the musclebound goons made another move towards me. This time I was the one to move away. MacTire would happily turn this entire street into a bloodbath if it meant he would win, and there was still a chance that Umbra would slit Nick's throat the second a werewolf crossed that threshold.

I knew from the alpha's expression that he wasn't willing to listen to reason, and he certainly wouldn't listen to me. I moved further away, grabbed Thane's elbow and half-dragged him to the edge of the crowd.

His eyes were still red but his fervour hadn't diminished. 'We can't stand here and do nothing, Kit. They could be draining the rest of Nick's blood as we speak. We can't keep delaying.'

'I know,' I said.

'Wolfsbane won't affect you.' His desperate gaze roved my face.

I smiled. 'I know that, too.'

He swallowed, aware of what he was suggesting. 'They'll probably kill you the moment you go in there.'

'They'll certainly try,' I agreed.

'We don't know how many of them are in there, but we know they're wealthy and well-prepared.'

'I thought you *wanted* me to go in,' I said calmly.

'I do.' He shook his head. 'I don't.' He cursed. 'I don't know.'

'It's okay, Thane.' Much like MacTire, I was prepared to risk a lot to save Nick – but I wouldn't need to worry about anyone's safety, not if I played my cards right.

Samantha marched towards us. 'I hope you're not thinking of doing anything stupid, Ms McCafferty.'

'*Moi?*' I splayed my fingers. 'I'm just a cat lady. What on earth could I do?' I looked at the imposing building. 'I can assure you that I won't do anything stupid. In fact...' I stopped mid-sentence.

Samantha tapped her foot. 'In fact what?'

'In fact,' a broad smile spread across my face, 'there's a lovely cat over there that I know. I'm going over to say hello.' Before she could stop me, I turned, crossed the road, stepped over the unbroken line of wolfsbane and crouched down beside She Who Hisses.

'Hey there,' I said to the glaring black cat. 'Fancy seeing you again.'

'McCafferty!' Alexander MacTire roared. 'Get your arse back over here!'

I grinned and waved at him. 'Just saying hello to the cat,' I called, then leaned down and looked at She Who Hisses' body. 'It's healing nicely,' I observed. 'Your fur will grow back in no time.'

Her yellow eyes stared at me balefully but she didn't run away. She didn't even hiss.

'You saw what was happening, didn't you? You thought you'd have a little nosy.' Her tail flicked. 'You'll help me?' I breathed. I hadn't expected her to, but goodness knows I was grateful. 'Thank you.'

Her ears twitched. 'Yes,' I said. 'After this we're even, though I didn't need repayment.'

She Who Hisses blinked once then stood up, twisted around and padded down the side street that led to the western side of Umbra's hideout.

I pulled myself upright and followed her without looking back.

TWENTY-SIX

She Who Hisses didn't want an audience any more than I did. Ignoring the shouts from the various werewolf factions behind us, I followed her as she sauntered down the side street away from the Umbra building. Finally she veered into a doorway and angled her head up at me. 'Yes,' I nodded. 'This will do.'

She Who Hisses sniffed.

I licked my lips. 'It will only hurt for a few seconds,' I promised. I reached down and plucked a small clump of fur from her back, taking care to stray nowhere near her old wound. 'Thank you,' I whispered. 'If you could stay close until I'm finished, I'd appreciate it.'

She tilted her head as if thinking about it then turned round, curled up in the corner and wrapped her tail about herself. Within seconds she was asleep.

I drew a deep breath and opened my mouth to swallow the fur. There had only been one occasion in my past when I'd used the fur from a feral cat to affect my transformation and it hadn't been a pleasant experience, but I'd been young and foolish then and I hadn't asked the cat for permission. I'd learned that lesson and never repeated my error. With luck, this time would be different; after all, She Who Hisses had come to me voluntarily. Even so, I crossed my fingers; Nick needed me and I couldn't spend the next six hours violently throwing up.

I dropped the fur into my mouth and swallowed. For one long moment nothing happened but then the goosebumps started – and hot damn they were intense. My whole body vibrated, buzzing as the magical electricity zipped through my bones and along my veins.

I sneezed three times in quick succession and grimaced at the burning sensation in the back of my eyeballs. A series of spasms ran through my muscles until finally my whole body started to levitate before tumbling and spinning in mid-air.

Relax, Kit, I told myself. *Just relax.* Although that would have been easier if it didn't feel like I'd been zapped in the heart with a bolt of lightning.

I collapsed and my new black-furred body landed next to She Who Hisses. She opened one slitted eye then closed it again.

I allowed myself a few moments of recovery. Finally I raised myself up to my paws, stretched and limbered up for what was to come. As I arched my back and pushed my front legs forward, I heard footsteps behind me. I hastily completed my cat yoga and turned to blink at the incomer.

'Hi, Puss.'

Thane's deep Scottish brogue had a different quality to my feline ears, but it was unmistakably him. His bright red hair appeared as an odd shade of grey, although his green eyes were more vivid than usual.

She Who Hisses opened her eyes again and hissed at him, even though he'd been the one who let her escape from my house. I didn't want her to run off so I padded away; fortunately Thane got the message and moved with me.

We stopped at the corner, leaving enough distance between

us and the ring of potent wolfsbane so that it didn't affect Thane. He crouched down so that his face was close to mine and lifted his hand. If he tried to stroke me, I'd bite his damned fingers off.

He smiled and lowered his hand. 'Just kidding,' he said. 'Unless you want me to rub your belly?'

I stared at him. I'd hunt him down at the next full moon and try that when he was in wolf form if he got any closer. He smiled again, although it was a half-hearted effort. He was worried. Then again, so was I.

He got down to business. 'I've looped around the building. There's an open window on the second floor on the other side. If you approach it from the opposite rooftop, I think you can make the jump.'

I purred to show that I appreciated the information; it would save me considerable time.

We took off. When we rounded the block onto a busier street where some werewolves had been posted to keep watch on the rear of the Umbra building, I noted that Thane was garnering some strange glances. Maybe they hadn't seen a cat hang out with a werewolf before, which was a shame. Their lives would have been far richer if they spent more time around felines.

A few of the wolves called greetings and questions, but at least they were no longer jeering at him. He acknowledged them with brief waves and nods but he didn't pause. Neither did I; we were on a mission.

The building Thane had mentioned was down a narrow street only two metres away from the Umbra one, although it was considerably taller. As soon as we turned down the street and were forced to walk next to the long line of wolfsbane, Thane started to cough and his eyes reddened, so we picked up speed until we reached the door. Now I understood why he had chosen to accompany me; it was a large heavy wooden structure that required a full-sized person to open and close it.

He reached out, turned the door knob and let me enter first. We seemed to be inside an office building; there was a businesslike atmosphere about the place, and several of the interior doors had name placards attached to them.

Voices drifted towards us. 'There must be a hundred wolves out there. Maybe more.'

'We should hand out business cards. From the look of things, they're going to need legal advice fairly soon.' Lawyers, probably independent practitioners who offered their services to a range of preternatural beings.

Thane paid them no attention as he strode to the wide staircase in the centre of the hallway. He took the steps two at a time so I picked up speed and darted past him; it wasn't a race but I was keen to get inside the Umbra headquarters. He seemed to get the message and moved more quickly.

He paused when we reached the second floor. 'Here?' he asked. 'Or would you rather jump from a higher vantage point?'

Higher. Definitely higher. I miaowed and continued upwards.

'I don't talk cat,' he grunted.

Yeah, yeah. He'd understood me.

On the next floor, Thane glanced around then opened the door to one of the offices without bothering to knock. A harassed-looking woman wearing a suit was sitting at an expansive mahogany desk that was strewn with papers. She half-rose and gaped. 'Who are you? What are you doing in here?'

'Don't worry, ma'am,' Thane said. 'We won't be here for long.'

'I'm going to call security!'

He ignored her in favour of placing both hands on her desk

and yanking it away from the window. 'Hey!' she protested. 'Stop that!'

Thane circled her and pulled up the sash window behind her. He pursed his lips. 'It looks quite far,' he said to me. 'Maybe this isn't such a good idea.'

I jumped onto the windowsill and peered out: yes, it appeared quite a distance from this angle but I knew I could make it. I could feel the power bunching in my muscles as I calculated the trajectory. It would be fine.

'What are you doing?' the woman repeated in a high voice.

'Two minutes,' Thane told her. 'Then we'll be gone.' As I eyed the leap he added in an undertone, 'Be careful in there, Kit. I'm starting to like you. Don't get yourself killed.'

I wasn't planning to. I chirruped once then, because the longer I delayed the harder it would be, I jumped out of the window.

I sailed confidently across the two-metre gap and it was only when the open window was within touching distance that I realised there was a problem: the Umbra window had been propped ajar and there was only a gap of around four inches between the sash and the sill. I was about to smack into the glass and probably tumble down to the street below.

I twisted, intending to adjust my angle in mid-air, but I miscalculated. With my legs and tail flailing, I almost missed the window completely; only my front paws managed to make it and curl around the narrow windowsill, while the remainder of my body dangled. I was forced to dig my claws into the old wood and cling on for dear life. It was all rather embarrassing.

The woman in the office wasn't any calmer now that I'd left the building. From my clumsy, precarious position, I heard her shriek at Thane, 'What have you done? This is animal cruelty!'

Under any other circumstances, I'd have laughed but I had my paws full trying not to fall. My body writhed and I felt myself slipping. That wouldn't do. I sucked in air and scrabbled upwards. I was a cat. I could manage this.

My progress seemed painfully slow even though it was only seconds before I hauled my furry body up through the gap beneath the window. Thane was trying to hush the woman, clearly concerned that somebody from Umbra would hear her and investigate, but I wasn't worried. The room I'd squeezed into was empty and the door was closed, so it was unlikely anyone inside would hear the shouts over the commotion the werewolves were making outside.

I shook out my fur and sniffed. I should have managed that jump better but at least I was inside and safe – for the time being. Unfortunately, though, now I knew why the window had been left open: it was because of the vile stench of faeces and urine coming from a tin bucket in the corner. Next to the bucket, attached to the wall, were a chain and a pair of hand-cuffs. Somebody had been held prisoner inside this room – and judging from the silver bound into the handcuffs it had been a werewolf.

My near-fall forgotten, I skittered towards the chains and bucket, claws scratching on the old wooden floor. If Nick had been held here, where was he now?

I avoided the bucket – I already knew what was in there – and I sniffed delicately at the handcuffs and the chain, trying to separate the different scents. My stomach tightened when I registered the familiar teenage smell. Nick had been tied up here.

I took several steps backwards and then I noticed the blood. There wasn't a lot of it but there was a distinct trail of drops and small splashes leading from the corner where I was to the closed door. There were also a few faint scuff marks that suggested he'd been dragged. Nick had been here, his blood had doubtless been harvested and he'd been hauled away. His absence meant that either he was dead or his captors had removed him to a safer place when MacTire and his unmerry band of werewolves had shown up at the door.

I prayed for the second option; the drops of blood were still wet enough to suggest it could be true.

With no reason to linger, I padded to the closed door. Its lever door handle rather than twisting knob meant I could open it without transforming back into human form. I jumped up and pushed it down with both my front paws. The door swung open and I slunk out.

At least this time there was a clear trail to follow. My nose twitched and I caught a glimpse of the next blood splash. I turned right down the hallway in soft, silent pursuit.

TWENTY-SEVEN

At first sight the house seemed deserted and that troubled me. What if Umbra were running a bluff and had scattered the wolfsbane to make it appear as if they were inside when they'd actually taken Nick and made their escape? That would have been the smart move – depressingly smart.

I slipped through the corridors and empty rooms, searching desperately for any sign of life. There was nothing on the second floor apart from a small spider furiously spinning a web in one high corner.

When I reached the first floor, I was greeted by the same emptiness and my anxiety ratcheted up still further. It was only when I reached the ground floor that I finally – and thankfully – heard voices from behind a closed door.

'How long till the witches get here?'

'MacTire will want the best, so that means the Wicker Witches. They're based at the other end of Coldstream. It's one of the reasons why Brassick chose this place. The earliest the Wickers will get here will be forty minutes, and it'll take them another two hours at least to dismantle the magic that's binding the wolfsbane to the ground. We've got plenty of time.'

My eyes narrowed. Both voices were male and both sounded calm; I didn't hear even a quiver of anxiety about the lupine forces massing outside. It was as I'd expected: Umbra, whoever they were, had planned this. They weren't afraid – and that meant they must have an escape route or they were as happy to die as Quack's killer had been.

'Will there be time to draw all the blood we need?'

My claws extended of their own volition.

'Absolutely. Don't worry about it. The demon will be ours soon.' There was a pause followed by a satisfied sigh. 'And when we have it, Coldstream will fall under our control. Victor's sacrifice won't have been in vain – we'll make him proud. By Thursday evening we'll be toasting his name with the finest whisky this city has to offer while every werewolf, witch and ogre bows down before us.'

They were delusional; these wankers believed they could control whatever damned demon they conjured up. And if Victor was the assassin who'd killed Quack, yes, they were clearly prepared to die for their cause. They must have had fish paste for brains.

'What about the Church of the Masked God? They must suspect something by now. They know we want a demon.'

'They can suspect all they like. We've been advertising our solstice event for days and everyone who shows up in Crackendon Square will be food for our demon. If any Masked God devotees or deacons appear, they'll meet the same fate. It's time we showed them what power really looks like. Coldstream needs a single, unifying leader if we're going to get rid of those fuzzy-headed faith dealers. They think they own the hearts and minds of this community but our demon will eat the hearts and we'll take control of the minds. Thursday is D-Day, my friend. We're going to change the world.'

I'd heard a lot of crazy talk over the years but this was off the scale. I almost felt sorry for the two bastards – but it wouldn't stop me killing them and I wouldn't regret my actions for a second.

My ears twitched and my tail waved wildly from side to side. She Who Hisses had served me well but now I had to stand on my own two feet. I retreated to one of the empty rooms and hawked up the hairball. Time to play.

My unexpected sojourn as a MacTire captive meant I had no weapons on me; although that wasn't a disastrous situation, it was one I needed to remedy sooner rather than later. With any luck, the two hapless fools in the room down the hall would be armed. I'd soon find out.

I straightened my shoulders, cricked my neck and cracked my knuckles, then strode back to the closed door, raised my fist and knocked sharply. The two voices inside that had been continuing their inane chatter abruptly fell silent.

I waited two beats and knocked again. This time there was a hushed whisper and the sound of footsteps. 'Who's there?'

I mouthed my answer, 'Your worst nightmare,' then side-stepped to where I wouldn't be seen immediately. A beat later the door opened and one of the men thrust out a gun. I snapped my hand across and wrenched it out of his shaking fist, twisted it and smashed the butt into his face.

He stumbled backwards, which wouldn't do. I thrust my hand out again, grabbed the front of his shirt and yanked it hard, pulling the shirt and the man through the door in one swift movement. With my left hand I closed the door after him, then I drew in a breath and met his shocked brown eyes.

I dropped the gun. Placing both hands on either side of his

bony skull, I twisted hard and broke his neck with far more speed and far less pain than he deserved.

His companion was already yelling from the other side of the door and I wished he'd shut up; I didn't want all his deluded buddies appearing because they'd heard a commotion. Finally he must have remembered that he was armed because he loosed off two shots in quick succession. Both bullets smashed through the wooden door into the plaster of the opposite wall. Splinters of wood flew in all directions and annoyingly at least two embedded themselves in my cheek.

Silence descended as the shooter tried to work out whether he'd hit me or not. Given the lack of sound, it was clear that anyone else in the building was oblivious to what had just happened. Luck was most definitely on my side.

I bent down, scooped up the dead Umbra goon's gun and checked it over. Silver bullets, as I'd suspected.

I pulled a face then listened hard, using my hearing to visualise the room on the other side of the wall. I heard a creak followed by another shot, which he blasted not at the door but at the inner wall. It didn't penetrate the heavy Scottish stone. At least that answered one of my questions: if I wanted to ensure my bullets hit flesh, I'd have to fire through the door and not the wall.

Ducking down, I wriggled forward commando-style until I was in position. I heard heavy breathing and another faint creak, then closed my eyes and pinpointed their location. When I squeezed the trigger, I was rewarded by a painfully loud shriek and a thud. That was when I sprang up and burst through the door. Nice: from the way he was clutching his leg, my shot had done exactly what I'd hoped it would.

Getting shot is nothing like it is in the movies, it's not a moment of pain and then you're able to run away from your attacker or can properly defend yourself, not unless you have a lot of experience and an astonishingly high pain threshold. For the first few seconds, you don't really feel much beyond shock. The burning agony doesn't hit straight away but when it registers, it's horrible. You can't catch your breath and your body vibrates with fire and pain. Before too long, adrenaline takes over and you can react more usefully but until that happens you're a vulnerable mess. That's why I was able to walk up to the man and calmly take possession of both his weapon and the situation.

He groaned.

I eyed his wound; it was unlikely that he'd bleed out any time soon, and with proper medical treatment he'd recover. But I wasn't interested in whether he'd be around to celebrate his next birthday, I simply wanted to know that he could still talk.

After another few seconds, he proved that he could. 'You shot me, you bitch!' Uh-huh: people always felt the need to state the obvious. I could practically write the script.

I patted him down, searching for any sign that he was carrying a similar suicidal poison to the man who'd killed Quack. There was some chewing gum in one pocket and a packet of crumpled cigarettes in the other. I popped a piece of gum into my mouth and held up the fags. 'These will kill you, you know,' I said amiably.

He glared and spat at me, his limbs flailing as he tried to punch and kick at me. I watched his attempts with detached interest. He was keen, I'd give him that. In my old job, I'd ensured my targets died as quickly as possible; I didn't spend time observing their pain or asking them questions. Occasionally clients had requested that I inflict as much trauma and pain as possible but neither EEL nor I would ever have agreed to such a thing. You could be a killer but you didn't have to be a dick.

This situation, however, was very different. I crouched

down and stared at the man dispassionately. 'What's your name?'

He glared at me, so I waved both guns in his face until my meaning was clear.

He bared his teeth. 'Liam,' he muttered.

Good. I didn't actually care what his name was but he'd broken the seal; answering one simple question freed him up to answer more.

'Who else is in this building?'

He didn't reply; instead his eyes promised dark vengeance. Yeah, yeah.

'How many Umbra fuckers are in this building apart from you and your dead friend?' If I had to keep repeating myself, I would get very irritated very quickly.

I waved the guns again and Liam looked away. 'Three,' he bit out. 'And you can't stop us! Our mission is sacred! We're going to put Coldstream on the map. We're going to change the world and nobody will get in our way! My death won't change anything – in fact, it will strengthen our movement.'

Good grief. I gave him a long stare then spun on my heel, walked over to his buddy and half-lifted the corpse into a sitting position. I raised my eyebrows in pointed invitation. 'How many others?' I asked again.

Liam's thin mouth tightened and fear flared in his eyes. Apparently he wasn't as keen on martyrdom as he liked to pretend. 'Five.'

That was better. I dropped the dead body. 'Where are they?'

'Downstairs,' he said. 'In the basement.'

'In the same room?'

He nodded reluctantly.

'What are they?'

He knew what I was asking. 'Vampire, witch, ogre and two druids.'

Interesting. 'Who's in charge?' Someone had to be running this shit show; I reckoned I knew who it was but I wanted Liam to confirm it.

This time he pinned his mouth closed and I sensed he wouldn't tell me, no matter how much I threatened him. He was scared of me but he was terrified of his boss.

'Never mind,' I said cheerfully. 'I'll find out.' I crouched next to him, reached out and stroked his cheek. He flinched. 'And the boy?' I asked. 'Where is he?'

'He's with them.'

'Is he still alive?'

Liam swallowed hard. 'Probably.'

As far as I could tell, he was being truthful. From the way he'd answered, the Umbra bastards were harvesting Nick's blood until there was none left. He was alive for now but wouldn't be soon. I had been right not to delay outside.

I leaned over Liam, hooked my arms underneath his armpits and started dragging him out of the room. He kicked, thrashed and tried to dig in his heels. The blood seeping out of his wound left a wide trail across the dusty floorboards.

'What are you doing?' he gasped. 'Stop!' He licked his lips and I knew he was preparing to scream loud enough to alert his colleagues.

I paused. 'Make another sound and I *will* kill you. Stay quiet and I promise you'll leave this building alive.'

'Go ahead and kill me then.' He sneered as he belatedly remembered that he was supposed to be a zealot whose life was nothing compared to his cause. 'If I die, the demons will reward my sacrifice tenfold when my soul joins them.'

I still didn't think he believed what he was saying because he wouldn't have answered my questions so easily if that had been the case. Liam possessed the bluster but not the follow through. 'Have you talked to them about this yourself?' I enquired.

This time he only stared at me.

'Maybe if I hurt you more, your reward will be even greater.' I tilted my head. 'What do you think? If I chopped off a hand or a leg, will that make your afterlife in the demon netherworld even better? Shall we give it a try and find out?'

Again he chose not to answer and I grunted with satisfaction that I'd finally managed to silence him. At least he was too confused with pain and his silly visions of a glorious death to ask me what I was really planning – or maybe he was just too stupid.

I adjusted my hold on his body and continued dragging him out of the door towards the front of the building. Some sort of trap had been rigged around the front door. I examined it; it was considerably more elaborate than the booby trap Thane had constructed at the Galbraith house. This one would not release magical herbs designed to hurt rather than maim or kill but a spray of tiny silver darts; they wouldn't kill me but I suspected that even one of them could kill a werewolf.

I glanced at Liam's face. He was gritting his teeth and sweat was running down his pale face. Although my bullet hadn't nicked any of his arteries, it might have hit bone and I knew from personal experience that the pain must have been intense. It sucked to be Liam – and it was about to get worse.

I released him for a moment to disarm the trap. As soon as it was safe, I opened the front door to reveal a hundred gaping werewolves on the opposite side of the street. I caught a glimpse of Alexander MacTire, who looked ready to explode.

I put a finger to my lips, indicating that I needed him and his furry minions to stay quiet. The rest of Umbra hadn't registered my intrusion yet, but the sound of dozens of furious werewolves shouting at me could penetrate even the best sound-proofed basement. MacTire's eyes narrowed in anger but he raised his hand to order everyone to shut up. I flashed a smile of thanks.

'What are you doing?' Liam whispered. 'What the fuck are you doing? You said you wouldn't kill me.'

I scooped him up again. 'Yeah,' I said. 'I did say that. And I meant it, even though you said you'd happily die.'

'If my death means that Umbra wins...'

I waved a hand dismissively, tired of his ridiculous statements about death that even he didn't believe. 'I won't kill you,' I repeated. 'But I can't make any promises about the were-wolves. What they do with you is their choice.'

With that, I shoved him out of the door with enough force that part of his body landed beyond the wolfsbane line. Samantha darted forward and took hold of him, placed a hand over his mouth to muffle his screams and pulled him away. I didn't know what would happen to him now, but I could imagine.

MacTire continued to glare at me. He didn't need to worry too much; at the far end of the road, I spotted a group of witches heading towards us. They'd start dismantling the wolfsbane and if they were the Wicker Witches, as Liam and his buddy had surmised, it would probably take them less than two hours to complete their mission.

But even if it only took them twenty minutes, it would be too long for Nick. I turned my back on the werewolves and closed the front door. Bring on the basement.

CHAPTER

TWENTY-EIGHT

I t took me longer to find the entrance to the basement than it should have done. I'd expected a handy door and a proper staircase leading downwards but instead, after searching every room, I finally discovered a small hatch in a narrow back room that revealed a rusty ladder that plunged into darkness beneath the building.

For a moment or two I eyed it warily, wondering whether Liam had bluffed and I was about to walk into a trap. Then I caught the brief hum of distant voices and realised he had indeed been telling the truth.

I turned around to lower myself. It was such a long descent that I expected to find myself in a dank space with pools of stagnant water and the occasional scurrying rat, but beneath the bottom rung there was soft carpet. It was too dark to see much but there was a narrow chink of light ahead. I stretched out my arms and my fingertips brushed the walls on either side. Rather than slimy mould, I felt flocked wallpaper. It appeared the Umbra basement was a hideout in every sense of the word.

I tiptoed towards the light that was emanating from beneath a door which, when I got close, I found was made of steel; no doubt it could be barred against intruders. The people inside that room must have known about the hundreds of werewolves gathering outside. Any whiff of danger to their safe space and they'd end Nick's life in a heartbeat before they made their escape.

I was certain that there'd be another exit, some sort of tunnel that could be reached only from inside the room. It was the only thing that made any sense. For their demonic plan to work, they had to escape with Nick's blood and make it safely to Crackendon Square.

I could still hear the murmur of voices. Unlike the wooden door upstairs, the steel distorted the sound so it was difficult to judge whether there were five people plus Nick beyond the door or where they might be. I didn't know who they were and I didn't know their capabilities so I needed to employ different tricks if I was going to be successful. But there were two things that I definitely *did* know: one, they were underground, and two, the light was electric.

I went back up the ladder to the ancient kitchen. When I'd been searching for the basement entrance, I'd spotted an old fuse box in the far corner above the cracked sink. I jumped up onto the rickety counter, lifted the cover and flicked the mains switch. Although the result was undramatic from where I was standing, I reckoned there would be dramatic curses coming from the basement room right about now.

I grinned humourlessly, replaced the cover and beat a retreat to the room where I'd found Liam. I took his buddy's corpse with me so that the hallway was clear. As soon as I entered the room, I flicked on the switch for the overhead light then closed the door, took up my position and waited for the footsteps. When I heard two sets, my smile widened.

Someone walked past the room towards the kitchen; the

second person opened the door to the room I was in. 'You've tripped the circuit, you idiots. What are you—?'

The woman appeared to be the witch of the group. She faltered when she didn't see Liam or his pal and that was when I stepped out from behind the door and smashed the gun butt into the side of her head. She crumpled to the floor without another a word; it was almost disappointing.

I ripped off her shirt to reveal a plain white tank top that I tore into pieces to gag and bind her in the unlikely event that she regained consciousness. I'd just tied the final knot when the overhead light flicked back into life.

I congratulated myself on my timing as I dragged the witch out of the line of sight of the door which I left open. Seconds later, I heard footsteps returning. This person was warier and seemed to sense that something was amiss and they paused outside long enough to worry me. Rather than waiting any longer, I stepped out to confront them.

The male druid's mouth dropped open. It only took a moment for me to realise that he'd hesitated not out of suspicion but to check his reflection in the grimy mirror hanging on the wall next to him. Unfortunately, his vanity didn't detract from his skill or his speed and, even as his mouth started to close, he reached into his pocket.

Unwilling to risk firing the gun in case the steel basement door was open and the remaining occupants heard the shot, I barrelled towards him, knocking into his body with such force that he was thrown off his feet. He landed on his back and I fell on top of him and reached for his hand.

I couldn't tell what he was clutching but I wrenched his wrist hard enough for him to drop it. I scrabbled around until I touched a small linen bag tied with string. I whipped my hand around and stuffed it into his mouth just as he prepared to shout for back-up.

Whatever magic mixture he'd created, it was incredibly potent. His eyes bulged and his heart rate, which I could feel through his clothes, accelerated. He grunted twice and started to shudder.

I moved back and pulled myself upright as blood dripped from the corner of his eyes, then seeped from his ears and dribbled out of his mouth. As I watched there was a gush of blood from both his nostrils. A dark patch formed around his groin.

'I see what this is,' I whispered, feeling nauseous. 'It's not defensive magic, it's something that will increase blood flow. You made this to help you extract as much blood from Nick as you could.'

He was in far too much distress to answer. 'You thought that you could do this to a teenage boy. To a *child*.' I might have been an assassin but I'd never hurt anyone like this – and I'd never killed anyone under the age of twenty-five.

The blood was running faster now, almost pouring from the druid's every orifice. I hissed as I bent over and extracted the herbal bag. It might already be too late – the toxin had worked so quickly that I wasn't sure its effects could be halted – but he was still breathing so I hoisted him up and hefted him into the room behind me to join the unconscious witch.

Three to go, Kit, I told myself. Only three to go.

I returned to the trapdoor and gazed down into the depths. There was more light now, which meant only one thing: the steel door had been left open as the remaining occupants waited for their two companions to return.

I no longer had to worry about being quiet because they'd assume I was one of them when they heard my footsteps. In a few minutes, I'd see Nick – or at least what remained of him. Clambering down the iron ladder for the second time, I tried not to allow a mental image of Nick's dead body to appear in my mind. There was every chance he was still alive.

I walked along the hallway with deliberately heavy footsteps. When the door was only about five metres away, a cool, cultured voice called out, 'What were those fuckers doing up there with the electricity?' My ploy had worked: whoever was there believed I was part of the group.

The voice also gave me a lot of information about Nick's abductors. The oddly clipped accent suggested it was the vampire of the team talking, and the authority in his voice told me that my earlier theory was correct: he was the one who was in charge here.

It made sense. Like the Fae, vampires are long-living creatures and some of them are thought to be hundreds of years old. Longevity tends to produce not wise Methuselah personalities but twitchy men and women who find day-to-day life tedious. A long life doesn't always encourage joy and wonder, it can promote boredom and cynicism and encourage vampires to do stupid things to liven up their existence – like trying to conjure a demon into existence.

Vamps' long lives also mean that they're often incredibly wealthy, with the sort of money that could cover the cost of forget-me-not spells and concentrated wolfsbane. And they know how to deal with blood and how best to extract it. Using your fangs alone is considered passé if you're a bloodsucker.

I coughed loudly, doing my best to sound like Liam or the vain male druid, but I knew immediately that my attempt wouldn't fool anyone. Leaping forward before the steel door closed in my face and locked me out for good, I burst into the room with both guns raised.

Liam hadn't lied. There were three of the bastards left and, as I'd surmised, there was the gaping hole of an escape tunnel behind them. Thankfully, Nick was also there, trussed up on a bed in the far corner. His eyes were closed but there wasn't time to confirm whether he was alive because his captors were coming at me.

Although the vampire was my biggest problem, the ogre was my most immediate one. She was huge, even for an ogre; her head brushed the high ceiling and her girth was equally impressive. She was also very quick and she threw herself at me as I entered the room. I emptied both guns in her direction.

The bullets wouldn't penetrate her thick skin but I wanted to slow down her lumbering progress because she could easily shove me out of the steel door with one hand. If that happened, I'd never get back inside and Nick would be lost forever. I'd caught enough of a glimpse of the complicated mechanism on the inner side of the door to appreciate its strength.

Two bullets smashed into the ogre's cheek and three hit her chest. She staggered backwards and grunted in pain. With both guns empty, I side-stepped just as the druid, an older man with a bushy white beard, started an incantation.

I moved in the nick of time as fire burst from his hands, and instead of engulfing me the flames smacked into the ogre. That had been a particularly foolish move on the druid's part because ogres didn't like fire and it would do far more to slow her down than my bullets had done. It wasn't what I'd been expecting but I took advantage of the situation.

I jumped, gaining height that even a cat would have been impressed by, and twisted a full circle in mid-air to gain momentum. When I scissor-kicked the ogre and my feet slammed into her chest, she stumbled backwards, lost her footing and crashed to the floor. The old adage was true: the bigger they are, the harder they fall.

As I'd planned, she squashed the druid who emitted a squeak of protest before her massive body smothered him. What I *hadn't* planned was the searing pain that came from forcing my limbs into a manoeuvre I'd not pulled off since my twenties. I also fell to the floor as bolts of pain flared through my joints. Shit: I'd not been as clever as I'd thought. I kept forgetting I wasn't the lithe, honed assassin I used to be.

Knowing that the fight was far from over, I tried to heave myself back to my feet but every time I pushed upwards, a shooting pain in my left hip made my leg give away. Three times I tried to stand and three times I collapsed again.

Given my opponents it was a wonder I was still breathing, but when I was finally upright I realised why they hadn't renewed their attack. Only a small scrap of velvet remained as a testament that the druid had existed. He was still underneath the ogre's huge body – and the ogre was so heavy that she'd probably killed him.

The reason that the ogre had not continued the battle was because the druid's fire had continued to attack her even after she'd fallen. Half of her face had been severely burnt, her skin was red raw and several nasty blisters were already forming. She'd squeezed her eyes shut in pain and it looked as if she'd completely lose the sight in her left one. She was probably unaccustomed to being attacked and the hurt was too much for her. She was moaning softly but making no attempt to move.

The vampire was different: he stayed on his feet, watching me through hooded eyes. He didn't try to help his companions; in fact, he appeared entirely unperturbed by their fate. He adjusted his cuffs and gazed at me calmly. 'I know who you are,' he said. 'You are the landlady.'

As superhero names went it wasn't the most exciting one but I lifted my chin as if I were proud of it. 'Yeah,' I said, with a touch of cat-lady defiance. 'I am the landlady. Let me guess,' I said, remembering what I'd overheard upstairs, 'you're Brassick.'

The corners of his thin, bloodless mouth quirked upwards. 'I am. Congratulations.' He clapped slowly and smiled mirthlessly. 'Why are you helping the wolves?' He sounded genuinely interested. 'They only care about their own.'

'I'm guessing that's why you only thought to create defences against werewolves and not someone like me,' I said drily. The vamp grimaced at his lack of forethought and I half smiled. 'What can I say?' I continued. 'I'm community minded.' I paused. 'And it's just as well since you're trying to raise a demon.'

I was rewarded with a flicker of surprise. 'Bravo,' he murmured. 'It sounds as if you already have all the answers.'

'Not all of them. Why the fuck do you think invoking a demon would be a good idea?'

He shrugged. 'I thought it might be fun and I had nothing better to do.'

I suspected this dick was telling the truth about his motives. I lurched forward, mindful of the shooting pain in my hip. It was time to end this for good and kill the bloodsucker before more damage could be done. Unfortunately, the fanged fucker was a step ahead of me and he was capable of some speedy mid-air leaps himself. He didn't even twang his hip as he completed them.

I registered what his plan was about a millisecond too late. He sailed towards Nick's unmoving body and hoisted him up. Nick's head lolled to one side but finally I could see his chest rising and falling. He was still alive. For now.

Brassick grinned again, revealing his pearly-white fangs. 'Let's see exactly how community minded you are,' he murmured. 'You can catch me and prevent a demon uprising or,' he paused for effect, 'you can save the kid.'

And with that, he raised Nick's arm to his mouth and ripped his skin with his fangs, making sure that he tore open an artery in the process.

CHAPTER
TWENTY-NINE

After Brassick let Nick's body fall and turned away to flee down the dark tunnel behind him, it occurred to me that he was genuinely curious about what I'd do next. However, I didn't have a choice: if I went after the vampire now, Nick would certainly die.

While I was concerned about what would happen if Brassick invoked a demon, the winter solstice was still days away and there was plenty of time to track him down again and stop him. There was no time left to help Nick. Besides, Brassick knew I was a landlady but he didn't know what else I was capable of, even though he must have started to work out at least some of my skills.

I'd completed a fair amount of emergency medical training when I was an assassin, and EEL had required me to update that training on a regular basis – it was surprising how seriously an organisation of assassins took their training modules and employee certification. It might have seemed somewhat idiotic, given that my goal was to kill rather than to save, but I had to know how to deal with wounded bystanders or any injuries of my own. I knew exactly how to deal with Nick's wound, even though he'd doubtless already lost vast amounts of blood over the past few days.

Ignoring the painful spasm in my hip, I spun towards the fallen ogre. Her eyes remained closed and she was wheezing but, despite her severe burns, I was worried that she might try another attack. When I reached for her garish flowery blouse and ripped it away from her body, however, she barely flinched.

'I know what happens when you pinch the thoracic nerve in an ogre's shoulder,' I said as I returned to Nick. 'Yours is exposed at the moment, so I'd stay down there if I were you. Some of your friends have proved so dedicated to your cause that they were willing to die for it. That might be true of you, too, but I bet you'd rather not experience the sort of pain I can inflict before your soul passes from this world.'

She gave a tiny squeak; she'd heard my threat. Good. I didn't need to worry about her.

I crouched next to Nick's body and tied a tourniquet around his upper arm to stop the blood flow. When I was certain it was secure, I gathered him into my arms. He felt like skin and bones; he'd definitely lost weight and I still wasn't convinced that he'd pull through.

'Hang on in there, Nick. Don't lose that stubbornness of yours. Don't let go. I've got you now.'

If he heard me, he didn't react. I braced myself, told my hip sternly that it'd had its fun and now was not the time to falter, then staggered out of the basement room and down the carpeted hallway. I still had to get Nick's limp body up the ladder and that would be far easier said than done.

I knew that the only way to get Nick up to the ground level was to place him in a fireman's lift. In theory that was fine, but his arm would be dangling downwards when I needed to keep it raised to minimise any more blood loss.

I decided that fumbling around to find a way to hoist up his arm wasn't worth the time I'd lose, so I tensed my muscles, got Nick into position and powered up the ladder. Thankfully my leg and my hip, although brutally painful, didn't give way. I heaved both of us clear of the ladder and adjusted Nick's position, then I half-ran, half-staggered for the front door.

I emerged blinking in sunshine that felt incongruous after the basement. A ripple of shock and horror ran through the werewolves who had remained in position on the other side of the street.

A baker's dozen of Wicker Witches were attending to the wolfsbane; clearly Alexander MacTire was prepared to spend whatever it took to get into the building. I knew from experience that these particular witches were far too concerned about their own safety to enter of their own accord; they didn't go anywhere unless they knew exactly what to expect, which was one of the reasons that they were the most successful coven in Coldstream.

All thirteen of them stopped what they were doing to stare at me, tensing in case I presented a threat, but as soon as they realised they weren't in danger they continued their work. Alexander MacTire was a different prospect. He ran as close to the wolfsbane as he could with Samantha at his heels. There was no sign of Thane.

'Nick needs immediate medical attention,' I shouted, stumbling past the magicked barrier. 'But he's still breathing.'

MacTire halted in front of me and held out his arms. I passed over Nick and he cradled his nephew in his arms as he hollered for help. Samantha gazed at me, bristling with tension. 'What about the abductors?' she asked, unable or unwilling to keep the snarl from her voice.

I was already turning away. 'Most have been taken care of. They're inside and incapacitated. There's still one left.'

'McCafferty! Wait!'

I didn't have time to hang around and answer more of her questions. I darted back to the house; I was going to catch up to that damned vampire even if it killed me.

I pelted back down the hallway with as much speed as my throbbing hip allowed; the adrenaline released by my success in getting Nick into the arms of his family was over-riding my pain. I raced down the ladder and through the underground corridor to the basement prison.

The ogre was trying to sit up but as soon as I went into the room she sagged. 'Make any move to escape,' I told her calmly, 'and I'll make sure you live to regret it.' Manoeuvring around her, I marched into the dark tunnel through which the vampire had made his escape. His head start was lengthy but it wasn't insurmountable.

I was only a few steps down the tunnel when it became clear that it was nothing like the basement; this was the dank, smelly, rough-hewn hole that I'd expected earlier. After I'd run about fifty metres, however, I emerged into a larger tunnel and realised I was wrong. There was more to this place than met the eye.

There had been whispers among EEL employees for years that the city's small population of vampires had their own way of getting around that avoided the nastiness of daylight. Some of my old colleagues had even made it a personal mission to find the hidden entrances to this supposed network of vamp tunnels. If any of them had found a way in, they hadn't advertised it – even within the organisation, being secretive came with the job.

I'd never cared enough to search because I didn't need to scuttle around underground to fulfil my contracts. I was a cat, not a mole.

As I looked around, I knew that I was in those vampire tunnels. The question was, which way to go next. I didn't know where the vampire had gone and there was no trail. I had a fifty-fifty chance of getting it right, so I chose to go left.

Mindful that I was still injured, I jogged rather than risking a sprint. For a while I knew roughly where I was, but soon the tunnel slanted to the right and forced me into a series of rapid twists and turns. Within fifteen minutes, I could have been anywhere underneath the city.

The darkness was disorientating. The ball of frustration grew in the pit of my stomach, especially as I had no idea whether the fucking vampire who'd orchestrated Nick's abduction had already managed to escape. I was beginning to suspect that was the case – until I heard a faint whoosh.

I picked up speed and moved towards the source of the noise. I'm going to get you, I vowed. I'm going to make you pay for what you've done to Nick.

The tunnel curved around yet again and I saw an orange glow ahead. I gulped in air – and that was when a hand appeared out of the darkness and grabbed hold of me. I swung hard towards my assailant, prepared to fight for my life with every iota of strength I possessed, but then a familiar face swam into the gloom together with the heady scent of vetiver.

'Friend,' Thane hissed at me. 'Not foe. Now keep quiet and stay here.' He wrapped his arms around me and drew me into the darkness next to him.

A moment later the source of the light appeared and it took me everything I had to suppress my gasp. Even after all the years I'd been in Coldstream, I could still be surprised.

It was a worm, but not an earthworm or a bristle worm or a roundworm. It was at least as long as Thane was tall, and its girth matched that of a shire horse. Some sort of contraption was attached to its head with a single glowing lantern dangling behind it, though the light wasn't for the worm's sake since it was clearly blind. It appeared to be for its passenger because, perched side-saddle on top of its back and casually reading a book, was a female vampire dressed in a long cloak and flowing dress.

Neither of them glanced at us as they passed by. Soon the whooshing sound faded and the tunnel was dark again. I shook my head, amazed; it wasn't so much the worm's existence that surprised me but that it existed beneath my feet and I'd never known about it until now.

Thane's voice was soft in my ear. 'It's how the vampires get around during the day if they need to. It's not so much of a problem at this time of year when the sun sets early, but in the summer months they'd be trapped in their homes for most hours of the day without these tunnels and those creatures. Anyone who's not a vampire isn't supposed to be down here without an engraved invitation.'

I shook off my amazement and Thane dropped his arms so I could turn and face him. 'What are you doing here?' I asked, though it wasn't an accusation. Actually, I was delighted that I was no longer alone.

'I got to thinking about that house. Whoever was in there and took Nick had another way out, and it made sense that the escape route would be through these tunnels. Besides, who else would have the money, time and inclination to do all this other than a vampire?'

Who else, indeed?

He continued. 'I've known about these tunnels since I found one of the older entrances by accident after I was thrown out of the Barrow pack. I know where a few others are located, but they're not easy to find and it's not wise to use them unless you turn into a bat and guzzle blood by the bucketload.' He shuddered. 'A vampire caught me the first time I came down here and it didn't end well for me. I've not been tempted to return since.'

I didn't blame him: it wasn't a good idea to cross a vampire if you could help it.

Thane looked at me anxiously, too afraid to voice the question aloud but desperate to know the answer. I put him out of his misery. 'Nick's alive,' I told him. 'I got him out. He's in a bad way, but with the right treatment he should be okay.'

I felt his body relax. 'Good work.' He passed a hand in front of his eyes. 'Bloody good work, Kit.'

I wasn't prepared to accept any praise, not yet. 'One of the kidnappers got away. That's why I'm down here.' I quickly told him all that had happened.

'What about Nick's blood? If they were harvesting it...'

'There was no blood in any containers so any that they've already drawn from Nick must have been transported elsewhere, probably closer to Crackendon Square in preparation for the solstice.' I paused. 'Nick is still alive, so they didn't get the thirteen pints of blood from him. Even if that vampire Brassick escapes, he hasn't enough to summon a demon.'

Thane's eyes met mine. 'He won't escape.' He tapped the side of his nose. 'Take me back to where you started and I'll sniff out the bastard.'

CHAPTER
THIRTY

There were no giant worms or vampires as we went back through the tunnels. I caught Thane's gaze drifting down my body and I knew he'd noticed that something was wrong with my hip, but thankfully he didn't comment or suggest that I hang back while he went after Brassick alone. Instead we jogged through the gloom to the intersection where I'd first emerged.

Thane's nose twitched and he made several slow circles as he absorbed the scent. I watched; my sense of smell was better than most, but I was no match for a werewolf.

I wished the knot of anxiety in my stomach would disappear. Although Nick was safe, these unfamiliar tunnels and my lack of preparation made me feel as if I had no control and that wasn't a sensation I was used to. I didn't like it one jot; I trusted Thane but it was hard to yield to his werewolf senses and let him lead the way. In many ways, I was as much of a lone wolf as he was.

'I can't catch any scent from the vampire,' he said after several moments.

'But?' I prodded.

'But I can smell wolf blood. It's faint but it's definitely here. It must be what they took from Nick.' He turned to the right. 'The scent leads that way.'

So I'd made the wrong choice earlier. My irritation with myself grew, even though there was no way I could have known which way to go. 'He's got an hour's head start.'

Thane shrugged but I could see the tension in his eyes. 'We'll catch him,' he said with a confidence that neither of us felt. He started to move away. I swallowed my ego and followed.

For the first few hundred metres there was nothing of interest. We stayed silent until we reached another intersection then I waited while Thane sniffed the stale air. There were two heavy looking iron doors on either side of the junction; although they were unmarked, I was certain that they led to vampire-owned properties. The only way to keep these tunnels exclusively to anyone with fangs and a penchant for O neg would be to control the exits and entrances and that made it likely that every doorway led to a private property rather than a public place.

'This way, I'm sure of it.' Thane pointed left but despite his words he sounded doubtful. I gave him a long look. 'The smell is fading and there's only a faint odour clinging to the air,' he admitted. 'There are a lot of competing scents and no spilled blood to track. It won't linger for much longer.'

'Then we'd better get a move on and find that fucker before the trail vanishes for good.'

'Amen to that,' Thane murmured. We took off once more.

One turn started to look much like another. I noticed notches on some of the walls, doubtless markers for the vampires who used these tunnels, but the dark surroundings and similarities between one section of tunnel and the next meant that I had little idea of where we were. At one point I was certain that we were doubling back on ourselves. It didn't help that Thane was stopping more often and seemed less and less sure of himself, though even the most skilled werewolf tracker would struggle down here.

We were forced to take cover twice as more giant worms and their fanged passengers passed by. The second time there was a procession as five worms carrying five vamps trundled by. One of the vampires lifted his head and his nostrils flared. I felt a shiver of fear that he had smelled us even when the strange parade had drifted past and disappeared.

I didn't like the prospect of being discovered. I could handle one or two vamps, but if the alarm was raised and a whole host of the bastards came after us, we'd never get out. The more time I spent underground, the more my thoughts darkened – and the more my damned hip hurt. Once all this was over, I was going to start training again. Just because I was retired didn't mean I had to grow weak.

We'd passed twenty-three iron doors when Thane finally stopped in the middle of a tunnel that, to my eyes, looked exactly the same as every other section we'd been through. He looked left then right, then pointed ahead. 'There,' he said softly. 'In there.'

I moved to the rusty door he had identified; there was no number or name to indicate what it led to. I squinted as I examined it carefully. 'Are you sure?'

He snorted. 'Yes, I'm sure.' I gave him a longer look. 'Alright,' he admitted. 'I'm mostly sure. Can you do better?'

That was a hard 'nope'. I pursed my lips and reached for the door handle. Although there was every chance that we'd set off a trap by opening it, we had little choice and I was keen to get out of the tunnel.

I twisted the handle and the door opened without so much as a complaining creak. Nothing exploded in my face and no vampire was waiting for me on the other side. There was no sign of Brassick, just a long corridor lit by a strip light. So far so good. I stepped across the threshold and Thane followed.

We walked more slowly and quietly now. Remembering the booby trap that Thane had set off at the Galbraith house, I took my time checking the way ahead. It seemed inconceivable that there was nothing to stop us but we continued unimpeded. By the time we reached yet another door, I was more confused than concerned.

The ladder at the far end of the hallway was made out of wood and I could see scuff marks from where it had been used by numerous pairs of feet. I craned my neck but couldn't see anything above me, so I beckoned Thane. He stepped past me and lowered his head to the wood. 'Smells like vamp,' he grunted. That was hardly a surprise.

'What about Nick's blood?' I asked.

'The scent is stronger now. This wanker is ours, Kit. He must have come this way – he's somewhere above us. We can take him down together.' He reached again for the ladder.

'Wait,' I said. 'This feels too easy.'

'Easy?' Thane raised a disbelieving eyebrow. 'We've been running around in the dark for hours. It might be the middle of the day, but there are still vampires in these tunnels. If any of them had spotted us, we'd be dead by now. Even Alexander MacTire would think twice about wandering through them.'

He'd think twice but he'd still do it. I shook my head. 'Something isn't right.'

'I'll go first. If there are any traps up there, I'll bear the brunt of them.'

I frowned. 'I don't want you to get hurt.' I didn't want *either* of us to get hurt.

Something shifted in his expression. 'Does that mean that you care for me?' he asked softly.

'I wouldn't go that far.'

He grinned. 'Perhaps if I get any booboos, you'll kiss them better for me.'

'I'll give you a fucking booboo,' I muttered.

His grin widened – until there was a sudden thump above us. We both stilled. 'If you have a bad feeling,' he whispered, 'we can find our way out of here and try to locate this spot from above ground.'

We'd never locate the right building that way, not without a map. I shook my head. It was up this ladder or nothing, and I wasn't walking away no matter how threatened I might feel. Nick was safe but that didn't mean this shit show was over. 'No,' I said. 'Let's do it.'

Thane nodded solemnly then started to ascend the ladder.

My heart was in my mouth when he reached the trapdoor that led to whatever was above. It was the perfect spot for either a trap or an ambush but he didn't hesitate; he flipped it open, hauled himself up and vanished.

I heard nothing, not a whisper, a shout nor an exclamation of pain.

Several seconds ticked past before his face reappeared. 'All good.' He winked.

I scowled back at him. 'Did you deliberately delay as a joke?'

'*Moi?*'

Ginger idiot. I returned his wink with my middle finger and he winked again. He'd clearly regained his humour now that Nick was safe. I wasn't impressed, even if he was disarmingly handsome when he smiled.

I hoisted myself up the ladder; my hip pain had eased, though I suspected that meant it would hurt all the more the next day. Unless Brassick really did have an ace up his laced sleeve and I didn't survive until the next day.

I pulled myself through the hatch. The basement we were in

was of a similar size and configuration to the last one, albeit without an unconscious teenage werewolf in need of a blood transfusion or a squashed druid, a wheezing ogre and a sniffy vampire. There were, however, dozens upon dozens of dusty bottles of wine.

Thane picked one up and examined the label. 'A 1926 Bordeaux,' he said, holding it up so I could see it. 'A good year.'

'You like wine?'

'You don't?'

I shrugged: I enjoyed wine but I knew jack shit about it. I chose my bottles according to how pretty the labels were and whether the names were interesting. I wouldn't have chosen the wine Thane was holding, not based on that font.

He returned the bottle to the rack and gestured to the woodworm-ridden door in the corner. I checked its frame carefully before inching it open. There was a soft creak and I caught a brief glimpse of a spider scuttling away from the corner.

Pursing my lips, I stepped across the threshold. A narrow set of stairs loomed above me. I could hear an old clock ticking and several thumping footsteps, followed by a mutter. I tensed. Was somebody else here as well as Brassick?

The footsteps moved closer and I realised that he was pacing the room next to the ground-floor landing while talking to himself. 'Everything is good, Brassick,' he said. 'Fine and dandy. There is nothing to worry about.'

I smiled humourlessly: he had everything to worry about. I glanced over my shoulder at Thane, who dipped his head to indicate that he was ready. Moving as quietly as possible, I climbed the stairs.

Brassick was still talking. 'There will only be one demon and it can't possibly eat all that much.' He paused as I reached the top of the stairs. He was in the kitchen, a large room with high ceilings. Although there were windows, they were shuttered against the sunshine.

My gaze hardened. He appeared to be decanting blood from a tin receptacle into empty wine bottles. That had to be Nick's blood. 'I wonder what a demon's favourite food is,' he mumbled.

'I expect that they're rather partial to vampires,' I said aloud.

Brassick's back stiffened though he didn't turn round immediately. '*You*. You followed me through the Understream? Really?' His astonishment revealed exactly why we'd managed to sneak inside so easily: the vampire was an idiot.

'You're braver than I thought you were,' he went on. 'If you'd been spotted by one of my kin, you'd already be strung up and suffering from a thousand cuts. Literally.'

I wondered if that was what had happened to Thane when he'd been caught down there. Maybe it was better not to know. 'That's what you call those tunnels? The Understream?' I asked. 'What are the worm things called?'

'Worms,' he said. 'What else would we call them?'

Ask a stupid question, get a stupid answer.

'What about the boy? Is he alive?' Brassick demanded.

When I didn't answer, he finally turned and his dark eyes met mine. He glanced over my shoulder and spotted Thane. 'Number Three,' he whispered, his face lighting with recognition.

Thane growled. Both of us knew what that number had to refer to: Thane was the third on Umbra's list of lone werewolves whose blood could be used to bring forth a demon.

'You killed Paul and Alice,' he snarled.

Brassick's brow creased. 'Paul was the tall wolf with the long hair? Yeah, he was Number One. Alice, I suppose, was Number Two.' He splayed his hands out in a mock-conciliatory gesture. 'We didn't mean to kill them but some of my colleagues were … over-enthusiastic about their work. Sadly, Number One died of blood loss. We tried to take a few pints from him but we misjudged how much he could stand to lose. Accidents happen.'

'And Alice?' Thane spat.

'Number Two put up more of a fight than we expected and she died when we tried to take her off the street.' The vampire shrugged his bony shoulders. 'You did well, Number Three. You managed to escape but we got two full pints from you before that happened. Your donation to our cause will make all the difference.'

Then he smiled. 'Not as much difference as Number Four, of course, but he's special. Teenage blood is so much more useful.' He smacked his lips. 'And tasty.'

That was too much for Thane and he pushed past me, quivering with a bitter lust for vengeance. Brassick's reaction was swift. He raised his arms and transformed into a cloud of black smoke before Thane reached him. His bat wings flapped rapidly as his tiny body rose out of Thane's reach.

I was already at the door, closing it so that Brassick couldn't escape no matter what form he chose to take.

Thane jumped up, sweeping his arm as high as he could in a bid to knock down Brassick's bat body.

'You can't get away,' I called. 'You might as well give yourself up and face the consequences of your actions.'

The bat fluttered left and right before descending, then there was another smaller puff of dark smoke and Brassick's human form reappeared. 'I can't do that, dear woman. What would the demon say?' He bared his teeth and displayed his glistening fangs. 'But if you won't let me take flight, let's fight instead.' And with that, he sprang at me.

Hand-to-hand combat wasn't my speciality. Most of my

work had been conducted from the shadows and from a distance, not close up, but there had been the odd occasion when I'd needed to fight with my fists and I knew I could hold my own. I was delighted to show Brassick exactly what I was capable of.

He swung at me with his right fist and I ducked to avoid the blow. I raised my leg to retaliate with a kick but, to my chagrin, Thane beat me to it. He grabbed Brassick by the scruff of his neck and hauled him back before my foot could connect, then slammed his fist into the side of the vampire's head.

It was going to take more than a single punch to bring Brassick down. He staggered back a few steps and reached for the drawer behind him, pulled out a long-bladed knife with a serrated edge and thrust it forward.

The blade sliced into Thane's upper chest. Although the wound was only superficial, there was enough blood to soak the front of the werewolf's shirt and his face tightened with pain.

Thane threw another punch, side-stepped to avoid the blade and blocked me from attacking Brassick. There was a smacking sound as the edge of his fist connected with the vampire's jaw. It was a powerful blow but Brassick did little more than smirk. He delved into his pocket and withdrew something. I tensed as he opened his fingers to reveal a small pile of herbs that he blew into Thane's face.

Thane's howl was like nothing I'd ever heard before.

'You didn't really think I wouldn't have kept some wolfsbane back, did you?' Brassick smiled. 'This really is extraordinarily powerful stuff.'

Thane's knees gave way and he fell to the floor. Shit.

I vaulted over his body. Brassick slashed the knife through the air, catching my arm and cutting through my flesh. Blood dripped from the wound but he'd not cut anything vital.

I took a step backwards and my hand stretched behind me onto the worktop until my fingers curled around one of the blood-filled containers. I smashed it against the marble, sending a spray of blood across the kitchen, then I jabbed the jagged glass at Brassick.

He waved the knife at me before angling it downwards: he meant to hurt Thane in the same way that he'd hurt Nick, to draw my attention away and force me – again – to make a choice. This was why it was better to work alone; I didn't have to worry about anyone else's health and wellbeing when I was by myself.

In an ideal world, I'd have brought Brassick to his knees then questioned him properly about his demonic plans, but Thane's vulnerability didn't allow for such niceties and there wasn't time to come up with a useful alternative. I needed to end this as quickly as possible.

I leapt upwards again, this time not aiming for Brassick but jumping onto the kitchen counter. I smashed more of the glass containers containing Nick's blood then kicked the sealed wooden shutters as Brassick stabbed downwards. 'Left!' I shrieked at Thane.

He rolled in the nick of time, although the kitchen knife still slid into his shoulder. He grunted loudly. I kicked the wooden shutters again and only then did Brassick register the threat. He abandoned Thane and turned to me. 'Wait,' he said. 'Don't—'

I didn't hear the end of the sentence as I kicked the shutters once again. The third time was the charm: the wood splintered and, although the shutters didn't bounce open, I'd done enough to cause the vampire mortal damage. A bolt of sunlight blasted through the crack and landed squarely on his forehead.

The results were almost instantaneous.

The patch of pale skin hit by the sunshine blackened and I actually heard it sizzle. Brassick's mouth opened in a silent scream and his eyes widened and momentarily glowed red. He dropped the knife as his body stiffened into a rigid, scarecrow-like figure then he jerked and, bizarrely, grinned. Before I could draw breath, his flesh burst into flames as if he'd been doused in accelerant.

I threw myself at Thane, grabbed his arm and dragged him out of the way as the vampire combusted. The last thing I saw before Brassick's bones turned to ash was him forming a circle with the thumb and index finger of his right hand. He used the middle finger of his left hand to slash through it, a burning facsimile of the red graffiti that Umbra had sprayed around the city.

A beat later, there was nothing left beyond a pile of burning ash and bone.

Umbra were finished.

THIRTY-ONE

I hadn't appreciated how much paperwork was involved when you killed somebody in Coldstream and their death wasn't conducted under the secretive guise of an assassin. Even though Brassick's death had been deemed both just and necessary, I still had to spend more time than any reasonable person would have considered worthwhile filling out forms and explaining my actions.

Thankfully, MacTire and his wolves had tidied up the scene at the building where Nick had been held captive, otherwise I might have been buried for good under the weight of bureaucracy and Captain Montgomery's desire to cross every t and dot every i. I'd also been forced into meetings with several high-faluting vampires who wanted detailed explanations about what had happened. They'd extracted several bound promises from me that I wouldn't breathe a word about the Understream tunnels and that I wouldn't enter them again without stamped approval.

Thane had been fortunate: he got to spend three days recovering in hospital instead of dealing with all the damned form filling.

The morning of the winter solstice was the first chance I'd had to relax properly since all this crap had started. It was cold but sunny enough for me to drag a chair into the front garden, sit with a cup of coffee and watch the world go by. Umbra had been, by both name and nature, a thing of shadows and darkness, which made me almost as grateful for a splash of winter sunshine as She Who Loves Sunbeams.

All five cats were gathered around me. There had been a minor stand-off as He Who Crunches Bird Bones and He Who Must Sleep vied for my lap, but in the end they both backed off when She Without An Ear nabbed it first. She curled up into a tight ball while I clutched my mug and resisted scratching her ears. I knew my place.

I was, however, touched that all five of them were still worried enough about me to stay close. It was almost like the old days when I'd sometimes returned home after a particularly gnarly assignment and they'd crowded me with warm feline concern.

I murmured inanities to them about the weather and my plans for the day. He Who Roams Wide sent me an arch look, judging my level of conversational skill and clearly finding it wanting. Before I could respond with a snarky comment about *his* conversation, he sprang up and hissed.

She Without An Ear tensed and dug her claws into my legs before leaping off my lap and disappearing. The others followed her lead, although He Who Crunches Bird Bones opted to hide under a nearby bush rather than retreat inside.

I gulped down the last of the coffee. By the time I'd placed the mug on the grass next to my chair, the gleaming black car had rolled up outside my garden gate.

I stayed where I was. I'd have been disappointed if I'd not received another visit from the MacTires but I was surprised that it was happening so quickly. I hoped that didn't mean bad news about Nick, who was still recovering in the furry fold of his uncle's pack.

Samantha was in the driver's seat, her expression inscrutable, though she did turn her head and nod slightly. That was probably as much an acknowledgement of what I'd achieved with Thane's help as I was likely to get from her.

The rear passenger door opened and Alexander MacTire stepped out. He was a different man to the one I'd seen last time. The pained angst and barely contained fury had vanished and in their place was a more sober man, one who'd been confronted by his vulnerabilities. I wondered if the experience would change him in the long term. Only time would tell.

He strode to the gate and paused, raising his eyebrows in silent question. Well, that was certainly different. 'You may enter,' I said, amused by my imperious tone.

He unfastened the latch and walked up the narrow path. I got to my feet and met his gaze. 'Morning.'

'Good morning, Ms McCafferty,' he replied. 'I won't take up much of your time but it was important for me to come by.' His eyes held mine. 'You saved Nicholas and for that you have my eternal gratitude and that of the MacTire pack.'

At least he wasn't blaming me for allowing Nick to get kidnapped. 'He's alright?' I asked.

'He's recovering.' MacTire licked his lips and lowered his voice. 'Thank you, Kit.'

There were several answers I could have given. I chose the simplest. 'You're welcome.'

'If there is ever anything the MacTire pack can do to help you, you only need ask. We owe you and we will repay that debt.' He paused. 'You have my sworn word.'

I sucked in a sharp breath; I hadn't expected that. 'Thank you,' I said. 'I appreciate that.'

He nodded and stepped back. 'I'll leave you in peace now

but there is someone else who would like a word with you, if you don't mind.' The car door opened again to reveal Nick.

He was much thinner than before; his face was gaunt and there was a haunted expression behind those familiar eyes. He would recover, though, both mentally and physically. I was certain of that.

I watched him walk through the gate. His progress was slow, as if it were a struggle to put one foot in front of the other. Alexander MacTire didn't reach out to help him because that would have been too great a sign of weakness for a wolf. In fact, that lack of action meant that I knew exactly what was going to happen next. Nick had made a decision about his future – and I believed it was the right one.

MacTire melted away and I barely noticed his departure; my attention was on Nick. I waited, giving him the same respect by not offering to take his arm. I wouldn't offer him my chair either.

As soon as he reached me, his face broke into a wobbly smile. 'Hi, Kit.'

I smiled in return. 'I'm glad that you're finally calling me that and not Ms McCafferty.'

Nick blinked rapidly as he held back his tears; damned werewolves and their need to hide real emotion. Crying didn't make you any less tough, quite the opposite, but I knew better than to tell him he could let his feelings show. It would only embarrass him and that would never be my intention.

'Thank you,' Nick said, once he'd composed himself enough to speak. 'You saved my life. I wasn't aware of what was going on but I have a vague memory of you coming into that room. When I saw you, I knew everything would be alright.'

'I'm amazed you were conscious enough to notice anything at all. They must have taken a lot of your blood. You're recovering quickly.'

'They were trying to fill an enormous conical glass flask – there was a mark on it that indicated the level they wanted to get to. I was literally watching my life drain away.' He dropped his gaze. 'That's what would have happened if you hadn't shown up.'

'You're a survivor, Nick. You'd have made it out of there.'

'No, I wouldn't.' He shuffled his feet. 'I owe you everything.'

I gazed at him for a long moment. He'd only been gone for days but he'd aged years.

He cleared his throat. 'I'm taking the oath this afternoon,' he said. 'I'm joining the MacTire pack. I won't be coming back here to stay.'

I wasn't even remotely surprised. 'I'll return your deposit,' I said.

His eyes widened. 'No! That's not why I'm here. Keep the money. I just wanted to let you know in person. It's the least you deserve. You helped me out when nobody else would.'

'Are you sure that you want to sign up for life with the MacTires?' He was making the right decision but I wanted to be sure he'd considered all the ramifications and he wouldn't live to regret it.

'Yes. My uncle asked me to wait before taking the oath – he wanted me to be certain I was doing the right thing. But it is. I don't want to be a lone wolf. I *can't* be a lone wolf.' He swallowed. 'I'm not sure if Thane will understand. He was my friend.'

'He'll still be your friend,' I said gently. 'And he will understand. He'll approve, too.'

'You really think so?' he whispered.

I didn't hesitate. 'I do.'

He Who Crunches Bird Bones edged out from underneath the bush, miaowed and wound around Nick's legs. The boy smiled and crouched down to stroke him. 'I should probably go,' he said eventually. 'But...'

'Go on,' I said.

'Can I still come and visit sometimes?'

I grinned. 'Always.'

He straightened up. 'Thank you.' He bowed as if I were some sort of queen, and my cheeks warmed in response. 'See you, Kit.'

I nodded. 'See you, Nick.'

He returned to the car, hesitated then turned around and waved. I caught a glimpse of the happy, cheeky teenager he'd been before he disappeared inside and Samantha drove away.

Dave's front door opened and he walked into his garden. 'Been curtain twitching?' I asked.

He scowled. 'Well, I wasn't going to come outside with all those wolves around. I suppose they won't be coming here any more.'

'You suppose right.'

He grunted. 'Shame. I guess you'll have to continue lowering the tone of the neighbourhood all by yourself.'

'I guess I will.'

Another front door opened across the street, and Mrs Miller appeared dressed in her Sunday best: a tweed two-piece complete with a matching hat. She'd even taken the trouble to pin a corsage to her breast. 'Happy Winter Solstice!' she beamed.

I smiled back. 'Happy Winter Solstice to you, too.'

Dave's scowl grew more ferocious. 'Whatever.'

She waved at us and turned in the direction of the tram for Crackendon Square rather than towards the Glebe where the Church of the Masked God was planning its more muted solstice festivities. I watched her departing back then suddenly froze.

'Problem?' Dave grunted.

'Fuck, yes,' I whispered.

CHAPTER
THIRTY-TWO

It took me four minutes and twenty-three seconds to run into the house, strap on all the weapons I could possibly need and change my clothes. It took me three minutes and forty-one seconds to sprint out of the garden down the street to the tram stop.

Frustratingly there was no tram in sight. I shoved my hands in my pockets and huffed. Would it be faster to run to Crackendon Square? Solstice was a public holiday in Coldstream, so the trams were on a reduced timetable; they could also be running late because of the large number of people heading to the square for the 'celebrations'. I clenched my jaw as I tried to decide.

'Hey, Mrs McCafferty!'

Mrs McCafferty? I turned my head and saw the kid, Adrian, with his mother and his brothers and sisters. 'Kit,' I said shortly. I hadn't told them my name so they must have asked around. 'I'm not married.' I felt a flash of guilt for my lack of friendliness and forced a smile. 'Happy Winter Solstice.'

He clearly hadn't registered my mood because he beamed at me. 'We're going to Crackendon Square for the party.'

My stomach tightened. 'No.'

There was enough force in my voice to make his smile falter. He stared at me wide-eyed while I switched my gaze to his mum. 'Don't go,' I told her. 'If you want to celebrate the solstice in public, head to the Glebe to see what the Church of the Masked God are up to. They need the support. But don't go to Crackendon Square.'

Her face had whitened, not as a result of my words but because of my tone. 'What's wrong?'

'Nothing,' I said. 'Probably nothing. But don't go to Crackendon Square. Trust me.'

Her eyes scanned my face. 'Alright.' She hesitated. 'Thank you.'

I nodded and ignored the pouts from the younger children. She grabbed hold of their hands and started to drag them away from the tram stop. One of them was starting to cry.

I swallowed hard and thought about all the other families heading to Crackendon Square. Thankfully at that moment a tram rounded the far corner and shoogled towards me. There was still time. I could still do this.

It was standing room only inside the tram and I was squashed between a tall bony man who smelled of blue cheese and a short, plump woman who had a garland of flowers in her hair. I cleared my throat. They were going to think I was mad but I had to try.

'Don't go to Crackendon Square.' I raised my voice so that as many people as possible would hear me. 'Something bad is going to happen and you shouldn't go.'

Several excited conversations hushed as people turned their heads towards me.

'Don't go to the square,' I repeated. 'Please. It's dangerous.'

There were a few snorts of derision. The tall man frowned down at me. 'You're from the Church of the Masked God, ain't

ya? They're only jealous that everyone has decided to go somewhere else for the solstice this year.'

I tried to stay calm. 'I'm not from anywhere. I'm just telling
you that going to Crackendon isn't a good idea. Not today.'

'Oh yeah? Where are you going, then?'

I ground my teeth. Damnit. 'Your lives are in danger!' I
shouted. 'Don't go to the square!'

There was a beat of silence before most of the members of
my unwilling audience started to laugh. My shoulders dropped.
It was what I'd expected but even so it was depressing. These
people didn't know me, they had no reason to believe my words
and they'd heard a million conspiracy theories over the years.
Coldstream tended to breed daft ideas and whispered rumours
– but that didn't mean that some of them weren't true.

'Shut your trap,' the man told me. 'We're off out to enjoy
ourselves.'

I wasn't going to convince them, so I'd simply have to try
harder once I reached the square.

I conjured up a picture of the square and the surrounding
buildings in my mind. The area would be packed. I was vertically challenged enough for it to be difficult to see anything,
and I doubted I could squeeze my way to the front of the
crowds. My best bet was to get up high; if I could scale one of
the buildings to gain a decent vantage point, maybe I could spot
the danger. The Paradigm Bank was my best bet: its flat roof
was high enough for me to see everything, and thanks to its
ancient outdoor fire escape it would be easy to climb.

I breathed out slowly. I had a plan of sorts; it wasn't ideal,
but it was the best I could come up with under the circumstances.

I pushed to the front of the tram. There were several loud
complaints and tuts, and I received at least two elbow jabs in
my ribs. 'Stupid woman,' someone hissed. I ignored them.

When we finally arrived I sucked in a sharp breath when I saw how many people had gathered. Hundreds, possibly thousands, were here to celebrate the solstice and see what the posters and flyers advertising the event had been about.

The tram doors swished open. I jumped out and pushed through the crowds to the bank building. As soon as I reached it, I veered around until I was at the bottom of the rusty fire escape. Ignoring the creaking of the metal, I sprinted up it.

I wasn't the only one who'd thought to come up here. I was furious at the thought that someone might get in my way and stop me from doing whatever was necessary – but then I realised that it was Thane.

He turned to face me as soon as he heard my footsteps. 'Kit.' He sounded relieved rather than surprised.

I hadn't seen him since he'd been carted away for medical treatment after the events at Brassick's house. He looked well, if a little pale. 'What are you doing here?' he demanded.

'I might ask you the same thing.'

He grunted. 'You first.'

I met his gaze. 'Brassick wasn't Umbra's leader.'

'Why do you say that?'

I waved a hand at the people below us. 'It's the middle of the day and Umbra's goal is to raise a demon. There's no way that its leader would miss the event, and there's no way a vampire could stand out there without burning up. Their big event takes place at *noon*. They could easily have arranged it for after the sun goes down in less than five hours but they didn't.'

A muscle throbbed in Thane's cheek. 'Perhaps Brassick wanted to watch the action from a distance. Perhaps he wasn't as convinced as his cronies that they could control whatever creature they invoke.'

'Perhaps.'

He eyed me. 'There's more?'

269

'Nick came to see me. He spoke about a large conical flask into which they were decanting his blood.'

Thane finally understood. 'And there was no such flask at Brassick's place.'

'I don't think this is over.' I folded my arms. 'What's your story?'

He looked away. 'The numbers.' He sounded oddly defeated. 'The numbers Brassick used to label us all. Paul was Number One. Alice was Number Two. I was Number Three and Nick was Number Four.'

Suddenly I realised what was worrying him. 'Lorna,' I breathed.

His jaw tightened. 'Brassick didn't mention her at all.'

'But she told us she'd been attacked just like you. *Before* you, in fact.'

He didn't answer.

'Did you go to her house? Did you speak to her?' I demanded.

'Nobody was home.'

'Maybe she's gone out of town for the holiday. Maybe Brassick forgot about her.' Even as I said the words, I didn't believe them.

Lorna had played us all. No wonder Umbra were sure they could control whatever demon appeared: they were using Lorna's blood to complete the invocation. She'd daubed her apartment block with graffiti, she'd pretended to be attacked and she was inexplicably wealthy. Maybe Brassick had bankrolled her or maybe it was the other way around. It didn't really matter.

'If she shows up here,' Thane said dully, 'we'll know for certain.'

No sooner had he finished speaking than a trumpet

sounded across the square. Thane and I gazed over the crowd. When I saw the figure step out of the building, I knew we were right: it was unmistakably Lorna. Blood was dripping from both her arms and splattering the stone cobbles. She was holding a large conical flask containing a dark, viscous fluid.

I reached for my gun.

'People of Coldstream!' She amplified her voice magically so that everyone could hear. 'People of Coldstream!' she repeated. 'Witches, druids, ogres, nymphs, shapeshifters, trolls.'

'Leprechauns!' someone yelled.

'Squibs!' shouted another. There was a ripple of good-humoured laughter.

Lorna smiled beatifically. 'All of you! Happy Winter Solstice!'

As the crowd roared, I lowered myself to the rooftop; I'd be more certain of my aim if I was lying flat. I reached into my pocket, pulled out a silencer and fixed it to the gun's muzzle. I didn't want to create panic in the crowd, and I didn't want to kill anyone other than Lorna.

'Don't kill her,' Thane said, as if he'd heard my thoughts. I squinted upwards at him 'We need to talk to her.'

I snorted. I was done talking.

'And if she drops dead,' he went on, 'she'll drop that damned flask. Between what's in it and her own blood, there'll be enough to bring forth a demon.'

True. I adjusted my aim. If I hit her shoulder, she'd be flung backwards. With any luck, the flask would land on top of her and remain intact. I inhaled. There was no point in wasting any time. I squeezed the trigger and took the shot. There was a dull *phht* as the bullet was ejected and I felt the jolt.

Nothing happened. Lorna was still smiling – and still standing.

'You missed,' Thane growled.

I didn't fucking miss. I never missed. 'She's using some kind of magical ward.'

'She's a werewolf, not a damned witch,' he snapped.

'Then there's another member of Umbra who we've not found yet. Someone in that crowd is powering the barrier magically.'

He hissed under his breath. 'I'll find them.'

'Be quick, Thane. Look for anyone who's focusing on the space around Lorna rather than Lorna herself, anyone holding a box.'

'I know what to fucking look for.' He was angry because his old friend and ex-partner had fooled him. I couldn't blame him; she'd fooled me too.

The noise of the crowd started to die down. Thane clattered down the fire escape while I held my position and waited, hoping he'd find the witch who was protecting Lorna.

She spoke again. 'Twice a year Coldstream comes together to celebrate the solstice, but we know deep down that we don't really have anything to celebrate. We are not a unified city. We keep to ourselves and our own communities. We don't help our neighbours. We don't have a governing body that has everyone's best interests at heart.'

That wasn't the speech all those people down there had been expecting and I could hear grumbles even from up here on the roof.

'The rest of the world ignores us! The rest of the world passes us by while we focus on ourselves and not on making Coldstream the best, most powerful city in the country. We could be so much more! The right leader can bring us together. The right leader can show everyone else that we are a power to be reckoned with.'

'Who's the right leader?' somebody in the crowd bellowed out. 'Because it's not you! It's not a damned werewolf!'

There was a wave of amused titters but many were listening carefully, taking in Lorna's words. I glanced to my left and spotted Thane's bobbing head. Thank goodness for that bright ginger hair that made him so visible. He was elbowing his way through the mass of people, searching desperately for any sign of an Umbra witch.

'You are correct!' Lorna answered. 'It's not me. It would never be me.'

Yeah, yeah. She *wanted* it to be her; she was going to use a damned demon to make it her. 'I am going to bring somebody here who can make Coldstream powerful!' she shouted.

I checked on Thane again. He'd stopped and seemed to be staring at something – or someone. He veered slightly left towards the fringes of the crowd. 'Come on, Thane,' I whispered. '*Come on.*'

'I am going to bring the leader we deserve!'

Another voice sounded from the crowd. 'Hurry up then!'

Lorna's smile broadened. 'As you wish.'

I clenched my jaw. For fuck's sake, Thane, do something!

He'd reached a man in a dark cloak who was holding something. Thane punched him hard in the jaw and wrestled the thing from him. I recognised it immediately as a witch's box used to contain all manner of magical material. That had to be what was powering the magic barrier that was protecting Lorna. Thane held it aloft, about to smash it to the ground.

I re-checked my position and my aim. Any second now. Any ... second ... now.

Thane hurled the box to the ground at the same time as Lorna dropped the flask. Blood gushed forth at her feet and I squeezed the trigger again, still aiming for her shoulder. This time the bullet found its target.

273

The barrier was broken. Lorna's body jerked backwards and I exhaled with relief, but I'd relaxed too quickly. The blood that had come from at least one lone werewolf – and quite likely more – was spilling across the ground in front of Lorna's feet. Shit.

A few people cried out in alarm probably more because of Lorna's collapse than anything else they suspected was happening, although thick red smoke was already billowing forth as the magic of the blood and the day coalesced.

I peered past it and caught a brief glimpse of Lorna struggling to sit up. Her lips were moving as she muttered some final incantation that would seal the deal and summon a demon. I adjusted my sights. I'd shoot her in the head this time if that was what it took to stop her.

Then I saw Thane flying towards her. An instant later, he vanished as he was swallowed by the cloud of scarlet smoke. That was when the ground started to shake.

The crowd were more alarmed now and there were screams and cries as the building beneath me juddered and swayed violently. More and more of the red smoke filled the square and there was nothing I could do. I couldn't see any targets, couldn't see beyond the damned smoke and the fleeing people.

There was a loud crack, as if the air itself was splitting in two.

I focused on the thickest part of the smoke cloud. I doubted that my bullets would do much against a demon but I'd certainly try. I *had* to try.

A breeze picked up from the western side of the square, not particularly strong but enough to clear some of the smoke. I concentrated on my breathing. Even if Lorna were dead, I couldn't allow a demon to take hold of Coldstream. This city wasn't perfect, not by a long shot, but it didn't deserve this. It didn't deserve the chaos that a creature from the underworld would bring.

And then the smoke gusted upwards to reveal a tiny creature sitting in the pool of werewolf blood. My mouth dropped open and I lowered my gun.

CHAPTER
THIRTY-THREE

Although plenty of people had turned and run, once the earthquake was over and the red smoke had dissipated hundreds still remained. Some were curious, some afraid to move – and some were laughing.

'Look! There's our new leader! That's who's going to unite Coldstream and make us a world power to be reckoned with!'

'Miaow!'

'Who's got kibble?'

'How about a piece of string?'

'Happy Winter Solstice!'

I ignored the amused shouts as I elbowed past a group of druids. Thane was by Lorna's side but she didn't appear to be moving. I left them and focused on the ginger kitten, which was now on all fours and licking carefully at the pool of blood around its little paws.

'Hey there,' I said. I bent down and scooped its warm body up with one hand. It let out a tiny miaow of protest as I examined it closely. One white tipped tail, four little legs with four little paws and a number of outstretched claws. A curved belly, quivering whiskers and intelligent green eyes. It was a cat, nothing more, nothing less. I checked underneath: a girl.

She wriggled free, darted towards Lorna and Thane and sniffed at Lorna's feet. Thane looked up at me. 'She's gone.' His voice was stiff. 'She must have used a lot of her own blood to start the invocation. Getting shot as well was too much for her body to take.'

The witch whom Thane had punched was out cold, his body sprawled on the cobbles less than twenty metres away. If there were any more answers to be had, he'd be able to provide them.

I gently touched Thane's arm.

'She betrayed us,' he said starkly. 'All of us. She manipulated everyone.'

I gazed at Lorna's wide-open eyes and unmoving body. Had she truly believed she would be helping the city of Coldstream by bringing a demon here, or had it been nothing more than a power play? There was little doubt that she had created Umbra; she knew what it was like to be on the periphery of society and she'd found other outsiders and persuaded them to join her cause with promises of power and wealth and ideological control. They'd fallen hook, line and sinker for her lies. But then again, so had I.

The kitten clambered over her corpse towards Thane and jumped up, clawing her way up his body and onto his shoulder. He jerked in shock. 'What the hell?'

'Cat distribution system,' I informed him. 'You have no choice in the matter.'

He straightened up and reached for the kitten, then he paused. 'Kit,' he said slowly, 'is this the...'

'It's a kitten,' I told him firmly. 'And she wants to be with you.'

She had already started to purr.

~

THERE WAS no market during the solstice and I had promised Trilby that I wouldn't bother them at their house without an invitation, so I hovered around the waterfront on the edge of Danksville. They'd be along sooner or later; they wouldn't be able to stop themselves.

I sat cross-legged by the river watching for monsters, but there were no signs of life. Even the Tweed's usual bloodthirsty creatures seemed to be enjoying a holiday.

'Hello, Kit.'

I didn't turn around. 'Hello, Trilby.'

'Happy Winter Solstice.'

Yeah, yeah. 'You knew, didn't you?'

They didn't play dumb. 'That Coldstream is already overrun by demons? Yes, I knew.'

'You could have told me.'

'Perhaps you didn't ask the right questions or come to the right conclusions.' They examined me dispassionately. 'You know that once the genie has been let out of the bottle it can't be put back in. Demons have roamed this world from time immemorial. It's true they can't escape from their own realm without help – but it's also true that there are millions of them here already.'

'*Hunters art they, first and foremost,*' I quoted. '*Natural predators equipped with sharp claws, keen senses, and a most terrifying agility.*'

'You see?' Trilby said. 'You had the answers all along. And as the book said, they do murder up to three thousand souls. Your own little furry family are all killers.' They paused. 'As, I suspect, are you.'

I wasn't going to give them the satisfaction of answering that last comment.

Trilby sat down beside me. *'Anyone who canst bind and command a demon shall wield power most formidable, far beyond the ken of mortal men. Such mastery over the infernal arts doth grant dominion over forces unseen, and with it the might to shape the very world to one's will.'*

I flicked them a side look.

'That makes you a demon lord,' they said. 'Demon lady, if that's what you prefer.'

I wasn't amused. 'People have died, Trilby.'

'I suspect they deserved it – and look at what you've learned along the way. You've been floundering for some time, but now you've found your path.'

'And what path is that?'

They clapped me on the shoulder. 'Helping the waifs and strays of Coldstream, of course. We need demon ladies like you to keep us on the straight and narrow.' They grinned. 'And now you know it as much as the demons do.'

'They're just cats.'

Trilby winked. 'They're never just cats. And that means you're never just a cat lady.'

I sighed, but then I smiled too.

ACKNOWLEDGMENTS

Thank you so much to everyone who has helped along the way with this book. This story was inspired by a single book cover, purchased on a whim from JoY Cover Design and later adapted by Covers By Juan, and which has been begging to be used for too long.

Karen Holmes, my fabulous editor has championed the story and worked on the nitty gritty of my writing which often contains so many redundant words until she wields her exceptional cutting skills.

Thanks must also go to all the wonderful ARC readers who've been so enthusiastic and helpful throughout so many book series. Last but not least, everyone who's ever written a review, bought a book or recommended one of my stories. I couldn't do this without you.

Helen x

ABOUT THE AUTHOR

After teaching English literature in the UK, Japan and Malaysia, Helen Harper left behind the world of education following the worldwide success of her Blood Destiny series of books. She is a professional member of the Alliance of Independent Authors and writes full time, thanking her lucky stars every day that's she lucky enough to do so!

Helen has always been a book lover, devouring science fiction and fantasy tales when she was a child growing up in Scotland.

She currently lives in Edinburgh in the UK with far too many cats (and dogs!) – not to mention the dragons, fairies, demons, wizards and vampires that seem to keep appearing from nowhere.

OTHER TITLES

The complete *The Thrill of the Hunt* series

Sure, I might be a low elf. But that doesn't mean I won't get up to high jinks.

I'm not particularly special. I'm certainly not perfect. I'm just another delivery driver with a smattering of elvish magic who's trying to make an honest living on the mean streets of Edinburgh.

Go me.

However, my world changes when I cross paths with Hugo Pemberville, the celebrated high elf who's well known for his accomplished work as a treasure hunter. He might be famous but he's also an arrogant idiot who deliberately destroys my life.

I'm not the sort of person who'll let anyone ruin me without a fight. But when I take my revenge on Hugo, I end up thrust into a treasure hunting adventure that I could never have dreamed of.

I'm determined to succeed against all the odds. Unfortunately, treasure hunting is more difficult and dangerous than I'd expected. I'll need all my wits about me if I'm going to survive.

But, hey, who doesn't love an under-dog?

Book One - Tattered Huntress

Book Two - Fiendish Delights

Book Three - Skullduggery

Book Four - The Salted Sceptre

The complete *FireBrand* series

A werewolf killer. A paranormal murder. How many times can Emma Bellamy cheat death?

I'm one placement away from becoming a fully fledged London detective. It's bad enough that my last assignment before I qualify is with Supernatural Squad. But that's nothing compared to what happens next.

Brutally murdered by an unknown assailant, I wake up twelve hours later in the morgue – and I'm very much alive. I don't know how or why it happened. I don't know who killed me. All I know is that they might try again.

Werewolves are disappearing right, left and centre.

A mysterious vampire seems intent on following me everywhere I go.

And I have to solve my own vicious killing. Preferably before death comes for me again.

Book One – Brimstone Bound

Book Two – Infernal Enchantment

Book Three – Midnight Smoke

Book Four – Scorched Heart

Book Five – Dark Whispers

Book Six – A Killer's Kiss

Book Seven – Fortune's Ashes

❧

A Charade of Magic complete series

The best way to live in the Mage ruled city of Glasgow is to keep your head down and your mouth closed.

That's not usually a problem for Mairi Wallace. By day she works at a small shop selling tartan and by night she studies to become an apothecary. She knows her place and her limitations. All that changes, however, when her old childhood friend sends her a desperate message seeking her help - and the Mages themselves cross Mairi's path. Suddenly, remaining unnoticed is no longer an option.

There's more to Mairi than she realises but, if she wants to fulfil her full potential, she's going to have to fight to stay alive - and only time will tell if she can beat the Mages at their own game.

From twisted wynds and tartan shops to a dangerous daemon and the magic infused City Chambers, the future of a nation might lie with one solitary woman.

Book One – Hummingbird

Book Two – Nightingale

Book Three – Red Hawk

The complete *Blood Destiny* series

"A spectacular and addictive series."

Mackenzie Smith has always known that she was different. Growing up as the only human in a pack of rural shapeshifters will do that to you, but then couple it with some mean fighting skills and a fiery temper and you end up with a woman that few will dare to cross. However, when the only father figure in her life is brutally murdered, and the dangerous Brethren with their predatory Lord Alpha come to investigate, Mack has to not only ensure the physical safety of her adopted family by hiding her apparent humanity, she also has to seek the blood-soaked vengeance that she craves.

The complete *Bo Blackman* series

A half-dead daemon, a massacre at her London based PI firm and evidence that suggests she's the main suspect for both ... Bo Blackman is having a very bad week.

She might be naive and inexperienced but she's determined to get to the bottom of the crimes, even if it means involving herself with one of London's most powerful vampire Families and their enigmatic leader.

It's pretty much going to be impossible for Bo to ever escape unscathed.

Book One - Dire Straits

Book Two - New Order

Book Three - High Stakes

Book Four - Red Angel

Book Five - Vigilante Vampire

Book Six - Dark Tomorrow

The complete *Highland Magic* series

Integrity Taylor walked away from the Sidhe when she was a child. Orphaned and bullied, she simply had no reason to stay, especially not when the sins of her father were going to remain on her shoulders. She found a new family - a group of thieves who proved that blood was less important than loyalty and love.

But the Sidhe aren't going to let Integrity stay away forever. They need her more than anyone realises - besides, there are prophecies to be fulfilled, people to be saved and hearts to be won over. If anyone can do it, Integrity can.

Book One - Gifted Thief

Book Two - Honour Bound

Book Three - Veiled Threat

Book Four - Last Wish

The complete *Dreamweaver* series

"I have special coping mechanisms for the times I need to open the front door. They're even often successful..."

Zoe Lydon knows there's often nothing logical or rational about fear. It doesn't change the fact that she's too terrified to step outside her own house, however.

What Zoe doesn't realise is that she's also a dreamweaver - able to access other people's subconscious minds. When she finds herself in the Dreamlands and up against its sinister Mayor, she'll need to use all of her wits - and overcome all of her fears - if she's ever going to come out alive.

Book One - Night Shade

Book Two - Night Terrors

Book Three - Night Lights

∼

Stand alone novels

Eros

William Shakespeare once wrote that, "Cupid is a knavish lad, thus to make poor females mad." The trouble is that Cupid himself would probably agree...

As probably the last person in the world who'd appreciate hearts, flowers and romance, Coop is convinced that true love doesn't exist – which is rather unfortunate considering he's also known as Cupid, the God of Love. He'd rather spend his days drinking, womanising and generally having as much fun as he possible can. As far as he's concerned, shooting people with bolts of pure love is a waste of his time...but then his path crosses with that of shy and retiring Skye Sawyer and nothing will ever be quite the same again.

Wraith

Magic. Shadows. Adventure. Romance.

Saiya Buchanan is a wraith, able to detach her shadow from her body and send it off to do her bidding. But, unlike most of her kin, Saiya doesn't deal in death. Instead, she trades secrets - and in the goblin besieged city of Stirling in Scotland, they're a highly prized commodity. It might just be, however, that the goblins have been hiding the greatest secret of them all. When Gabriel de Florinville, a Dark Elf, is sent as royal envoy into Stirling and takes her prisoner, Saiya is not only going to uncover the sinister truth. She's also going to realise that sometimes the deepest secrets are the ones locked within your own heart.

The complete _Lazy Girl's Guide To Magic_ series

Hard Work Will Pay Off Later. Laziness Pays Off Now.

Let's get one thing straight - Ivy Wilde is not a heroine. In fact, she's probably the last witch in the world who you'd call if you needed a magical helping hand. If it were down to Ivy, she'd spend all day every day on her sofa where she could watch TV, munch junk food and talk to her feline familiar to her heart's content.

However, when a bureaucratic disaster ends up with Ivy as the victim of a case of mistaken identity, she's yanked very unwillingly into Arcane Branch, the investigative department of the Hallowed Order of Magical Enlightenment. Her problems are quadrupled when a valuable object is stolen right from under the Order's noses.

It doesn't exactly help that she's been magically bound to Adeptus Exemptus Raphael Winter. He might have piercing sapphire eyes and a body which a cover model would be proud of but, as far as Ivy's concerned, he's a walking advertisement for the joyless perils of too much witch-work.

And if he makes her go to the gym again, she's definitely going to turn him into a frog.

Book One - Slouch Witch

Book Two - Star Witch

Book Three - Spirit Witch

Sparkle Witch (Christmas novella)

The complete *Fractured Faery* series

One corpse. Several bizarre looking attackers. Some very strange magical powers. And a severe bout of amnesia.

It's one thing to wake up outside in the middle of the night with a decapitated man for company. It's another to have no memory of how you got there - or who you are.

She might not know her own name but she knows that several people are out to get her. It could be because she has strange magical powers seemingly at her fingertips and is some kind of fabulous hero. But then why does she appear to inspire fear in so many? And who on earth is the sexy, green-eyed barman who apparently despises her? So many questions ... and so few answers.

At least one thing is for sure - the streets of Manchester have never met someone quite as mad as Madrona...

Book One - Box of Frogs

SHORTLISTED FOR THE KINDLE STORYTELLER AWARD 2018

Book Two - Quiver of Cobras

Book Three - Skulk of Foxes

~

The complete *City Of Magic* series

Charley is a cleaner by day and a professional gambler by night. She might be haunted by her tragic past but she's never thought of herself as anything or anyone special. Until, that is, things start to go terribly wrong all across the city of Manchester. Between plagues of rats, firestorms and the gleaming blue eyes of a sexy Scottish werewolf, she might just have landed herself in the middle of a magical apocalypse. She might also be the only person who has the ability to bring order to an utterly chaotic new world.

Book One - Shrill Dusk

Book Two - Brittle Midnight

Book Three - Furtive Dawn